Penguin Books
Alter Ego

Patrick Watson first came to prominence with the television phenomenon *This Hour Has Seven Days*. By then, however, he had already established himself as a skilled film producer and television journalist. His internationally acclaimed film *The Seven Hundred-Million* was the first ever made inside Communist China by a North American director.

Known principally as a probing interviewer through *The Watson Report*, the dramatic *Witness to Yesterday*, and specials like his prize-winning *Speer: The Last Nazi*, Patrick Watson is also an aviator, screenwriter, teacher, and insatiable investigator of life, art, music, morals, society and change. *Alter Ego* is his fifth book.

Patrick Watson

Alter Ego

A Novel

Penguin Books

Penguin Books Ltd, Harmondsworth,
Middlesex, England
Penguin Books, 625 Madison Avenue,
New York, New York 10022, U.S.A.
Penguin Books Australia Ltd, Ringwood,
Victoria, Australia
Penguin Books Canada Ltd, 2801 John Street,
Markham, Ontario, Canada L3R 1B4
Penguin Books (N.Z.) Ltd, 182–190 Wairau Road,
Auckland 10, New Zealand

First published in Canada by Lester and Orpen Limited 1978
Published in Penguin Books 1979

Made and printed in Great Britain by
Richard Clay (The Chaucer Press) Ltd, Bungay, Suffolk
Set in Linotype Plantin

For Cliff

Crucial to the art of Karate is the *kata*, an exercise performed alone, beginning and ending upon the same spot. In the *kata* there is no victor, no vanquished: the opponent is your self.

I

All this took place within a very few seconds.

The noise from the kitchen startled Daisy Nelson, not because it was in itself an alarming noise – in fact it was a homey, familiar sound that she used to find comforting. But it startled her this time, the soft clunk of something shifting in the sink full of dishes because, despite her resolve not to allow it to happen, she had sensed her husband behind the sound, had almost turned as the faint crockery percussion struck her ear to call out, "Rob?" and then, before the word was formed, had thrust her fist hard against her lips and shaken her head in a gesture of anger and impotence.

She should have been prepared for it. More than one friend at the funeral, and afterward over coffee and whisky and sandwiches in her own living room, had warned that she might suffer the illusion that he was still alive, that she might hear his voice, hear him moving in another room. Their telling her this had made her feel sick, had forced into her mind the scene at the morgue, identifying Rob's body. It had been a farewell so final, so violent in the stillness of the mutilated corpse, that she was certain no illusions could persist. They said, "Oh yes," she would probably hear him in the house as other widows were said to do; instead she saw him on the slab, felt nauseated with the memory, was afraid if she spoke she would vomit so she pressed her fist against her lips hard and shook her head. She wanted to say firmly to them, "Never. That will never happen to me." But all she could do was try to suppress the nausea and shake her head, and they thought, "Poor thing," and patted her arm and poured more coffee.

And now, in the empty house, she stared at the mirror over the mantelpiece, at the reflected reality of her compressed mouth and tired grey eyes, trying to make the imagined sound of him in the kitchen go away. Mouthing the words without voicing them she said, "I am only thirty-one years old, God! He was a faithless bastard. I have time."

The little house on Moore Avenue was silent again. Behind the house Daisy could sense the sheer mass of Toronto's Mount Pleasant cemetery, closed and locked now, Rob's raw grave invisible half a mile away among a forest of squared stone, under the bare elms, cold. Daisy shivered, folded her arms and hugged herself for warmth. In front of the house a small park, deserted, was heavy with shadow. The street was empty. She could hear nothing.

Daisy clung somewhat precariously to a tough-mindedness, to a realism she had to work for. She was proud of this, more as an accomplishment than as an instinct; she had had to overcome an inclination to romanticism to achieve it. Her role as courtroom lawyer was an important device in maintaining it, as well as being a career. Now she was angry at herself for having slipped, for having so nearly permitted the – romantic, she thought bitterly – approach of the illusion that he was still alive, that she had found it necessary to stop a word – his name – from forming on her lips. And now, although she had demanded privacy half an hour ago and shown her friends abruptly out, she regretted the pride that had driven her to do it.

She glanced a moment at the phone on the desk in the darkening corner of the living room. She had found relief for a few moments in washing the dishes, but had stopped after a while, leaving them half done, and had come back into the carpeted room feeling suddenly helpless. Then, a few minutes later, came the sound that made her sense Rob, alive in the house, followed by her anger at the weakness that allowed the thought.

After a moment she found the anger comforting; there was a hot reality to it. She yielded to it and said aloud, freeing her throat at last, "Damn them all!"

Her anger warmed her. Anger at Rob for his neglect of her, for his absences, his unrepented affairs with other women, for this last irreversible desertion which was, she told herself, probably the result of the same impetuous carelessness that had led him to spoil so many things between them; fruitless anger at the dishes in the sink where they must now be settling as the rinse water leaked away and settling, made a noise like a bottle opening, a noise – there it was again – that damnably made her *feel* Rob's presence in the empty kitchen where he always seemed to stop off and sit and drink a couple of glasses of scotch or rum before he made it into the rest of the house. Then he became loose and funny and did sharp-edged imitations of the Prime Minister or someone else in the news, until she was yawning through her laughter and they went up to bed ...

She closed her eyes on the memory. But tears would not stop welling through the lids, and then the lids were sore from too much wiping. She let the tears run down her face. She sobbed a loud sob with the word *love* choked in it. When her mind brought Rob's stocky drunken body arcing over her in playful love, the image was shredded by the lacerations on his dead chest, by the voice of the police inspector explaining that Rob's fingertips had been destroyed so that there were no prints. She was unable not to recall the swollen, pulpy, unrecognizable face while someone pried open the eyelids and she nodded, yes, at the opaque pupil of the left eye, and then looked again at the familiar scar across his dark, hairy belly, and nodded again, yes; and then forced herself to say aloud, "Yes, this is my husband."

And now the impossible sounds in the kitchen – the soft closing of the refrigerator door, the clink of a glass – sounds she would have heard had he arrived home late and stopped to get a glass first before coming to her, with "It's me, Babe," and one of his new stories or a lie to explain his lateness or a scheme for a trip they might take or ...

She squeezed her sore eyelids closer together. She was losing her mind, succumbing, hearing those phantom sounds as people had said she would and she had been so sure she never would.

And then, distinct in her ear, close, no illusion, a voice said, "It's me, Babe."

She opened her eyes at the mirror.

Rob's face stared back at her from the glass, a crinkle over the black eyepatch, a mixture of compassion and humor. Her knees buckled, but his hands grabbed at her, spilling cold scotch

9

on her back as he eased her to the floor. She was still partly conscious. In the midst of the sickening sense of madness, the swirling, floating away from reality, she said to herself, "His eye is *laughing*, the bastard!"

She fainted completely.

There was a time of confusion, of children laughing, of deep, fast-flowing water somewhere, physical warmth on the back of her neck, her ears ringing, glittering sunflecks on a bright stone wall, the smell of apples.

The fingers kneading gently at her temples. She knew the fingers. She knew their owner was a corpse and the tips were destroyed. She was too frightened to reach for the hands. She fought to keep her mind from breaking. She was terrified to open her eyes and be deceived. Her heart ached to believe but her mind demanded verification. She opened her eyes. The man's face was still crinkled. She recognized the expression: he was trying to reassure her.

"Rob, I saw you ... your body ... !"

He shook his head. "It was something else, Babe. Another body. I'll tell you about it but it will take time. You have to believe me."

"I saw your eye!" she whimpered in bewilderment. "I saw the scar on your belly!"

Daisy lay on the floor. The man had put a sofa cushion under her head. He was bending over her, still gently massaging her temples. She grabbed at his hands, pulled herself up to a sitting position, drew him to the light by the low reading table and studied the hands. She turned them over and stared at the fingertips. She could not even remember the whorls and circles of her own prints, let alone his, and yet these hands *were* Rob's hands – broad hands, dark hair furring the outer edges of the backs. The lopsided thumbnail was Rob's thumbnail.

She searched his face. He waited patiently and said nothing. She lifted the eyepatch. An opaque pupil looked out. She lowered the patch. She reached for his belt buckle. He rose to his knees and opened it for her. She drew down the edge of his shorts and looked for the scar. By now she knew she would find it and she did. Scepticism and the struggle to be sane collapsed within her; resistance snapped like a cut cord. She fell into his arms and a thin wail flowed from her lips and filled the room.

"Shh, shh," he whispered. "It's all right now."

She gave in to her wish to believe. She sobbed relief and she sobbed the anguish she had withheld from their friends at the funeral, his television friends mostly, whom she did not trust enough to grieve with. But still her mind stayed partly watchful, even flooded like this with the release of weeping, and she knew that his shushing her was not just reassurance; she recognized the subtle tone of instruction; he was telling her not to make too much noise. She stiffened slightly. He noticed this and drew back and said, "Let's eat something and then I can tell you about it."

Suddenly she felt hungry for bacon and eggs. She smiled tentatively at him, and they moved to the kitchen.

All those weeks of silence.

Daisy glanced furtively at the man settling himself in a familiar way at the kitchen table and sticking his finger into the glass of whisky to turn the ice cube around and around. She tore the plastic cover from a package of bacon, and when she looked back at him, his gaze was on her and for a moment she was not sure whether she felt guilty for watching him or angry for being watched. She came back to the table and sat down. He took her hand. She stared at him, examining his face. He waited.

The weeks of silence. "Don't expect to hear from me for a while, Babe." She remembered his voice on the phone that August night. "It's getting so intense, now. I'll be able to tell you what this has been all about in a couple of weeks. Hang in; it's more important than you could imagine. A couple of weeks."

She had accepted the embargo at first, telling herself, "This is the last one, the last 'Hang In Babe' – if this doesn't end it then I will." He had asked for a couple of weeks. She had waited four. And then, in a mixture of righteous anger and deep anxiety she had phoned him, and reached a recording, and had then gone to Montreal, to the house where Pinch had been keeping Rob from her, she felt resentfully, so much of these last five years. The house was locked and silent. She went to the university where nobody could say where Pinch was, and then finally to the police.

There followed the days of searching, the stories that Rob had been seen here, seen there, stories that raised her hopes and dashed them again and left a terrible wake of silence. Silence. The grinding of the old electric clock on the kitchen wall. The quiet telephone, the uncommunicative streets, the nights of standing at her bedroom window, staring at the brown grass under the yellow streetlight in the park across the way, as if she could summon a man to appear out of the shadows and stride, familiarly, toward the house.

And then the morning, three days ago, when she had opened her door to a huge sergeant of detectives and had known what he would tell her.

This afternoon she had buried her husband. Now he sat opposite her across the rough oaken kitchen table, puddling the circles from his sweating whisky glass the way he always used to do, and trying to look reassuring.

The smell of coffee when Daisy opened the can soothed her and she bent her face over the dark grounds to bathe for a moment in the waves of fragrance. The physical comforts in the room were very strong. They tempered her bewilderment. She grew cautious. She could not completely suppress the spasms that filled her lungs, but she stared at the man who sat there and spoke and looked and yes, even smelled like her husband, and she said, "I'm ready."

"All right," he said, "It begins with Pinch."

2

"My name is John Alexander Haig. I have a stone I would like you to appraise, and if the appraisal is satisfactory I may wish to sell it."

Abram Backer placed his hands lightly on the glass-topped desk and spread his fingers. He regarded his visitor thoughtfully and tried to place the accent. Scottish in it somewhere, he thought, and American or Canadian. The man was in his fifties, pale, lean, a sandy moustache neatly trimmed, the eyes light blue, intense, confident. His three-piece suit was not fashionably new, but it became him excellently. The cuffs and elbows of the jacket were slightly worn. He held an attaché case easily on his lap. It too was of fine quality, but old and scuffed from use. Backer assumed that the diamond would be in the case, and that it would be in a box of its own.

All these observations Backer made in a single scanning sweep. He was a careful student of the outward signs of personality. He noted that the man was tense but not anxious, and he concluded – he could not have explained why – that this customer was likely to be whatever he said he was, although he might not say a great deal.

Outside on the hazy Amsteldyk Road motor-scooters and 2CV delivery vans sputtered faintly, scarcely heard through the thick walls and heavy wooden doors of the old building. A pale sun shone through the high arched windows and cast a shaft of light on the table.

"I flew here to Amsterdam from Rome yesterday," Haig volunteered. "I am hoping to go home to Montreal in a day or two. I would like very much to conclude a transaction before I depart, but if it is clearly in my interest, I am prepared to stay longer.

"Or even," he added in a measured way, "to leave the stone in the right hands if time is required to realize the maximum from its sale."

Haig pronounced words as though he were reading them with care from a dictionary. The word "interest" had been spoken in three clear syllables. The cadences of the man's voice, the faint Scottish roll to the "r's" and the tight, precise vowels had a curiously relaxing effect on Backer.

"I might say," Haig went on, lifting the attaché case and placing it gently on the desk between them, "that I have made very careful inquiries and that I am perfectly satisfied that you are the man with whom I should be dealing."

Abram Backer opened his lips slightly in a polite smile. "This is 1970 not 1937, Professor Haig," he said. "Amsterdam is not overrun with refugees seeking to sell their stones, nor contaminated with merchants whose knowledge of diamonds is somewhat less exact than their knowledge of the quickest way to profit from frightened human beings. So. I think you would have been hard-pressed to find someone in diamonds now in Amsterdam who was not utterly reliable."

Haig's eyebrows had gone up at the word "Professor;" Backer noticed this and said, "I think I was right to call you Professor?"

Haig nodded, not surprised but amused.

There was no hurry between the two; the cloistered afternoon had no sense of urgency. Even Haig's remarks about his hope to fly home in a few days had not seemed pressing. He unlocked the clasps of the attaché case and drew up the lid.

Backer said, "Just as the facets of a stone are no accident, you understand, they reveal the basic crystalline structure quite exactly, so the surfaces of a man ..."

With a smile and a shrug, he peered into the attaché case. It looked like a display case for trivial antiques. There were two old fountain pens in a clip fastened to the bottom and beside them, in a wooden frame to keep it from rattling about, a small bottle of black ink with a bit of stained rag around it. A block of white notepaper had its own space assigned, so did a bundle of sharp pencils bound together by a wide rubber band. A rub-

ber band was also wound around a small safety razor in a clear
plastic box, a comb and a pair of very old silver nail scissors.
There was a miniature electronic calculator of an advanced make
but so hand-rubbed from use it looked antique, a pair of needle-
nosed pliers held in a leather loop that was stitched to the lining
at the back of the case, papers in the lid, a small tin tobacco box
marked 'postage stamps' in faded orange enamel, a number of
other unidentified paper and leather packets, and, in the middle,
an incongruously new royal-blue imitation-velvet jeweller's box
the length and breadth of a passport and about four centimeters
deep.

Before Haig lifted the jewel case from its place Backer said,
"I have to accept that you have, as you said, made careful inquiries, but I confess to being puzzled why you came here to
Amsterdam if you want a quick sale and a good return. You
must know that Amsterdam is no longer the center of gravity of
the diamond business?"

"I know that," Haig said. "The centers are Hong Kong, New
York, Tel Aviv and Antwerp."

"And London," Backer said.

Haig nodded.

"And yet you came to Amsterdam and you came to me."

Haig nodded again.

"And I am not even the biggest in Amsterdam."

"I know."

"Really, only two of us came back after the war. Antwerp
was liberated more than a year before Amsterdam. Most of the
diamond men who returned to Europe went to Antwerp. Asscher
came back here to the factory his father had built on the Tol-
straat. I came back to my grandfather's place here on the river.
There's nobody else who counts. I'm wondering why you came
to me?"

It was said politely but not without a kind of professional
scepticism that tacitly announced Abram Backer to be very much
on the *qui vive*, despite his inclination to trust his visitor. Haig
read the tone of voice accurately and was not offended; he knew
the importance of protocol in the diamond trade. Rather than
answer, he lifted out the unimpressive jewel case and opened it.

He folded back the corners of a piece of soft grey cloth to reveal an astonishing sapphire blue diamond, big enough to fill a dessert spoon, cut in the pillow-shaped Emerald style, each of its facets concentrating hard blue fire from the pale yellow Dutch sunlight. Having revealed his treasure, Haig lifted his eyes to watch the diamond merchant's reaction.

Backer had gone white.

His hands gripped the edges of the table so tightly that the knuckles of the first joint of each finger paled over the tendon. His eyes darted from the stone to Haig's face and back to the stone in confusion which he struggled to hide. He still smiled, but it was a frozen, spastic smile. These spasms lasted for five or ten seconds – a long time in a silent room – and then he made an effort to recover, licked his lips hastily, removed his hands from the table and wiped them together covertly underneath it, pulled down the bottom of his vest, cleared his throat, and said, "It is an amazing stone, an *amazing* stone."

"I know," Haig said quietly. "If we were to draw the drapes now and darken the room, it would phosphoresce for several seconds. In ultra-violet light it is quite an unexpected golden color and on a high-voltage plate it gives off a brilliant white light. I was sure you would be impressed by it."

This little lecture gave Abram Backer time to collect himself; he wondered whether Haig, in some kind of intuitively courteous way, had meant it so.

Backer lifted the diamond gingerly from its case. Haig looked for, and saw, the way the diamond expert slid his fingertips smoothly over the stone to feel the temperature – diamonds, being better heat conductors than glass or crystal, always feel cold – and to check the characteristic greasy feel of the true gem. What he found seemed to perplex him even more.

"So," he said. "So. I am very much intrigued. I cannot tell you how intrigued I am. I am quite curious to begin my examination right away, if you permit?"

"That's what we're here for," Haig said with a hint of alacrity.

Backer carefully replaced the stone in its box and started to carry it out of the front room to the workshop at the back of the suite of offices. He turned for a moment and said, "I assure you it is perfectly ..." But Haig cut him off with a cheerful wave of his hand. "Get on with it, Mr. Backer. I'm just as curious as you are."

Left alone in the reception room, Haig strolled softly back and forth across the polished floor. He glanced at the miniature surveillance television camera mounted high in one corner, and was tempted to wink at it. Instead he turned away and chuckled. When Haig chuckled the sound was subterranean and diaphragmatic. His mouth closed and the chuckle sounded as if he were saying "*hut hut hut hut hut*" deep in his belly.

From behind the workshop door he could hear a telephone being dialled. The door opened and a young woman entered and, for a moment, Haig caught the sound of Backer's voice, muted, urgent, the words indistinguishable. He knew what was likely being said, and, in any event, he did not understand Dutch.

"*Verstaat U Nederlands?*" the woman asked.

Haig shook his head.

"*Koffie?*"

Haig bowed in reply. "*Ja, Danke.*" he said, knowing it was German but hoping it would sound more courteous than English. The girl smiled and retreated.

The sun had fallen too far west to penetrate the high windows any longer, but the room still glowed with the polish of its fine old panelling. The sounds from the back of the suite were muted almost to silence now. Haig sat down on a carved chair and drummed his fingers again. He began to look a trifle impatient, but still cheerful and intensely curious. Presently the young woman returned and switched on two wall lamps that warmed the room with a yellow suffusion. The telephone rang in the back, faintly, and was instantly answered. Haig could make out Backer's voice and it sounded excited. Then there was silence again, not even a clock ticking to measure the time.

Haig leaned back in the chair, slid his lower body forward until his head rested on the arched back and closed his eyes. He imagined he could smell the coffee. He felt strangely at ease and began to doze, so that perhaps ten minutes later when the door opened and a very real smell of fresh coffee came with a breeze from the back rooms, he was startled and confused for an instant.

"I apologize to be so long," Backer began, "but I suppose you understand why, and in any case I am going to explain it to you. Please ..." He motioned to the girl who was standing beside him. She put a tray down on the table without a word and once more left the room. Haig looked hard at Backer's face. He saw confusion, mostly. The color had returned to his cheeks but he was sweating and shaking his head involuntarily so that the dark hair swung back and forth.

"Mr. Haig," he said finally, "I have been in the diamond business for thirty-one years. I began as an apprentice to my father when I was eighteen and my father was apprenticed to his father. I *know* diamonds, but ..." He paused.

Haig made a single muffled *hut* in his belly and said, "But you are not going to tell me that you have never seen such a specimen as this, because in fact you have."

Backer sighed. "Do you have any idea how perplexing this is to me? Do you realize that my first impulse was to call the police? I am very glad I did not, by the way. Please."

He began to pour the coffee. It was a steaming black mocha, ground only moments before. Haig added a lot of cream, drank deeply, offered his cup again and waited. Backer sighed again.

"The *Pietra della Reconciliazione*," he said.

"This is not the *Pietra della Reconciliazione*," Haig said firmly.

"My grandfather directed the cutting of the *Pietra*; you probably knew that?"

"Yes."

"It was the largest stone and the finest stone ever to come through his hands, although he had been one of the men who worked on the Cullinan in 1908, on commission from Edward VII of England. But the *Pietra* was entirely his own work."

Haig remained silent.

"The *Pietra della Reconciliazione* was that rarest of stones, a sapphire blue diamond of the finest water, cut in the Emerald manner and having a table measuring exactly 11 mm on the small axis and 17.7 mm on the long."

"A perfect example of the Golden Proportion," Haig said.

"Well," said Abram Backer, "your stone is a genuine sapphire blue diamond. I'm almost certain of it, but I'm going to send it to my lab, if you agree, for confirmation. It is cut in the Emerald manner with a table of 11 mm by 17.7 mm and it has a weight of exactly 101 carats."

"The weight of the *Pietra*?"

"Exactly."

Haig waited.

"You can see why I was about to call the police. I was sure by the feel of it that it was genuine. And *I knew that stone!* Professor Haig, I have my grandfather's original sketches. I have the original black and white photographs taken right here in the factory. I have the color photos taken by Winston's in Rome in 1959. I scarcely needed to consult those photographs, you understand, but I did. To be certain. I have studied the *Pietra* very often.

"Now. A real diamond man does not need any lab to tell him whether or not a stone is genuine. He just puts it under a loop and looks at it, you understand?"

"What is a loop?"

"A jeweller's glass. Ten power. I know this is a genuine stone, and yet I am going to send it to my lab. I suppose you know why?"

"Go on," Haig said, interested.

"I telephoned to Rome, to the Medici Museum, where the *Pietra della Reconciliazione* has been since 1946. I spoke to my friend the assistant curator. I bear in mind that you have told me that you came from Rome yesterday."

"Yes."

"Yes. Well, I of course had to verify that the stone was ... alive and well, so to speak."

"And he told you that it was perfectly safe and on display where it has always been."

"He did. He told me that it had been removed from the museum only ten days ago, under armed guard, for some private family ceremonies, the family of the owners, the original owners. That made me suspicious until my friend said that he had personally supervised the laboratory examinations when the stone was returned, in the presence of several notaries, and again personally supervised its return to the display case and the reactivation of the electronic protection devices."

"So you are satisfied this is not the *Pietra*."

"The trouble is, it *is* the *Pietra*."

"And yet it can't be, can it?"

"No ... no. That's why I have to let them have it for a day downstairs in the lab. I could begin right now except that my laser man has gone to London to do a job for Christie's. He'll be back tomorrow morning."

"Laser?"

"We have a new technique of laser photography. It reveals the crystalline structure of the stone very clearly. Plastic – what we used to call 'paste' – has no crystalline structure. So. Can you wait? Would you like to observe the procedures?"

Haig scratched his left ear and looked out into the dusking street. Curious though he was about their photographic techniques it would be better to leave them alone with the stone for a day.

"I can wait," he said. "And thank you but I think I will spend the day walking in your extraordinary city. I don't know it at all and I'd like to. We university people spend too much time in labs anyway."

He smiled comfortably and noticed that Backer seemed relieved at his decision.

Haig said, "By the way, since both of us are certain that the lab will verify what you already know, I wonder if we could talk now about a transaction?"

"I will wish to make some inquiries about you, while the diamond's being examined. I hope you understand."

"Naturally. I'll give you all the help I can."

"Well, then. Yes, I suppose we could discuss a price. It will be a great deal less than you might have got at public auction in Zurich, or even in London, you know."

Haig smiled at Backer. "You must be wondering why I came to you, Mr. Backer, realizing you would immediately think the stone was the *Pietra*, when I could have gone to Hong Kong, say, where the stone might not be known. Well, we both are aware that any splendid diamond like this one, sold anywhere in the world under false pretenses, or carrying a trail of suspicion, would create trouble for the man who sold it – am I right?"

Backer nodded.

"I came to you so that there could be no doubt at the beginning that I was trying to pass off ... some other stone. What doubts there might be have to be settled first."

After a long silence, Backer said, "Then of course you understand that it is very unlikely that the stone can be sold again in this form."

Haig winced. "Do you mean it will have to be recut into smaller stones?"

"No. That would lose too many carats. I will have to modify it slightly, and that will diminish its value. Also, you realize that if I buy it from you, I will give you only about seventy-five percent of what I think I can get for it. Otherwise, it will not be worth the effort."

"Of course. But if you buy it, you'll be sure it's all right, and I won't hear about it again?"

"Yes. It will still be a very valuable stone after I have modified it. You will lose perhaps forty or fifty thousand dollars. But that is inevitable unless you are willing to submit to a prolonged public scrutiny concerning the origins of this stone ..."

"I won't be able to satisfy such a scrutiny. I can assure you that I have the stone legally. Tomorrow, you'll have confirmation from the lab that it's not a fake. Couldn't another diamond have been cut from a rough stone to the same pattern as the *Pietra*?"

"Nobody who knows diamonds would believe it. You could come close to the pattern, but not with this absolute precision – the exact weight, the dimensions of the table ... I cannot explain it and I take it that you *will* not, Mr. Haig, and so ..."

"Then what will it be worth when you have modified it?"

Backer made some sketches and then began to jot down figures. He pushed a slip of paper towards Haigs.

"The larger figure is what I think you might get if you can wait until I have completed my work on it. The smaller figure is what I am prepared to guarantee you. I could have the money for you within a day after the lab work is done."

The two men bent over the figures silently in the darkening

room. Backer rose, left the room, returned with a cut crystal decanter and two tiny cut crystal glasses.

"Whisky?" he asked.

"I don't drink, but thank you very much." Haig frowned at the numbers another minute or less and then said, "I'm sorry; I don't know why I took so long; pure old fashioned greed, I suppose. The smaller figure is quite adequate. I have to get back to work as soon as I can."

For a moment Haig flirted with the idea of asking Backer to have dinner. He needed someone to talk to. The trouble was, what he needed to talk about was the one thing he could *not* talk about, perhaps not even to Rob Nelson – not yet – although Nelson's discretion was quite exceptional, would have been excellent in a priest or a lawyer, and was unbelievable in a journalist. At least he could tell Rob about the Medici Museum ... up to a point. The rest of it he hardly believed himself, any more than Backer had believed in the stone when the grey cloth had first been unfolded. He could wait, he decided. The stone would be back from the lab tomorrow, the money would change hands, then he'd fly home and be in his own lab by Sunday.

He provided Backer with names and telephone numbers in Montreal where his character and reliability could be verified. Backer gave him a receipt for the stone. Haig saw that it contained a description, with weight and measurements, but there was no mention of the price that had been agreed on.

"Shouldn't I have some kind of conditional letter of agreement of sale?" he asked.

"Professor Haig, in the diamond industry a sale is agreed to orally and then we shake hands. It is our tradition."

Haig smiled broadly. He reached out his hand. "Then it's agreed," he said.

"So." Backer courteously opened the door and Haig started slowly down the stairs, began to trot as the door closed behind him, and was taking the stairs three at a time before he reached the bottom. He slowed to a decorous amble as he came out into the yard and passed the security hut, where the guard recognized him and nodded as he went by. Then, once out in the Amsteldyk and out of sight of the Backer establishment he ran half a block at full speed, stopped in front of a shop window, and, looking at his reflection in the glass, grinned at himself fiercely: "Pinch my boy, you're going to make it! You're going to make it!"

Then he walked quickly back to his hotel, past the bluff-bowed barges with their rudders folded alongside like huge walrus asleep in the Amstel River, *hut-hutt-hutting* every few blocks deep in his throat.

3

"What would I do," Daisy Nelson asked herself, "If some guy came to me to take his case, and started off with a story like this?"

In the watchful part of her mind, Daisy found it curious that she should yield so readily to Rob's familiar wizardry as a story-teller. She thought it interesting that he, in such bizarre circumstances, instead of coming quickly to whatever point he was leading up to, should use the old tricks of suspense and imagined dialogue that had always made him a popular dinner guest.

Then she remembered the funeral of her father's closest friend who had been killed gliding, and how, at that funeral supper, another member of the gliding club had told a hilarious story with himself as the butt, and how the grieving family had laughed louder than the guests, who were embarrassed because the story was about crashes and near-crashes in a glider. And she recalled seeing clearly at the time how badly the family needed a story, needed an involvement in adventure to take them out of their grieving, and she saw that this was happening to her now, the same need, the same escape.

Still, she was irritated with Rob's enthusiasm for story-telling when the circumstances called for lucid explanation. Shuddering with the effort, she told herself, "treat him like a client." It was a way of grasping for sanity.

"You could have saved me the pain of your death!" she said sharply, gulping air to help steady her. "Why do I need all this background? You're working on me, aren't you; trying to get on my good side after what you've done to me, is that it?"

"Babe, Babe! You're not in court now, never mind the cross-examination! Give me some time."

"Time!" she burst out, "Time! You're having too good a time, that's the trouble. It's another spellbinding Rob Nelson story, goddam it, but it doesn't explain how you could be dead this afternoon and alive tonight!"

Then she heard the echo of her own words, and their meaning overwhelmed her with fear and vertigo. She fought for control but her face was stricken. Seeing the desolation in her eyes, the man moved tentatively toward her with his hands open, his arms partly stretched out offering an embrace. She shook her head and held him off with her eyes.

"I want you to hold me," she said brokenly. "God, you know how I do. But I'm too afraid, and you're not helping me to understand!" She yelled the last words at him with the explosion of another sob.

"Shhh, shhh," the man said. "I told you it would take time."

"Anyway, what are you shushing me for," she said, a little more firmly. "I noticed that before."

"We've got to get out of here before it gets light. Both of us together. That gives us about eight hours. I don't think it will take that long to tell you all this, but I'm not taking chances on any short cut. If you're going to believe it, you'll have to have it all. I want to make damn sure you've got it all because I want you with me when I go. And you're not going to go with me till you're sure, are you?"

She shook her head and bit on a sodden Kleenex. "Go where, by the way?"

"If you say you'll come, then we can discuss that. Meanwhile, I don't want nosy neighbors running in to see if the widow's got hysterics and needs a needle, okay?"

Although the words were insulting, the tone was not. Rob — if it was Rob, and she was increasingly comfortable with the idea that it was — said it directly and with an unpretentious kindness. His compressed smile was now a smile she liked; it had a vulnerability to it. It was different from the big smile of the storyteller, the showoff smile, the conning smile; this was a smile that asked something back. So one more time — how many one more times had there been? — she made herself a compact to go along with Rob, to give him another chance.

"Solid, reliable Daisy," she thought, "with a weakness for incorrigibles, especially when they were supplicating."

But aloud she said, feeling like taking charge as much as the night would allow, "I need some more coffee, and you better go easy on the sauce."

He looked regretfully at his whisky glass and pushed it away with one finger.

As she moved toward the stove, Daisy perceived something in his manner now, his posture, something intent, urgent and patient at the same time. She said, "What you're going to tell me is immense, isn't it. It's bigger than ..."

"Yes."

She peeled the top off a fresh can of coffee. The man said, "Can I go on? Can you stick with it? Not too many fantasies cutting in and making it hard to listen?"

It was a characteristic insight, she thought; no one else knew her so well. "It's all right if you keep talking," she said with some gratitude. But the wariness had not completely left her. "Can I ask questions?"

"No, it's too soon for that, I think. Well ... maybe not. What questions?"

"How much did Pinch get for the stone?"

"Just under two million. One-point-eight."

"Dollars?"

He nodded. Daisy blew hard through her lips.

"Why did he need it so urgently?"

"Okay, that puts us back on the main line so I'll have to do some more filling in."

Daisy sat down to wait for the water to boil and the man went on.

"You know Pinch never made full professor."

"I think I knew that. Didn't publish enough?"

"That's right. Just a minute, let me show you something." He headed for the living room, stopped half-way through the door, reached his hand around to find the light switch, switched it off, crossed the room, closed the window drapes firmly and then went to the desk in the corner and pulled out a file. He showed Daisy the file, marked HAIG, J.A., and thumbed a paragraph on the top sheet of notes. "Read that."

She read: B.A. McGill 1933. B.Sc. Toronto 1935. Ph.D.

M.I.T. 1939. "Electronic Diffraction Patterns in the Analysis of Crystalline Molecular Structure" (Unpublished).

Publications: "Practical Wireless Transmission of Three-Dimensional Images" 1946; "Structural Instability in Diamond and Some Other Crystals" 1948; "Laser Diffraction and Molecular Analysis" 1950, "Laser Energy Quanta Measurement" 1952, "On the Theoretical Possibility of the Teletransmission of Physical Objects" 1954.

Daisy said, " 'The Teletransmission of Physical Objects;' does that mean what it says?"

"Yes it does."

"Moving objects themselves, not images."

"Yes."

He looked a little odd, almost as if he were blushing. Daisy decided to let it pass rather than interrupt his sequence of the story, and so she said, "What happened between '39 and '46, was he in the army?"

"National Research Council. Mostly submarine detection research and all top secret. It got him started on 3-D television, as a matter of fact."

"Then nothing for the past twenty-two years. Why?" Asking questions; that felt much better.

The man shifted in his chair. He had lost his embarrassed look; it had stayed faintly in his eyes only a moment and then vanished. He said, "That's an important part of it. When I first met Pinch I was working on *Sputnik and After*."

He had met Daisy through that film too, and for a moment she wondered awkwardly whether he had forgotten. She had been in the film, a 1958 television documentary on scientific education which was a huge North American issue after the Russians showed, by successfully orbiting the first man-made satellite earlier that year, how far ahead of the United States they had advanced in their science.

For a moment she saw quite vividly her high school science classroom, a TV film créw visiting for the day, with lights and a big brown camera. There was a stocky production assistant who eyed her with a frankness that made her ears hot, a young man who seemed to be the only one in the group besides the cameraman who had any real confidence in himself, and who kept quietly advising both the writer-interviewer and the director in an adroit way, not offensively, earning himself nods of gratitude and agreement. "He must be making them think *they* thought of it," she had perceptively mused at the time. It was four years later, when she was nearly twenty, that she and Rob met again and fell in love and were married within the month. She nodded out of the reverie.

"Sorry," she muttered, got the coffee, poured, and listened.

The man said, "I was square enough then that I thought Pinch's ideas about scientific education were a bit far out. And I wondered why he took any interest in me, a young production assistant on a documentary crew. I went around McGill asking some questions: 'Was it legit? Was he queer? What was his track record as a teacher?' I bought a few drinks for some of the other physics professors and picked up what I could. My producer was going to practically star Pinch in a network film, and I had the feeling he was strange, and people might come along after and say, 'You blew it using that nut.'

"What I found out was that the 1954 paper about teletransmission had brought Pinch instant ridicule. In the scientific community, he'd been pretty hot stuff until then. People couldn't believe it wasn't a hoax. But, when they found out that Pinch meant what he said – that there was a theoretical basis for investigating the possibility of sending objects from one place to another by radio waves – they were outraged."

Daisy said, "It's not very surprising, is it? Except that Pinch is so, well, solid. And sensible and straight-ahead."

"And good-humoured."

"Yes."

"Which is what saved him. Tough Scots' common sense. Freethinker's common sense. Plus an immense intuitive capacity, a doggedness, to follow through on his own hunches. If it hadn't been for . . ."

He stopped and sipped the scalding coffee.

Some vagrant current of air in the house brought to Daisy's nostrils the scent of funeral carnations. She had to make an effort to keep at bay images of a body on a slab, a coffin, the funeral's bitter emptiness. She tried again to focus her attention on the man's words, to set aside her doubts about her motives. She said, "If Pinch is so determined, why didn't he publish any more on this ... on the transmission of objects?"

"You're ahead of me now. The thing really is ..." Recalled excitement was making his face glow; he was immensely amused in the telling of it. "The thing really is: Pinch had already done it!"

"Done it! transmitted objects by radio?"

"By wire, at that time, radio not long after. This is where the diamonds come in."

"He used them to transmit? As samples, as test objects?"

"Not at first. In the beginnning he was working on 3-D picture transmission. He had all the early work on TV available to him and he'd gotten the idea that the laser might have properties that would make a 3-D image possible without wearing polarized glasses – like holographs."

"I don't know about holographs."

"Never mind for the moment. Here's the important thing. Pinch began to develop another form of radiation; he's tried to explain it to me, and I'm getting pretty sophisticated in it, but he never wanted to let me in on the way the amplifier was constructed, so I'm only one-third of the way through the door on a theoretical level: it's a high-energy field radiation.

"Try this," the man said. "The molecular structure of a crystal is sort of nodes and spaces. The field radiation causes the nodes to give off an echo. But it just passes through the other parts as though they were transparent, and then the target sends the signal to a computer that works out the mass and depth from the relationship between the 'opaque' nodes and the 'transparent' linkages. If the radiation is too intense, by the way, the nodes can be weakened and the color or mass of the stone will change. That's what that paper about instability grew out of. I can't explain much more."

"I couldn't handle much more."

"You don't need it anyway. The important thing is, this radiation was pretty potent, and Pinch was using cheap diamonds, industrials, because they could stand the heat and produced a good 3-D picture. Then one of the diamonds disappeared after he tried to transmit its picture three-dimensionally with a new form of this radiation."

"Evaporated?"

"That's what Pinch thought at first. He was very excited. Possibly he'd created a ray-gun. He'd spent enough time on military projects that he could recognize an interesting weapon when he saw one, and if this non-laser thing could volatize a diamond, it might be something important for the defense department. Then he went looking for the remains of the diamond inside the photo-chamber – it was a closed metal chamber. The object to be photographed was on a fine tungsten alloy target in this chamber."

"And?"

"And he vacuum-cleaned the inside of the chamber and put the vacuum cleaner filter under the microscope and there was nothing. No carbon particles, no diamond particles, no ash, nothing. There'd been no transmitted picture. The target hadn't received any pattern."

"It might have just burned, carbon dioxide, nothing to see."

"Pinch thought that for a moment too. But this chamber was airtight. Absolutely sealed. And when he opened it there was no rush of gas. If it had been full of volatized gaseous carbon, or CO_2 or both, the door would've damn near blown off."

"So where was the diamond?"

"All over the outside of the chamber."

"All over the *outside*!"

"In the form of carbon molecules: some of them free, some of them embedded in the steel shell of the chamber, some of them alloyed with the steel. It was a hell of a detective story that led to finding them, but that's going to take too long. What matters is, Pinch realized there was only one way they could have got out through a non-porous substance: they had to have been transmitted electrically, broken down into electrons and protons somehow by this new form of beam, and then reconstituted on the outside of the chamber, which is pretty highly charged after the beam is turned on. Anyway, let me compress it a bit.

"Pinch worked almost entirely on his own for the next sixteen years, until he got me involved. The man's patience is incredible. Most of those sixteen years were years of failure. It only began to come together about the summer of '69. The reason he didn't publish anymore was the university didn't want his publications after that crazy paper. That's what *they* say. And he'd been burned. The ridicule and the rejection made him realize he had to work in secret or he'd be in real trouble. He didn't want anybody to know what he was up to before he could demonstrate, because, so far, he didn't really understand what it was he had hold of. Knew he could do it – faith mostly – but didn't know why."

"People must have had some idea what he was working on."

"No, because that's when he moved the lab to his house. That's why we were always working at the house. He continued teaching me because he had to eat and buy materials, but he never did any more research at the university, and if he hadn't had tenure already they would've fired him."

As the man went on to describe how Pinch had finally found a way to collect the secondary radiation, the pattern of nodes and linkage, and the matter-turned-to-energy of the disintegrating diamond, and then to reconstitute the stone intact on a second target in a second chamber, Daisy's mind began to wander.

She had heard Rob's voice saying something about the huge amounts of money Pinch's invention could generate. The reference to money, now, in this context with so much at stake between two people, with a life and a death to be explained, seemed bizarre to Daisy, and its inappropriateness triggered off another uncontrollable memory search by her tired brain, which seemed intent upon throwing up images and sounds designed to make her anxious.

Rob's parting words as he left to work full-time with Pinch had been that he would bring back "the only really important documentary of my life," and "make our fortune." Daisy was cynical about money. She knew Rob to be a bit weak in the head about fast money. There had been hints about a mysterious source of investment funds. Now something about those funds swirled indistinctly in her brain and made her uneasy; something about people in New York ...

Early in 1970 Rob had thrown himself with his customary impulsive, unexamined enthusiasm into a film about organized crime in the US. And now Daisy recalled snatches of conversations overheard during the first months of his full-time involvement with Pinch; conversations which had not made sense at the time but, as she heard them again in memory, and remembered how Rob hastily changed the subject when she would come into the room where he was on the phone, seemed to be connected with the people in New York whom Rob had been so excited to be associated with and whom Daisy had refused to meet as she would refuse to touch something fetid.

And then helplessly she saw again in her mind the livid body on the slab at the morgue, and she felt nauseous and realized that she had lost the thread of Rob's story, and instead of apologizing burst out at him.

"Why the hell did you keep me in the dark all this time! When did I ever betray your confidence? Why couldn't you have told me what was going on? And who was that man, that ... your double in the morgue? I can't concentrate on all this stuff about diamonds until you clear up who that person was and what it's got to do with us now!"

She glared at him. He moved toward her. She shook her head menacingly but he came and knelt on the floor beside her chair. She sat rigid as he put his arms around her. He felt the hardness of her back muscles and knew the signal but he stayed on his knees anyway and lifted his left hand to knead the tightness across her shoulders. She wondered if he had ever thought, during those weeks of her lonely waiting, how she must have been physically yearning for his fingers on her shoulders, at the base of her neck, to undo the knots of muscular tension that gripped her so implacably as her anxiety grew day by day. Once at a conference in the boardroom during that time, she had found herself leaning back toward a man who was standing inches behind her chair talking to someone else across the table, hoping he would reach out and massage her shoulders. Now, despite her anger, she could hold out no more than a moment; then she yielded to the soothing hands and began to cry softly and then came into the man's arms.

"Babe, you know it is me all right. Don't you."

"Of course I do Rob, of course I do. But I'm still in bad shape. Can't you tell it faster?"

Then she sat up straight and scared. "You said we had to leave here before morning," she whispered sharply. "Everything's not all right, is it!"

"Not yet, no."

"Then tell me about that other man! Are his friends after you? What's going to happen if we don't leave? Where are we going?"

"All those things are tied together. The answer to the other man won't make sense until you've heard the rest. I can't tell you yet. You'll see why. I can't let things get out of order."

"Rob, for God's sake!"

"Trust me."

"Trusting you hasn't always been very satisfactory."

"I've changed. Anyway, the only times you were disappointed in trusting me were when your instinct told you not to but you did anyway."

She was silent.

"There are no women involved in this thing."

Only over a woman had he betrayed her. Never in anything else.

"Such a gulf has opened between us," she thought, "stayed open for so long, how can I believe the betrayals are over, or believe anything he says?" But as his hands continued to send waves of relaxation from her shoulders throughout her body, and the roughness of his cheek worked against her temple like a hard towel and the smell of him close was like a drug, she told herself that perhaps she didn't have to trust his words, perhaps she didn't have to rely on the truth all the time. If she knew that when the lines *were* open between them, the flow was unique, then that was enough. Her body slumped still more softly against him.

But when he said, "What does your instinct tell you now?" her mind interfered again, and she stiffened very slightly and answered: "To be careful."

"Then you shouldn't rush me," he said.

"Rob, that's an intellectual goddam thing to say."

"Maybe it is. But all the same," he whispered, "don't rush me. You've got to hear all of it."

She sighed and drew away from him gently.

"Go on then," she said flatly.

He really was more serious this time. She could tell by the set of his body in the chair. He was more committed to saying what he had to as fully and as fast as he could, and to getting through to her. She knew that this was what she needed to believe, but she believed it anyway. Not without watchfulness. She even regretted having yielded to his hands; it had been an interruption more than an interlude. Seriousness now matched seriousness. She was demanding of him that he strip away from his narrative everything except what counted absolutely. She knew that she was slipping into a kind of mental second wind. She felt more alert and optimistic than she had for months. Even though, as his voice went on with a quiet urgency, she was again aware of other currents of remembered conversation, other voices running through her mind in counterpoint to Rob's, voices of strange women on the telephone, Pinch's voice, once a tough New York voice saying Nelson better call back fast if he knew what was good for him, Rob's refusal to explain.

She was mentally standing back from the scene at the kitchen table. She listened to the man telling her how Pinch had learned to send the diamonds from one chamber to another without damage; how he had gone on to work with more complex substances until he was able to transmit complicated structures including cellulose and finally dead protein; how when he tried to work with minute living organisms – paramecia and amoebae – they would disappear from the first chamber and reappear in the second chamber intact, but invariably dead for no discernible reason. Yet she remained outside herself, no longer drawn into the telling, and she found satisfaction in her immunity. She began to doubt the story now. And because the man relating it appeared to be telling what he believed, she coldly asked herself if he was sane.

Her mind was satisfied that this was her husband; no impostor could know what he knew, smell as he smelled, display the exactly minute gesture and tone and style, find a file on the desk in seconds, find the trigger in her back muscles that broke for a moment her resolve to stay distant. So it was Rob, alive; yet she felt lonelier than she had when she thought the dead body on the slab to be him.

She drew in a deep breath. The man paused in his telling. "You all right?"

"Yes. Get on with it."

She could listen to him carefully, critically, ask useful questions, supply a missing word when he groped, and at the same time pursue a line of private reflective inquiry as important to be engaged in as was Rob's story to be told. Even though the need for her private inquiry contained more than a tincture of fear, there was satisfaction in being able to carry it forward.

As the story unfolded and she was told how much of this man, her lover, her husband, had been kept secret from her for so long, she was left feeling as though she existed alone on a dead planet in a deserted quadrant of the universe. And yet she felt strong; she could survive in that sunless place, she thought.

After a while she interrupted him. "Listen, I don't know what it is you're leading up to, but I think I'm afraid to hear it."

He opened his mouth and made a protesting gesture, but she stopped him again.

"I know I've got to hear it and I will. But even if it comes out all right, whatever it is, and even if I believe you, I'm not sure I'm ready to go away with you."

He winced.

Daisy said, "My whole life has been turned inside out twice in the last three days. It's nearly killing me but I don't think it's going to. Something else has just begun to happen in my head."

He looked impatient but said nothing.

"I'm feeling very strong in spite of it all, Rob. And not very close to you right now. Very alone and very strong and very cautious. You came in here tonight almost laughing, do you know that? Do you know how that made me feel? You used to try to laugh it off when I'd get a poisonous letter from some bitch at the network who thought you were about to run off with her and took it out on me when you came back home again. You laughed when they told you you'd probably lose the sight of your eye."

"Of course I laughed. I laugh when I'm in a tight spot. It gives me a chance to get on top of things, to grab for a foothold ..."

"Yes, it gives *you*. You were always very quick to see what a situation could give you."

There was a heated silence. Daisy sensed the man's anger and his guilt and she was not without sympathy, even though she was determined to be hard on him for as long as it took to establish some new ground rules.

She perceived the change in the air outside the house. A creeping dampness. She heard the faint breath of the pilot flame in the stove and the sound of a distant airplane. She smelled coffee and whisky and Rob's sweat and her own sour body smells after a day of too much strain.

He said tightly, "You always blamed me for what happened to my eye, didn't you."

"I never said that."

"No. But you blamed me. You did your best by me all the way, but in the end you felt it was my fault. You felt I'd somehow done something to you. Isn't that right?"

"If you hadn't been so careless and so arrogant you would have believed the lab technician and let him handle that sodium. Instead you had to jump in and fool with it yourself and bend over it to line up your bloody camera shot. But what you were really doing was proving that you knew better than anyone else on that set."

"Daisy, I've heard all this before! Do you still blame me for that? You blamed me for a lot of things."

"You did a lot of things."

"You could have walked out on me."

"I nearly did. Several times."

He waited.

She looked up at the dark window and then at the electric clock grinding quietly on the wall. She said, "Time is crucial now, isn't it. Do you think this is a waste of time?"

He made a grimace but didn't answer.

"We never said any of these things to each other," Daisy said quietly.

He answered eagerly, "If you'll come with me, we can say all the things we never said."

"You've made promises before."

"And I broke them. And you still stuck with me."

"Because you were the only one I wanted to stick to. Because when we were really *on* together, I felt totally alive. Because you made my body sing and I think you sang with me then, didn't you."

He agreed with his eye but said nothing; he looked terribly anxious.

"And I kept on hoping. As angry and as lost as I got sometimes, I kept on hoping you would grow up and stop doing things that made me feel so far away from you."

The man said, "It's different now. A lot has happened. You'll see. Let me go on."

As he began to talk again, intensely, taking her with him through the bizarre experience he had lived in these last silent weeks, her flicker of doubt about his sanity returned. Not because of his manner; she knew the manner and it was in some ways the best of Rob Nelson: thinking it out carefully, telling it cleanly now. No, his manner was lucid enough. But the story was less and less acceptable; she could not stop herself thinking: *"If he believes that he's telling me something that really happened, then he must be out of his mind."*

4

Some considerable time after the onset of their collaboration, Rob Nelson and John Alexander Haig sat over the remains of a late afternoon tea-and-store-bought biscuits in the professor's bleak grey stone house on the north side of Pine Avenue, near the hospital and the campus, on the slopes of the Montreal mountain. There was a fire burning low in the brick fireplace. Orange flicker from it dappled the panelled walls. The mood was companionable, although the tone of the conversation was not. A listener unacquainted with the normal style of discourse between the two would have heard hostility in the words they said to each other, and would have missed what was really going on.

"You should never have introduced me to her. It was none of your business."

"You were pleased enough to be introduced. And I know she spent last week with you when I was in New York. I saw her stuff in the bathroom. You can still smell her perfume in the kitchen, on your coat, all over the house. I thought things were going great. I was really pleased. Now you say she's not coming back."

"I told her not to."

"You *told* her! Jesus, Pinch!"

"Actually, I asked her. It was very hard."

"But why?"

"Because ... Rob, I asked her to leave because she wanted to stay. You wouldn't understand that."

Rob snorted. Haig stared into the fire and looked miserable. The last light was dying in the street outside. If the scientist had been looking at his friend instead of trying to penetrate eternity in a shifting pattern of orange and blue and yellow flame, he might have been surprised to see how grave the tough young face had become, how wet the blinking eye seemed for a moment. Or perhaps he would not have been surprised.

Rob cleared his throat. "As a matter of fact, I understand it better than you ever will," he told Haig. "You lose your nerve. You can't commit because you're always thinking of where it'll lead. You're always figuring results. You don't know how to give in to it, lose control."

The scientist chewed at the edge of his moustache for a while. Then he said, quietly, "The bed's not always empty, as you are well aware. And God knows it's an unexpected loss of control that's going on right here for me to discuss my private life with someone like you who has an absolute marvel of a wife and can't be faithful to her three months running."

"What the hell do you know," Rob said, good naturedly.

"I disapprove, all the same."

"You?"

"I'm not married," Pinch said stonily.

Rob stared at his friend with a mixture of affection and impatience. Haig was leaving for Rome that night. Rob had flown in earlier in the day from New York to see him off. Daisy was expected from Toronto to spend the long holiday weekend with Rob in the Laurentians; she would pick them up at eight-thirty in a rented car and drive them to the airport in time for Haig's flight. Then Rob hoped he and his wife would head for an inn in the mountains and a long and much delayed renewal, and he found himself impatient for that and impatient with Haig's deviousness about the real purpose of his trip to Rome, and with all this impatience and distraction he was becoming bad-tempered as well.

Finally, although he knew that breaches of protocol irritated Haig, Rob said, "If I'm going to become your collaborator, don't you think you should give me a progress report?"

"Where did you get the idea you were to be my collaborator?" Haig asked. "I thought we were agreed on a contract: I do the research, you film the experiments ..."

"Videotape the experiments," Rob corrected.

"Right, videotape it all as part of the scientific record of my work, and the tapes belong–"

"To both of us."

"But with my control," Haig said firmly.

"Come on, Pinch! This is all agreed, and I say we're going to be collaborators. You didn't need me just to tape the work; you could have done that yourself. You want another perception involved all along. You're just fencing. Tell me what's going to happen in Rome."

"Robbie my dear, nobody can predict the future, not even me."

"Cut the crap, Pinch."

Haig chuckled, *hut hut hut hut*. But then he looked serious over his glasses and reached across to squeeze Rob's arm. Rob waited.

Haig said, "For the first time in months I'm beginning to feel profoundly optimistic about the work."

Rob was baffled. "You've always been optimistic. Otherwise, how the hell could you have kept on all these years?"

"Because I had to. But what I didn't tell you – and Robbie I'm sorry I didn't tell you because it looks like not trusting you – is, I'm out of money."

"I knew you were interested in getting some backing for the next stretch – all that new equipment – but you never let on."

"I was ashamed. Isn't it strange, the old things that hang on in your psyche? You see, McGill has fired me. I haven't even got living money."

"You had tenure."

"But I wasn't teaching; I wasn't publishing; tenure isn't absolute."

"How did you keep going at all?"

"I mortgaged the house. And now that's nearly used up. I was getting very desperate. Until I thought of your friend from New York."

"Who?"

"Appolinari."

"Did you give him a demonstration?"

"At first he was sceptical. But he did agree to come to the lab to see for himself."

"That's a very tricky customer. You know who he works for."

"Don't be redundant. You told me all about those people

when you were shooting *Rackets Don't Make Noise*. I'm a pretty tricky customer myself when the chips are down."

"No you're not."

"I mean I can handle myself."

"I wish I thought so."

"All right, Rob. Try this." Haig looked a little testy. "You know them. You know what they would want. Full control, eh? Nothing for me but a royalty. That's not how he described it, but that's what I saw. Those are very tough, greedy men, but I'm tough too, and hold all the cards. They know I could go public, and this time they're greedy enough to want any share they can get their hands on."

"So?"

"I said I'd only go on if they could get international financing, a lot of it, from people who know it's high risk and who'll come in for the money, with me still in control."

"How much?"

"I'm asking two million."

Rob didn't blink. "I meant how much do they get back?"

"That depends."

"I know, 'It depends,' but suppose everything works and the project starts to earn. What do they get?"

"Seventy-five percent."

"*Seventy-five percent!* The hell you're tricky – you've been had!" Rob was red-faced and furious.

"Easy, lad. It's not signed and sealed. I've got a card or two to play yet. The thing is, I've still got control. It's my project, and I keep the books."

Rob looked glum. "Why Rome?"

"Because Appolinari's people have been trying to tie into big European money and this is going to be their *entré*. He's got five investors interested. It's my work that's turned the trick, do you see it now?"

"Who are they?"

"A Swede, a German, a Frenchman, two Italians, all looking for high-risk, high-return, world-shaking investment. They want a demonstration. They want it there, on their turf, and I'm going to give it to them."

"How? You can't take the lab with you."

"I can take part of it. I airshipped the chambers yesterday. Obviously I can't take the whole amplifier so I'll just take the crucial parts: the circuit boards and the laser matrix. They only weigh a few pounds and I'll take them in my baggage. I've an agreement from Appolinari to set me up for a month before I have to show my wares. He's got an empty store in a deserted shopping plaza. I'll have enough time to buy what I need and build an amplifier and test it before the big day. A month tomorrow they're gathering. And Appolinari has quite a sense of showmanship. Have you heard of the *Pietra della Reconcili-azione?*"

Rob shook his head.

"It's a big blue diamond; one of the world's finest. Appolinari and one of the Italian investors share a cousin who belongs to the family that owns it, or owned it. They gave it to the Medici Museum about twenty years ago. Now, when I told Appolinari I would use industrial diamonds for the test, he got the notion that the whole thing would be much more effective if they could get the *Pietra* out of the museum for a few hours and use it. It's absolutely distinctive, do you see? Couldn't be copied. Couldn't be mistaken for something else. Industrials all look the same."

"And how are they going to get it out of the museum?"

"Borrow it, under guard, which makes it better from the point of view of security in the test. You see, the investor in question – from the family who owned the diamond – is also chairman of the Board of Governors of the museum. Appolinari thinks we can get a million dollars from these men. And Appolinari is going to look after the security while I get things ready. He's bringing a few of his professional friends from New York."

Rob said seriously, "I hope you know these men are very dangerous. I'm glad you haven't borrowed any money from them!"

Haig looked evasive and Rob groaned. "If anything goes wrong, Pinch."

"It won't."

"Some of your early diamonds vaporized."

"Appolinari doesn't know that. He's seen the industrials transmitted half a dozen times. He described the process to Ginori – that's his contact in Rome. Either they travel or they don't. Nothing will go wrong, Rob!"

"But if it did, Appolinari would think you stole the stone. He's a mean one, Pinch. When I was working on the film, he told me if I ever led him up the garden path I'd better have my life insurance paid up."

Haig curled his upper lip under his lower teeth and tried to bite his moustache.

Rob said, "Suppose they steal the amplifier?"

"Ach, Rob! Nobody but me knows how to set up the system and operate it; that's my safeguard. And if anything should happen to me, you'll be hearing from my lawyer. He has copies of all the design work and a kind of operating manual that would be comprehensible to only two or three men in the world, that I know of. It would be up to you to decide who carries it on. I've made you my scientific executor. I trust you'll accept."

Haig reached across the table and took Rob's hand in both his and pressed it hard. Rob returned the pressure but he did not speak. The two men sat in silence for some minutes. Their thoughts were broken by the door bell. Rob went to the window. Daisy was below, looking up at the window. Rob shook the curtain to attract her attention, and waved and blew a kiss. He turned back to the room. "Let's go," he said to Haig, and helped him on with his coat.

They accompanied him to the airline concourse, Haig and Rob walking ahead, Rob carrying Haig's worn brown attaché case and occasionally looking at the tall scientist with a respectful affection.

Daisy thought, "There is no one else in the world he looks at like that." She wondered if what she felt was a touch of jealousy. She knew that her curiosity about their relationship was still unsatisfied.

On a sudden impulse she reached forward and took Haig's sleeve and stopped him.

"Listen," she said. "I've just thought of something I want

43

you to do for me. When you get back from Rome, I want you to make some time and stay with us in Toronto for a few days and ..."

Haig, misunderstanding, interrupted her. "Now Daisy, you know I'm no good for just visiting. I'd be pacing up and down and you'd be off at court all the time intimidating some poor policeman and ... you understand."

"Pinch, it might do something for all of us. You and me and Rob. We need to know each other better ... Rob's always coming to you, and I am sometimes, but Pinch, the picture changes when you're on the other guy's territory. You've got Rob a hell of a lot; I think you should let me have you for a while – in the office, come to court with me? That's what *I'm* all about. We could do some important things together."

They came to the security gate.

Haig bent and kissed Daisy's cheek. He shook Rob's hand firmly and walked through the gate. On the other side, while a woman examined his passport, he frowned and fooled with his moustache.

Daisy called, "Pinch!" and threw a quarter across the gate at him. The guard looked annoyed and wagged his head reproachfully but Pinch caught the coin and held it up to the guard.

"For me, Pinch," Daisy called. "Throw it in the Trevi Fountain. I'll do the rest."

5

"Signor Haig, I am the Director of Security of the Medici Museum. My name is Alessandro Cossato." The heavily accented English, spoken in a surprisingly high voice for so evidently hardened a man, had a musical lilt.

Haig shook his hand and motioned him into the lab, an apparently deserted store built into an abandoned row of commercial buildings in the side of a low man-made hill. Appolinari had decided it was so shabby and unlikely a place that no one would suspect what was going on inside. A couple of dubious Renovation in Progress signs had been put up to account for the few comings and goings.

"I understand that there are security considerations regarding your laboratory too, Signor Haig. I am sure you will appreciate the strictness of my own program and so on and so on."

"Please tell me how I can co-operate?"

"Certainly. I have brought two men with me, and I would request your permission to examine the premises before the delegation arrives, which is to say, right now."

"Signor Cossato, as long as your men do not touch or interfere with my electronic equipment, you are quite free to look over the place."

"You do understand that these precautions are for the purpose of protecting you. It is not that we have any suspicion of you, sir."

"Of course not," Haig said, playing along.

"On the other hand, it is, if I may say it, a most unusual incident for the object in question to be removed altogether from its proper place of public trust."

"No doubt," Haig said graciously. "But then, the close involvement of the Conte di Ginori must relieve the museum of any really deep anxiety about moving the stone?"

"Signor Haig," Cossato went on, in a conspiratorially quiet voice, "I have been told by the Count that the stone will be closed in a chamber of some description?"

Haig indicated the sending chamber on its waist-high pedestal, the polished stainless steel shell gleaming in the electric light. The door was open, the clasps hung down and the matte red interior looked like a dark mouth inside.

"And ... perhaps I did not understand His Excellency perfectly, but there is to be a movement of the stone from this chamber to a second chamber?"

Haig pointed to the matching vessel, twelve feet across the room, its interior blue instead of red but in every other respect visibly identical. A heavy shielded cable led from each chamber to its own large instrumented electronic package, a transmitter on the first, a receiver on the second, each with its short dipole antenna and each with a separate amplifier and set of large transformers that were the bulkiest parts of the whole apparatus.

"I am not a scientific man, Signor Haig, but I do not see any way in which the object in question can be removed from the red chamber to the blue chamber."

"There is nothing to see. It moves by radio."

There was a pause. Cossato then said. "You will not think me impolite if I say that I do not exactly believe this ... ?"

Haig shrugged. "Did you believe television?"

"I think," Cossato said, "that you will not misunderstand if I insist that after the demonstration you stay here with me until the object in question is returned to the museum and the necessary examinations are done to verify that all is as it wishes to be?"

"I'll understand perfectly well."

Twenty minutes later a rattle of footsteps sounded on the stairs, and suddenly the room was filled with men. A large uniformed museum guard with holstered pistol entered first. Behind him, Vito Appolinari, in Navy pinstripe and white cuffs, came in like a boxer on his toes, his eyes darting everywhere – at the guard's pistol, at the equipment, at Haig. A whiff of carnation entered the room with him and hung about his dark, intense head. Then came five well-dressed men, two of whom Haig had already met, then two more armed guards, one of them carrying a locked steel box fastened with a chain and a single handcuff to his wrist, and then a thin young man in a slate-colored lab coat, who was the museum's gemologist. The room was very crowded. Haig was introduced to the prospective investors and shook hands with all five. Cossato supervised the unlocking of the case and made it clear to everyone that only the young man in the lab coat would be trusted to handle the stone. Haig asked permission to examine it. "After all, I'm going to be held responsible for its safety while the experiment is in progress," he said levelly.

Cossato raised his eyebrows inquiringly at the tallest member of the investor group, a hawk-nosed, quiet, white-haired man in a grey silk suit. The Conte di Ginori said graciously, "But of course, Cossato."

Haig quickly and efficiently proceeded with an examination. He directed the gemologist to place the stone on a small jeweller's scale and noted the weight – 101 carats – and the temperature, shown by a delicate electronic thermometer with a diode readout that fluctuated constantly, fluttering its red numbers between 22.403 degrees C. and .405, .400, .398 ...

Haig took a Polaroid camera and photographed the stone from two angles. He indicated with signs that the gemologist should apply two small electrodes to it, one at each end of the longer axis. The man looked at Cossato, Cossato looked at di Ginori. Di Ginori nodded, Cossato nodded. The man applied the electrodes. A needle indicated the impedance offered by the stone to the current.

Haig turned to the group.

"Gentlemen," he said, "I am ready to proceed. I feel it only fair to tell you that for a period of micro-seconds, there will be an emission of Xrays from the apparatus, but it will be quite low in Roentgens and will probably not even fog film in a metal-bodied camera, though unshielded film might suffer slightly."

There was an air of prurient curiosity in the room. Haig

addressed the man in the lab coat. "I shall ask you to place the stone in the transmitting chamber, and then station yourself by the receiving chamber" – he pointed – "so that you may extract it as soon as the transmission is achieved."

"And how long will that take?" di Ginori asked politely.

"It is virtually instantaneous, Count. Perhaps you would do us the honor of being the one to open the clasps on the receiving chamber after I close the switch. You will find them hot, but not unpleasantly so. You will see that they are quite cool now."

The count moved to the blue-lined chamber and ran his hands admiringly over the beautifully-worked steel. "I should be proud, Professor Haig. I believe that this is a historic moment for Italy, gentlemen, and that we should all be gratified to be present."

The room was silent. Cossato's face wore a look of the profoundest doubt. The gemologist placed the stone delicately in the red chamber. He looked terribly anxious. He watched like a poised snake while Haig closed the steel door of the gallon-can sized chamber and spun the heavy wingnuts to secure the clasps.

"All right, gentlemen?" Haig said.

Di Ginori smiled broadly, "Please, sir," he said.

Haig felt his heart beating very hard. He scanned the faces. They were all watching him. He picked up a small transmitter box with a telescoping antenna collapsed so that only three inches showed outside the box, said "Now!" and pressed the switch.

There was a loud crack from the receiving antenna.

"Good God!" Haig said in a choked voice. The shielded cable joining the amplifier to the receiving chamber was smoking and the chamber itself appeared suddenly discolored, streaks of blue suffusing the gleaming steel.

"Quick, open it?" Haig shouted.

Di Ginori went to spin the wingnuts and swore sharply as his seared fingertips rebounded from the scorched steel. He fished out a handkerchief and spun the nuts again. The door of the little cylinder swung open. A puff of smoke came out.

It smelled of burnt paint. Di Ginori thrust his handkerchief at the gemologist. "Presto!" he shouted.

The gemologist laid the handkerchief over his hand and thrust inside the chamber. Back came the hand again. The folds of the handkerchief opened. The stone appeared to have made its historic leap intact. He shook his head. "It is not even warm!" he said in astonishment, speaking for the first time.

There were fourteen men in that little room, and thirteen heads crowded for a look at the *Pietra della Reconciliazione*, the first named object in history to move through space by radio waves. The gemologist placed the stone on the scale. The weights were still in the balance pan from the first weighing. The needle rose exactly to the mark; the weight had not changed. One of the investors drew a magnifying glass from his breast pocket and looked hard at the flashing blue stone. Then he passed the glass around. Everyone wanted to look through it, even the guards.

Haig, his heart beating harder than ever, his mind whirling with confusion at the totally unexpected and never-before experienced explosion within the receiver, at the heat that burned the shielding on the cable and discolored the receiving chamber, felt an insane need to use his hands. He stepped back against the transmitting chamber and for no other reason than to be physically busy reached behind him and twirled the wingnuts, staring at the crowd bent over the scale. The wingnuts on the transmitting chamber were cool, quite as they should be. Still reaching behind him absently, his mind racing to try to understand what had happened, he passed his hand over the inner walls of the chamber – they too were cool – and then across the tiny chamber floor. He stiffened. His fingers encountered a cold, facetted object. His heart seemed to stop. His fingers closed around the object, withdrew it from the chamber and slid it quickly into his left-hand trousers pocket. No one was paying any attention: for the moment everyone else in the room was hypnotized by the brilliant blue diamond.

Di Ginori had picked up the Polaroid camera and was focussing on the stone, grinning furiously. Finally he turned and saw Haig standing back and misread the expression on the scientist's face. "A moment of triumph, sir! Come over here! Let us shake your hand. Cossato, take the camera. Take pictures of Professor Haig and me. And all the group," he added as the others buzzed and moved to get close to the scientist and share in the glory of the moment.

Cossato's face was pale and his mouth would not work properly. He still could not believe what had happened. He waved his fingers vaguely at one of his men who took the camera and lined up a shot of the happy investors with a bewildered Haig in their midst.

Di Ginori, still beaming, said. "I have to say, though, Professor, that the heat was somewhat greater than you had led me to anticipate. Was something not quite right? Did you not seem alarmed for a moment? I must say, I was alarmed myself, until the gem – ha, ha – quite wonderfully appeared. I am so full of wonder at the success of this thing that the little smoke seems quite in the remote past. Was that a normal emission of heat? Or ..."

Haig tried to think of something to say. He forced a confident smile and muttered something about voltage irregularities in the Roman power supply occasionally peaking above normal.

More Polaroids were taken and autographed by Haig and the investors and pocketed by di Ginori "to be framed for history when it is possible to reveal what has happened here today."

Everyone present was sworn to solemn oaths of secrecy.

The gemologist replaced the *Pietra della Reconciliazione* in the steel travelling vault and Cossato supervised the locking and the securing of the chain to the armed guard's wrist. More wringing handshakes all round; an appointment to meet in di Ginori's offices later that afternoon to discuss a business agreement; the exodus of the stone, of the perplexed gemologist, of the guards, two of them with their hands on their pistols.

Cossato and Haig were alone in the room.

Cossato had recovered his poise. "You were very alarmed for a few moments when the smoke went up, Signor Haig."

Haig said with an effort, "It doesn't usually get so hot. Once before a stone was discolored. But it was a synthetic and they're much less durable. You can see why I might be anxious. But it was all right after all."

"We shall see," Cossato said slowly. "They still have to test it."

It was noon before one of Cossato's men came back from the museum to report that tests were complete; the stone was undamaged and unchanged in any way by its decomposition and passage through space and reconstruction in the second chamber. Cossata seemed a little disappointed, but he summoned a good grace after a moment, shook hands with Haig, and left the room with a look of doubt still pulling at the edges of his face.

Haig was due in di Ginori's offices at half-past three. He went to the middle of the room, under the bright light over the jeweller's scale, and withdrew the object from his left-hand trousers pocket. He stared at it, immobile for a good three minutes. Then he shook his head suddenly and snapped into action. He put it on the scale, took his notebook and made a note. He tested the impedance and took the temperature. He looked around the room for something to put it in, then shook his head again and popped it back in his pocket.

He opened up a small cloth packet of tools and went furiously to work on the equipment. He withdrew a large glass tube, like an Xray tube, from the back of the transmitter and another from the receiver. The second tube was blackened and smoke-filled. Haig disconnected the heavy transformers. He carried the tubes upstairs to the back of the store, put them down, unlocked the door, checked outside, retrieved the tubes, carried them to a garbage can and dropped them in. Then he brought out the transformers and dropped them hard on the tubes at the bottom of the container, smashing the tubes completely. He struggled to move the garbage can across the dusty floor and out into a small courtyard, a good hiding place since the store, from the front, appeared to be right up against the hill behind it, while an irregularity in the hill had allowed access to the back of only the last three buildings in the row, and here was parked a small station wagon, into the rear of which Haig rolled the garbage can.

Back in the basement he slipped the circuit boards out of the transmitter and receiver, packed them into a small suitcase and locked it. He stared at the two instruments for a moment, shrugged, disconnected them from the cases, then emptied the electronic cores on the floor and jumped on them until they were an unrecognizable mess. Checking the courtyard first, he took them up to the station wagon and stuffed the jumbles of wire and transistors into the garbage can which lay on its side in the back of the wagon.

He returned to the kitchen, found two small wooden packing cases, brought them to the makeshift laboratory, put the two steel chambers in their fittings in the cases and nailed them shut.

Then he swept up, washed his face and hands, patted the hard object in his pocket several times, took it out, stared at it, wrapped it in a handkerchief, put it back in his pocket, sat on a chair to catch his breath, and stared at his watch. A quarter past three.

Footsteps on the stairs at the front, followed by a banging on the door – Appolinari's men.

"Sorry, boys," he said unlocking it for them. "I didn't want anyone coming in while I stripped the gear." He gave the customs slips to one of them and instructed him to airship the two crates to Montreal on the next available flight. "There's a garbage can in the back of the wagon," he said. "Dispose of it somewhere far away from here. In the river tonight. I'm going to di Ginori's now. I may not be back."

Haig threw his few clothes in his bag, methodically checked the contents of his attaché case, ran upstairs into the street, hailed a taxi, stopped at the bus station long enough to put his suitcase in a locker, and then, twenty minutes late, but composed and smiling, was clinking champagne glasses with Appolinari and di Ginori and the others, in a richly furnished office looking out over the thickening moist haze of a still, hot Roman afternoon.

6

"I said, 'If you want to move a house, either you have to have a very big vehicle and a lifting system or else at enormous expense, you take it apart, stone by stone, and move the stones.'"

Rob Nelson looked at Haig while he said this and made a vague wave of impatience. "Pinch, get on with it. I want to know what *they* said!"

Haig's face reflected mischief.

They were sitting on crates in the lab on Pine Avenue, each with a heavy mug of tea. Haig was not to be rushed; he was enjoying the teased creases in Rob's face. He held up a cautioning hand. "Then I said, 'Suppose the stones are locked together by a sort of secret lock, all in the same way, and you suddenly discover a key to that lock, and they all unlock, one by one? Matter is like that,' I told them. 'Molecules hooked into each other, and we have here the key that will open those locks and unhook those hooks all at once without disturbing the sequence, and all the energy needed is that which it takes to turn the key.'"

"Pinch! Cut out the poetry, will you! How the hell did you put them off, that's all I'm interested in. I've got practical reasons to want to know."

"Appolinari?" The older man sustained his flickering mischievous look a moment longer and then relented and leaned forward and spoke seriously. "I couldn't let them know that I didn't really want their money after all; for one thing I wasn't sure about that myself. I had to go to Amsterdam and get that object in my pocket looked at first. For another, with all that money lust in the air, I didn't want to risk getting anybody's back up."

"How much were they going to offer?"

"I'm not sure. Oh, we could've had the million. Or better. Most of the investor group had their pens out. The German prospect, von Borchardt, had already run his own financial prospectus. He's in transportation. When I came in, they were talking about how much they could make by selling short the air freight companies; von Borchardt wanted to know how long it would be before people could be transported by radio so they could make a killing selling short the airlines!"

"To say nothing of selling stock in Haig Industries."

Haig *hut-hut-hutted* softly. "They were already working on a prospectus, as a matter of fact. It hadn't taken them long to figure out the implications. I was impressed. A world-wide system of transportation with zero pollution and no more energy required to take you from here to Tokyo than what it costs to run a TV for half an hour. End of traffic jams and accidents. End of city crowding. End of airplane noise, end of . . ."

"End of airplane business!" Rob interjected. 'End of Boeing. End of Douglas, DeHavilland, General Motors, Ford! Christ, Pinch! Had you really thought about sending people?"

Haig shot him a queer sideways look, which Rob missed. "I just told them to forget about sending people. Too much radiation, I said. Now, the thing is, di Ginori is shrewd, not just about money. He knew I was frightened by that explosion in the lab. I could see that he was holding back, and that played into my hands. You see, he wanted me to reassure him, and I was evasive enough to worry him even more."

"From what you've said about him, he wouldn't let you keep being evasive."

"That's right."

"So you must've told him you weren't really ready yet."

"I said it looked like there were still design problems and that we'd had a pretty narrow escape with the *Pietra della Reconciliazione*. That shook them up. The checkbooks started going back in the pockets like a conjuror's trick. I said a factor had turned up that I'd never encountered before and it had to be ironed out if we were serious about going into business, else we'd have a bunch of lawsuits on our hands if we lost shipments of similar value. Appolinari was pretty red under the ears, Rob, but what could he do?"

Haig ripped off a half-dozen *hut-hut-huts*, but Rob looked worried and screwed up his face and tugged his eyepatch down a fraction.

"He'll get restless. You don't know those people like I do."

"I've paid him off, all his costs for Rome plus a hundred percent. I've promised him that when I'm ready for investors again he'll be the first to know."

"Where does he think you got the money?"

"I said I mortgaged the house. Which is true, if he checks. I never wanted to deal with Appolinari in the first place but I didn't know how else to keep this work going. All I took from him was enough for the demonstration in Rome. It's paid back. I have complete control. Financial, scientific, everything. I've used those people and I'm free of them."

Rob said disgustedly, "How you can pull off a stunt like that and still be so staggeringly naive, I'll never ..." He stared at the sink and chewed the edge of his teacup and the scientist blinked at him for a minute and said nothing.

Rob shrugged. "He'll turn up here. He's not going to let this thing slip out of his hands, is he? Probably want to see your lab notes."

Haig put his finger tips together and looked at the ceiling. "Then we'll have to get a set ready for him," he said after a while. "A fake set, of course, so he'll think we're stuck with our heat problems; that we haven't been able to progress beyond the transmission of diamonds. Anyway, it's time to get back to work."

Rob agreed, to keep the peace, knowing that while some day there would have to be a reckoning, they could buy time now and face the dangers later.

He returned to Toronto on the noon plane. Without making a formal announcement, he went on half time at the network, which was easy since few producers in his section ever worked that hard. Life in the department was tranquil and discursive. Instead of the tireless whirlwind of productivity he had uniquely been, an embarrassment to his indolent colleagues with their commitment not to making programs but to maintaining their careers, Rob, like the rest of them, now came to work only a couple of days a week. This relaxed his fellow-producers and acted as protective coloration for Rob, an apparent member of the Corps of Bureaucratic Survivors. He considered quitting television altogether, but what if Pinch's project failed? He'd better protect his flank, he thought. Once out, with new blood coming along all the time, it might be hard to get back in.

The devious part of his tactic was the invention of a program reason for his absence. The head of Documentary and Public Affairs was one of the few people in the network whom Rob respected and likely the only one who might wonder why Rob was not as productive as before. So Rob started saying that he was ready to begin research on his long talked-of and long postponed major series on the history of science. No one could remember that he had never talked of any history of science, so they nodded and said "Ah, yes, of course," as if recalling something important. Rob had, after all, been spending a lot of time with that odd Haig fellow at McGill.

Consequently, when he asked for it, they assigned a small budget for travel and research, on the History of Science. Now it had an administrative reality. With a docket and a number, Rob could put in modest bills for the Turbo to Montreal and for the contracting of some freelance research here and there, which meant handouts to some of his struggling younger film-making friends. The camouflage had a credibility that should allow him, with the odd pro-forma appearance in the network office, to spend most of his time with Haig for about two years, he thought. "Which should be enough," both he and Haig said then.

And if anyone did ask what he was up to, he simply said, "Research, you know. Full time. Doing the *magnum opus* now."

At first Daisy found the separation not only tolerable but welcome. Morley Stone, a senior partner at her law firm, Nickle, Nicol, Marcus and Hruska, had taken her in as his junior on a fraud and conspiracy case. With the travel entailed – the client was a northern Ontario mining company – and the late hours, she found her temporarily single status just another component of her exhilarating new professional environment.

At first. After a few weeks, after the headiness of the case had worn off, she began to feel a strong need to share with Rob what she was doing, to consult him, to have the perspective of his humor and cynicism, the always useful input of the journalistic questions he inevitably asked her and made her ask of any case in which she became involved. She began to have corrosive doubts about the story of a secret project with Haig. She suspected that there was yet another love affair and that this time it might be serious.

And yet, she told herself, the mysterious project *could* account for his absence and his preoccupation. It did not have to be what she found so threatening: a woman who could take not just his body – that was tolerable from time to time and she herself had enjoyed a few "digressions" since their marriage – but his attention, his mind, his imagination. She always feared that his dreamy distraction when he was "in love" again meant that he would finally drift away from her, permanently, and that she found deeply frightening.

But she could not speak to him about it.

"Stick to the evidence," she scolded herself. After all, he phoned her often and urged her to phone, and every time she did call he was at the lab. And, once in a while, she would get away from the law firm for a weekend, and go to Montreal, and the three of them would dine grandly or go to a movie, and then Rob would return with her to Toronto on the Sunday night, she to dive back into her case and he to pay his dues with a ritual appearance at the network.

Thus, as the weeks accumulated and became months, although she still suspected that Rob was not living a monk's existence in Montreal, Daisy came to accept that it was really Haig's project that kept her husband away from her. Then her curiosity about the nature of the project became difficult to contain and her resentment at being excluded from knowing about it took on a dangerous tint of bitterness and self-pity.

Rob, for the first time in his life, felt he was touching excellence. He told himself, a bit ruefully but not tragically, that he had come to believe his own press notices over the last years. Though the documentaries had rolled from his editing rooms with impressive frequency and to almost unvaried critical acclaim, Rob knew the work was far short of the brilliance claimed for it. Out of the early drive for recognition and a sense of personal power there had grown, in recent years, an urgent need to participate in and contribute to something ... some Work that would meet his own standards of excellence.

He had, in occasional moments of self-examination, wondered if it was possible to satisfy one's own standards: wouldn't the judgment always be moving ahead of achievement? And yet he thought he saw people in other fields who knew they had created something good, who took satisfaction in the completion of a project. The idea of a Work obsessed him then.

He had been looking, looking, looking for excellence, and with Haig perhaps he would find it; not necessarily achieve it for himself, but at least be involved in it.

The first part of the work was the development of a strategy against the possibility that Appolinari might demand to see what progress had been made in solving the problems that had supposedly arisen in Rome. Haig was impatient about this but he was also secretly pleased by the intrigue of it and so he accepted Rob's word for the need of a camouflage.

Once having agreed to create a dummy operation, they built two more small receiving chambers like the one that had nearly blown up in Rome. They deliberately overloaded the current flow into these chambers to discolor their steel shells with heat. The first one responded as expected, the second one blew its door off and nearly suffocated the two men with vaporized paint and carbon particles.

Before they abandoned the diamonds and the basement lab, Haig made several attempts to repeat the event that had made him rich in Amsterdam. He failed. He could not even formulate a satisfactory theoretical explanation. It had something to do with a transmission feedback. He suspected that the particular electromagnetic properties of the great blue diamond played a role but he had no grounds for this hunch. And that was about as far as he could go. He concluded that it was beyond him, at least as long as his mind was really seized by a very different purpose, which it now was.

For in the attic of the old grey house, he and Rob were building a second lab. They brought materials in at night through the back alley. At the rear of the house was a tiny two-person lift that had been boarded over years ago when it stopped working and the former owner had been using the lower floors only. Rob and Haig used a wrecking bar to pry out the nails. They cleaned and greased the gears and cables and installed a silent new electric motor in the basement and thus carried in their equipment unobtrusively and easily.

It was a very different lab from the old one which bespoke geology, electronics, metallurgy – the work of the minerals and electrical disciplines. The new lab was distinctly biological. There was an array of stainless steel sinks and taps, microscopes, a small industrial refrigerator which barely fitted into the lift, and a bank of animal cages of various sizes. Two much larger stainless steel cylindrical chambers began to take shape along with their extensively redesigned transmitters and receivers.

And it was in this lab, in the seventeenth month of the recommencement of the work, that they finally succeeded, after several hundred failures, in transmitting a moldspore from one chamber to another by wireless, and, in a Petri dish, watching it marvellously come to life and in the space of a few hours cover the amber agar with a tracery of fine white lines.

They had proved that at least one very hardy form of life could survive transmission through the ether, and they were exhilarated. They celebrated that night, and Haig agreed to try a glass of smooth, blood-thick *Côte Rôtie* that Rob had chosen. He claimed he did not like it much, but he drank two-thirds of a second glass. And he agreed that they needed a rest, both from the work and from each other; so Rob flew to Toronto on the late plane that same night.

It was one-thirty in the morning when the taxi dropped Rob off at Moore Avenue. The house was dark and the car was in the garage. The city was still and humid, unusually hot for late September. Some distant flashes charged a vague bank of cloud with pink, far to the north, too far to be heard. Rob slipped in the back door and quietly got some ice out of the refrigerator. He pulled out a bottle of scotch, noted ruefully that there were only about six ounces left, poured it over the ice, and sat and sipped in the kitchen, letting the silence of the house slowly transform itself into a musical ground of familiar comforting sounds: the barely discernible grinding of the electric clock on the wall, the soft blowing of the pilot lamp in the gas stove, an electric hum from somewhere unidentified. As his heartbeat slowed and the knots of tension in his body eased away, the sounds came creeping in, one by one, reinforcing the sense of home.

He went into the living room and looked in vain for another bottle of whisky, and then, feeling suddenly weary, put out the lights and climbed the stairs as quietly as he could.

Daisy was sprawled awkwardly on the bed, the sheet thrown back, her thin nightgown clinging damply to her in places. She was breathing heavily. He eased himself silently onto the bed. He bent over her face and, in the light from a streetlamp that was filtering through the leaves of their tree on the front lawn, thought how tired she looked.

The windows were wide open but the curtains hung limp. The air in the room was heavy. Rob could smell whisky as Daisy exhaled, a heavy, sour smell, unfamiliar on her breath.

He lay back and stared at the ceiling. For the first time, as far as he was aware, his wife had apparently drunk herself to sleep. He knew why. He knew that even more uncertainty and loneliness lay ahead of her. It was some time before he went uncomfortably to sleep.

At seven o'clock Daisy groaned and got unsteadily out of bed, shuddered to the bathroom holding her head, and vomited dryly. He heard the medicine cabinet open and a rattle of bottles as she searched for the codeine pills. When she came back into the bedroom her eyes were barely open, and it was only as she crawled onto the bed that she realized Rob was there. She groaned again and eased herself gently onto the pillow and felt for his hand. He gave her fingers a light squeeze.

"Listen," he whispered.

"Oh, Rob. I've never done that before. I'm so hung over!" Her eyes were squeezed shut, her mouth half open and her nose plugged.

"Listen," he said again, trying not to cause any unnecessary vibrations with his voice, "Did you take a 222?"

She showed him two shaky fingers and did not speak.

"Good. They'll work in about ten minutes and you'll go back to sleep and when you wake up your head'll be a lot better. Now . . ."

"But I've got to get to the office," she whimpered.

"No, that's it, Babe. You wouldn't be any good like this. And how long is it since you took any time off from this damn fraud case?"

Daisy groaned and pressed her hands over her eyes.

"You've never taken any time, have you?" he persisted.

She moved her head slowly from side to side.

"And is there anything vital happening this next couple of days?"

A pause, then she slowly indicated no with her head and whispered, "But . . ."

"I'm going to phone Morley and tell him you're under a lot of strain and you need a few days off."

She nodded weakly and the lines in her face relaxed a bit.

"You can go back to sleep. When you feel like driving, we'll go up to the lake and stay through to Monday."

"What about the network?" Daisy muttered.

"I'll go in for a few minutes this morning. As long as somebody sees my body there, that's enough."

He waited a moment. Then he said, "Okay, Babe?"

But she was asleep again.

At noon he left her soaking in a cool tub, and went out in the sweltering streets to fill the car with food and wine for the weekend. The sky was hazy over Toronto. There were some big buildups of clouds in the distance and the occasional faint roll of thunder, felt more than heard.

By half past two they had left the city behind them and were speeding north. The tires hissed on wet pavement still steaming from a small storm that had passed by only minutes before; they could see piles of gleaming cumulus and dark underbelly not far to the east.

It was normally a three-hour drive to Canopy Lake but

this time they took it easy, the way Daisy had always wanted to and Rob had been too impatient for. At Orillia they left the highway and threaded their way along the back roads, the oiltopped network running between fields of tall yellowing uncut corn, or past parched stubble or the black earth of early fall plowing.

They stopped a while for draft beer and some thick roast beef sandwiches on home-made white bread in an old village hotel, and so by the time they reached the turnoff to Canopy Lake it was dusking, still hot under lowering skies, although a spatter of rain was falling, and the dirt road that skirted their side of the long, crooked lake was deserted, the rain drops squirting puffs of dust out of the wheel tracks. They avoided Mac's Marina, having agreed without discussing it that the fewer people they met that weekend the better.

A mile from the turn into the marina, and still four miles from where the road narrowed almost into the vanishing point ending at the well-concealed Nelson cottage, was a public campsite, and in the campsite fairly close to the road, a half-ton truck with a camper van in the box. On the door of the cab was neatly printed

LUCAS RANKIN

Preacher

Petitcodiac, N.B.

Tied across the side of the camper was a cotton banner proclaiming

FIRST ANNUAL TRAVELLING FALL MISSION

Behind the truck, where a grove of birches framed a quick glimpse of the flat calm water, they saw for an instant one or two human figures at a picnic table, a gasoline lantern already lit in the middle of the table, but they were by in a moment and felt grateful that the preacher, if that was who it was, had not even looked up as they passed.

They saw no other cars the rest of the way and the few cottages they passed seemed not to be open. When they pulled in to the overgrown drive at their own small, weathered cedar house, itself almost invisible until you came upon it, and stopped the car, the silence was like a bath.

Rob carried their parcels into the cottage and turned on the power and Daisy busied herself putting things away and making up the bed. When she came out onto the porch to look for Rob, he was standing on the beach taking off the last of his clothes and gazing out at the placid lake.

The water was a single silver-grey surface stretching un-rippled a mile and a half to the black far shore which it perfectly mirrored. Daisy watched the naked, stocky figure step easily into the water and wade slowly out across the shallows. She ran back into the cabin and slipped out of her clothes and picked up a long towel and a bar of soap and, wrapping the towel around her, ran to the beach, feeling weak-limbed and driven.

Rob was further out in the shallows, kneeling now, the water at his shoulders, his back to the shore, his arms spread. Daisy dropped the towel on the sand by his clothes but held on to the soap. She entered the water silently, holding back a shocked hiss as she met the cold, dropped to the surface as soon as there was depth to float, and glided toward the kneeling figure. He heard the ripples and turned his head as she slowed to a stop at his back and brought her knees forward like a bird landing, and found the bottom with her feet and crouched against him shivering, only partly with cold. Her knees brushed against him.

Daisy looked embarrassedly into Rob's eyes. She wondered why this rush of desire should leave her so unexpectedly timid. She said foolishly, "I'll wash your back. I brought soap."

He nodded lazily at her and stood up. The water line was at his navel. He took the soap from her and lathered his arms and belly and crotch while Daisy leaned against him and shivered once or twice again.

But his skin felt very warm.

Rob handed back the soap and bent forward slightly, gazing at the water. The sky was darker now and the water nearly black. Patterns of white bubbles floated slowly outward from the focus of their two bodies. From behind them, the single light in the kitchen of the cabin sent dancing yellow flashes off the ridges of each ripple as it spread away from their small movements.

Daisy rubbed soap over Rob's back and shoulders and then, with a delicious reticence, moved it down the midline of his back until her hand dipped beneath the surface of the water. She leaned her cheek against his neck now and made wide smooth circles back and forth across the swelling of his buttocks. As her hand moved between them then and she sensed his recognition of her intentions first in the tilt back of his head against her own, and then in the quick surge of tautness that her fingers encountered as she brushed forward between his legs with the sliver of soap, back and forth, back and forth, her shyness left her all at once, floated away from her in the lines and swirls of soap on the polished surface of the lake, and she nuzzled him hard and made a low, urgent rumble in her throat and reached her hands in front of him, twining in the hair there and stroking.

Rob swayed with the rhythm of it, back and forth, back and forth, and turned and took her solidly in his arms. He felt the cold hard points of her breasts against his chest and closed his eyes and let out a long relief of breath. She let the weight go from her feet and lifted them and wrapped her legs around him, holding about his neck and pulling hard against him so that he might easily have entered her there in the water, but she stayed only a moment like this and then raised her hands and dropped through his slippery arms into the lake.

She slipped below the surface and turned like a fish and plunged to the bottom, feeling her breasts brush lightly along the rippled sand as she pushed hard with her hands against the water toward the shore.

He was beside her as she came up for breath, swimming easily to her right.

They stood up and ran the last few yards, splashing loud claps of water before them. Scooping up the big towel and the clothes, they ran shivering into the house.

She stood by the bed as he dried her with the long towel. Standing in front of her, facing her, he swept it over her shoulders like a cape and held the two ends and drew it back and forth. She leaned back against the pressure of it and felt the warmth of its rough massage moving down to her thighs, as he stared at her and an expression of wonder and a sleepy smile settled upon his features. Then he gathered the towel in front of her again and patted at her neck and arms and breasts and then knelt and dried her belly and between her legs and the front part of her legs and then dropped the towel and pulled himself softly to her on his knees. He buried his face now, slowly, softly searching with his tongue, and Daisy as slowly and softly sank backward on to the bed and crooned and opened to his searching and then shortly drew him up, holding his pelvis just above her with both hands, to hold back just a moment. He understood and touched her only lightly and took his own weight and she freed a hand and reached under and stroked a moment with finger tips and then her palm, taking his wetness now that formed warmly with each seeking movement of her fingers spreading it over him until she knew that she could wait no longer and so drew him down to touch her again, where she was flowing almost now, or so it felt, out of a hot line like a blade along her perineum.

She said, choked, "I want you to be huge in me," and drew him in and felt her throat hurt with the joy of it and, amazed, felt tears from him on her cheek and rocked with him and rocked him until at last he cried aloud and shuddered a long shudder and became lost in her hair and her arms and she floated up and out over the dark lake in her mind and then they clung together and slept a while and awoke with a drugged awareness that they were still linked together, hot now because the house was closed and still containing the day's heat. Their bodies were radiant.

Rob stuck his tongue lightly in Daisy's left ear. He said happily, "There's something about that lake tonight. Want to go back out and see what it does this time?"

She smiled a slow sleepy smile. Then she said, "Whither thou goest, I goest.

"And comest," she added with a laugh as they jumped out of bed, grabbed fresh towels and headed again for the dark shore.

They stayed in too long this time, romping and laughing and

diving with a delicious sense of danger down to the invisible bottom. The sky was a dark unity now. Haloes formed around their vision from the one light on the porch. A soft rain gave the water's surface a lambent glow in the light from the cabin. Soon, because the water really was cold, they were covered with gooseflesh and shivering and so they ran back and dried each other in a hurry and rummaged out sweaters and woollen socks and made a fire. They cooked hotdogs on long sticks and drank steaming cocoa with rum in it and went to bed and made love again simply and quietly and were soon deeply asleep.

Rob was wonderfully gay and affectionate all that long weekend; he felt Daisy was bewitched; happily he moved into her spelldom. Once they paddled in their canoe out to the islands and took food with them and a bottle of white wine which they let down to the bottom on a string to cool while they fished and caught three small bass. Daisy swam while Rob cooked the fish, and they drank all the wine and made love long and noisily on a blanket in the sun and swam again, and snoozed.

Rob found himself on the verge of telling his wife everything that was going on in Montreal, and wanted to badly, and had some seemingly lucid argument ready about why it was all right to do so – that Haig's enjoining him to total secrecy could be rationalized away – until in his imagination he started recounting the argument to Haig. Then Haig, in his mind, looked stern and shocked and so Rob brought himself up short and closed his mouth again when he had been on the brink of starting the story, so eager to see the wonder and excitement in her wide grey eyes when he told her, so longing to amaze her because he still believed that amazing her was one of the important pleasures he had to offer her.

Daisy, for her part, found herself falling in love again with her husband. The satisfaction of his work with Haig had given Rob an easier confidence than before, and the success with the spore had made him buoyant. All weekend he was tender and funny and in a mood to be fascinated by his wife. And so she came closer to making peace with the unnamed task that kept him away from her in space and time, since he seemed so close now in spirit and body.

She put off reckoning with the end of this weekend romance and went so far as to tell herself that life could not get much better.

And, indeed, it was soon to get much worse.

7

In the next weeks, certain that his new circuitry was producing the stability he needed to transmit, unharmed, the vulnerable elements of life, Haig tried to proceed beyond spores to tough seeds of grasses and grain plants: seeds that could survive centuries in storage, the hardy kinds of corn that germinate after a thousand years in an Aztec funeral jar. Haig tried and Rob recorded. The transmitted kernels and tiny spheres of clover and slivers of a dozen fine grasses were planted and watered and all of them rotted and the microscope showed not the least sign of germination having begun.

Rob wearied now of his charade at the network. Haig persuaded him to accept a salary from the project, and Rob asked the network for and was given indefinite leave without pay and began to spend five days a week in Montreal, sometimes n ore.

Haig grew morose. Rob cancelled several trips back to Toronto. Daisy tried to be patient. But the edge she heard growing in Rob's voice was only a hint of the frustration in that lab: because there was no reason for seeds to fail. There was nothing they could see, at any rate.

It was Rob who led them to the next breakthrough.

"Mold spores are more heat-resistant than these seeds, aren't they?" he asked Haig one night.

"Yes, Robbie. But the temperature in the receiver never rises above 40 degrees centigrade. That couldn't kill anything, laddie. Not you, nor me, nor corn, nor clover, nor my p-neumatic cousin Molly's aspidistra. It can't be that."

Haig, when he was frustrated, spoke with a more discernible roll of his parents' Scottish burr. And his perverse pronunciation of silent consonants – the *b* at the end of *bomb* and the *k* in *knight*, a trick of speech that did not belong, was exaggerated, and irritated Rob.

"Why can't it be?" Rob said acidly. "Why can't it be some sort of p-sychic heat! *Any* heat!"

Haig looked over his glasses at the pronunciation of p-sychic, and then went back to frowning crossly at the ceiling.

"At least do me the courtesy of answering. Why can't it be heat?" Rob felt he was barking up a wrong tree; he just needed perversely to annoy Haig.

Haig snapped at him. "Listen Rrrobbie. Who is it that checks the recording thermometer each time? You do. And photographs it? You do! So stop badgering ..." his anger faltered and he ended on a weak, whispered, "me."

And then, "I'm sorry, laddie. For a microsecond I was bloody mad at ye."

Rob looked at him.

"For a microsecond?" Rob asked.

Their eyes met. It hit them both in the same instant.

"Aye," Haig whispered.

"That thermometer takes nearly a second to show a response, right?"

"That's right," Haig whispered still.

"And the whole process of reconstruction of electrons and neutrons and protons and all that happens instantaneously?"

"No, there's no such thing as instantaneous in physics, not that I've been able to demonstrate, anyway. But fast. Damn fast." Haig's voice was back to flat Canadian. "We've got to quit transmissions until we've built a new kind of thermometer – a thermometer that can register a change so fast ..." He didn't finish.

"Because something might be cooked all over in that – what? – milli-millisecond it's being reassembled in the chamber? Every molecule cooked as it comes together. Like a microwave oven. And we'd never know. With a temperature that moldspores can handle and seed corn can't?"

Haig stared at him.

"By God, man! We *know* what that temperature is! Molds can survive 90 degrees centigrade. Seeds can't take anywhere near that. We have to build an extractive cooler, something to take out a precise quantity of heat just at the moment of transfer. Let's get to work, Rob. Let's do it."

After that night Rob did not go home again for nearly six months. It took almost that long to design and build and test the sophisticated electronic cooler that would, for the tiniest fraction of a microsecond, extract from the receiving chamber, by subtractive radiation, as much heat as was being induced in the reconstitution of the transmitted object. In the end, in order to calibrate a reliable hot/cold control system, they had to build a thermometer after all, to test the cooler. This part of the work was an unbroken grind; there was steady progress, no brick walls, no breakthroughs. The two men were tired much of the time, happy most of the time, absorbed all of the time. Weeks went by and Rob and Daisy did not even speak.

Once or twice she called and pleaded with him to tell her what was going on.

"I can tell from the sound of you that you're tired and you're happy," she said. "Well I'm tired and unhappy. And I think this goddam rotten useless secret project of Pinch's is going to kill us, kill the marriage. How can you stand it? I *hate* you for standing it. Do you understand that?"

"Babe, listen! I love you as much as I ever did. But this is something magnificent that we'll be able to share one day if I can keep it secret and it might all blow to hell if I don't," Rob said, with just a touch of impatience.

"You know what I'm bound to think. Why can't I come down there?"

"Because Pinch couldn't stand it and I couldn't either!"

"Just for the weekend Rob!"

"We'll be working through the weekend."

"Please? Please, Rob!"

He gave in.

It was a terrible weekend. The cooler was ready for its first tests. Haig didn't want to be away from the lab and was gruff with Daisy for the first time in their acquaintance and then repentant and apologetic afterward. She knew that both the men's minds were somewhere else. To make amends they took her out to a funny, wicked satirical review upstairs at the *Café André* and yet even though Rob and Haig laughed and laughed despite themselves, Daisy sensed the restlessness between the laughs. Making love, later that night, Rob tender again and fierce at the same time, she suddenly opened her eyes to him riding her and saw that his mind was elsewhere. She rolled from under him and pulled away with a whimper and stalked into the bathroom and turned on a cold shower and got into it, and Rob did not ask her why because he knew, and was ashamed, and could not help it.

In the morning they were polite to each other. Daisy said she understood but warned him that understanding was one thing and the ability to tolerate it was another.

The taxi honked outside. Daisy stood in the little hall, her face turned sideways, light from the kitchen tracing her profile.

He said, "I'll call you, and ..." She turned coldly then and put her hand out as though to touch his lips, but did not, and said, "No Rob. Don't say anything."

That week Rob and Haig planted seeds again upstairs on Pine Avenue, and two weeks later, under the banks of gro-lites, there were tender shoots of corn, then timothy, and soon, oats, and later a row of young Scotch pines – a single dark green spear for each.

And then, two months after that, and after more than two hundred attempts to send not seeds but living plants, attempts that had ended in either desiccation or frost-damage, they imported from Brazil a mature, bearing frost-resistant Brussells sprouts plant, put it in a huge pot in the newest, largest transmission chamber, retrieved it intact from the receiver, and, after keeping it watered two more weeks to see that there were no ill effects, had a *bravura* feast in the kitchen downstairs of steak, a bottle of *Côte Rôtie* and Brussells sprouts, *all of which* had travelled through space and were very tasty and very filling.

Now it was time to try animal life.

The paramecia were no trouble. And then earthworms. Earthworms came wriggling out of the receiver by the hundreds;

some were dissected, others set to breed, and the new breeds transmitted in their turn.

But the first mouse they tried died of a heart attack before the receiving chamber door was re-opened.

Rob and Haig speculated about emotional shock.

"But what would it feel?" Rob wondered.

"Perhaps there is something about sentient life that knows it has ceased to be, even for an instant. That's the one thing that I've been worried about; that the mind will not be able to stand it." He looked at Rob with anxious affection. "I don't know if I can stand . . ."

Rob waved the concern away. "It's too soon to worry, Pinch. Anyway, I'm sure training can prepare the mind."

"But how do you train a mouse not to worry?"

"Let's try."

They simulated transmission. They devised a way to change the interior color of a simulated receiving chamber, to produce the temperature changes, and to apply restricted amounts of radiation so that the physical effects of the instant before and the instant after transmission were approximated. Then they rewarded the mice with food. They kept the training up until the mice were asking to be let into the simulation chamber.

On October the nineteenth, a live mouse, paw-printed, blood-tested, weighed, Xrayed, voice recorded, odor-profiled and videotaped in maze-running, feeding habits and sexual responses, was put into a new transmitting chamber big enough for a man to squeeze into so that the mouse looked curiously grand running around on the dull red floor, where it was happily waiting for the walls to change to blue and a spoonful of bacon-scented pellets to appear. Rob locked the door and looked at the polished steel exterior with a curious feeling in his gut.

"I think it's going to be all right, Pinch. We'll have to start thinking about modifying that lock for an inside release."

Haig looked at him with that expression of concern that Rob had seen many times in the last few weeks. Then he checked the cooler controls on the receiving chamber, closed the blue-lined door, made a note, checked the time, nodded at Rob, pressed the small switch, and nodded again. Rob moved quickly to the receiving chamber and snapped open the lock. Inside the blue-walled cylinder there was a very agitated and very live mouse, which settled down to normal activity within an hour and repeated all its behaviour patterns exactly and lived a normal life for two more weeks until Pinch killed it carefully and examined it, in vain, for any signs of vascular or neurological damage.

Rob perceived something interesting about Haig on the day of the autopsy: he postponed killing the mouse. For nearly an hour after coming up to the lab, Haig fussed aimlessly, going over notes, checking parts of the equipment that had nothing to do with the morning's work. The small dissection table had been prepared the night before. The microscope was out of its case, standing on the side of the dissecting board with a vinyl hood over the lens. There was nothing to do but inject the creature. As Rob watched Haig's busyness, he felt that Haig would probably ask him to administer the injection; he so obviously did not want to do it himself. But finally Haig stood up with a sigh, went quickly to the table, prepared the syringe, and took up the mouse gently. Once the tremors of the animal were over, his mood changed and it was all method and practice and competence again, but Rob never forgot Haig's squeamishness.

From mice they proceeded to rats. The rats were very easy to train and proved good "travellers." Later, as they enlarged the size and spectrum of their menagerie, they kept some well-trained rats in the lab as test-pilots to check out the equipment before each transmission.

They tried cats. The cats took longer to train and to settle down emotionally after each trip. One male was quite odd for several days, spat at the cracks under doors and took to gnawing its tail until the bone showed and infection set in. Another became withdrawn and inert for the rest of its life of three weeks before Haig, again with reluctance, injected the quick death and performed the post-mortem.

They bought a pair of mating chimpanzees, Fred and Peggy. They trained them for two months. Fred was slow to feel at ease in the simulation chamber, but Peggy caught on fast. Within a week she began to come out of the chamber happily after the tests, grab her reward banana and jump on Rob for a hug and a kiss before she ate it. They decided to give her her first real trip. But unspoken between them was the possibility that the intelligent animal might be permanently damaged, mentally; both were deeply anxious about this.

Chimpanzees are excitable, mischievous and affectionate primates. Rob predicted emotional storms after the transmission. It seemed possible that Peggy might be hostile to her mate – or vice versa – after the trip. Haig and Rob bought thick gloves and leather aprons in case the strong ape should turn on them in her post-transmission confusion and fear: Peggy, when annoyed, had once bitten through the rung of a hardwood chair.

The chamber doors were now fitted with modified locks. A simple push on a polished disk on the inside of the door would swing it open. Peggy and Fred were trained to push on the disk when the color changed from red to blue.

It was Friday morning, January the fourth. Neither man had slept well. Both had grown too fond of the big, demonstrative apes. As a kind of compensation for what was about to happen, they gave the animals a luxurious breakfast. It proved too much. Peggy became sleepy after the meal and refused to enter the chamber. Haig and Rob waited, fidgeting and striding up and down. They played a vacant game of chess to pass the time until the chimpanzees brightened again.

It was noon before they found Peggy in a co-operative mood. Rob showed her the banana she would be rewarded with upon leaving the chamber. Peggy jumped up and hugged him and licked his ear and pulled his eyepatch down. Then she chattered happily and took his hand in all innocence and allowed herself to be led to the red chamber. Fred sat on Haig's desk shredding a wad of note paper, watching the proceedings nervously. When the red chamber door was locked, the male chimp ran to Haig, pulled at his arm, grabbed the waistband of his apron and jumped up for a hug. Fred weighed a hundred and twelve pounds and Haig grunted. Fred looked deep and inquiringly into Haig's eyes.

"It's all right, Fred," Haig said, trying to sound calm. But there was a quaver in his voice and Fred did not believe him.

He jumped down, ran to the transmitting chamber, pounded on it and called to Peggy. The door opened; Peggy had pressed the disk. Haig and Rob stared at each other.

"What now?" Rob said.

"Play time," Haig said.

They played for twenty minutes – painting, hugs, hide and seek, but no bananas.

Finally Rob felt it was time to try again. While Haig distracted Fred with a banana, Rob led Peggy inside. Fred had busied himself in a corner of the lab with his banana and then forgetfully headed for the toilet.

"Now!" Haig whispered urgently. He forced himself to carefully make the temperature checks on the blue chamber. Rob watched him intensely, urging hurry with his eyes. They heard the toilet flush.

"Now!" Rob said, and refocussed the videotape camera for the third time.

Haig was visibly agitated. He picked up the control box with a shaking hand and dropped it on the floor. Fred reappeared at the door of the toilet. Haig scrambled for the little control box which had slid under the edge of the desk. Fred looked around the lab for Peggy and gave a yell of alarm. He began to run toward the red chamber. On the floor, Haig's fingers found the control button. Without even rolling over to watch, he pressed the button and said, "Please" between his teeth.

Fred reached the red chamber and pounded on the door. It stayed shut. But, marvellously, the door of the blue chamber opened.

Peggy stepped out.

She looked around, a little puzzled for a moment. The stand with her banana on it, which had been directly in front of her before the door closed, was now twelve feet away from her and Fred was behaving strangely beside it. Peggy rushed across the room, knocked Fred down with a hammering left backhand, and grabbed her banana. Then she ran to Rob and jumped up for a hug and a kiss.

That night Haig drank a whole bottle of *Côte Rôtie* himself, and Rob drank two.

"We'll give Fred a trip tomorrow," Haig said. "I want them each to each have ten trips each. Do y' see? I feel terrible but I feel great. This will surprise you, laddie, because you think of me as the cool, detached – ah – experimenter."

Rob wagged his head owlishly and was going to say something about killing mice when Haig went on, "But the fact is, I've been really afraid.' He shuddered and picked up his glass again and gulped it down. He gazed at the empty bottle.

"I dinn realize how fond of Peggy you were getting to be. Fond of her, you know?" Rob was slurring heavily. "I mean I was ready to divorce Daisy and marry Peggy and buy Fred out with a crate of bananas. But I thought – I dinn know you were competing with me." He laughed foolishly.

Haig looked at Rob with moist eyes. "It wasn't Peggy I was worried about, laddie," he said. "It was you."

8

It was three o'clock in the morning. In the house on Moore Avenue the kitchen window was fogged. And in the cemetery behind them, Daisy knew without looking, the fog was slowly drowning the head-stones.

"I'm going to make more coffee," the man said. "You still with me?"

She looked at the misted window. "I guess I am," she said. Her limbs and her back had begun to ache slightly. Her head felt fragmented; she had a sensation of planes, of some taut white material running in two or three layers across the inside of her skull, dividing her brain into different levels. Not a pain, but a sensation of partition. Despite the exhaustion of her body, her heart was beating fast and strong, a little too strong. She knew that even if the story should come quickly to its end, she would not sleep. She was experiencing a dark, void, formless anticipation about what he would tell her next, and a thread of fear had begun to grow like a fine line of mold in her throat.

"Am I going to hate you when you tell me the rest?" she asked him suddenly.

He fussed with the coffee pot and did not answer but shook his head in a way that indicated not a denial, but a kind of resigned uncertainty.

"It's been going on for five years, Rob."

He looked at her with an opaque expression. He is frightened too, she thought with a sudden understanding.

"Not really five years," he said. His voice was rough and dry. He ran cold water in a coffee cup and rinsed out the stale coffee and drank a few sips of the water. "I was home for six months before ... before the last ... session."

"You always had to calculate the time," she said reproachfully.

"I only knew you were away. Most of the time it seemed. You were away even when you were here – on those awful weekends. You didn't want to be here."

"Some of the time I didn't. But you must begin to see what it was that ..."

"And it scares hell out of me."

Water boiled up suddenly in the spout of the kettle. He seemed to welcome the interruption. With his back to her, he said something she couldn't hear over the fluttering kettle.

"What, Robbie?"

He turned. There were tears on his cheeks. "I'm scared too, Babe – that you'll turn away from me, see. I'm going to ask you later and I'm going to ask you now to hold on, to ... to stay in touch with me through this next part. Because ... because it's going to be damn hard."

He sat down. Water spattered through the coffee into the pot below.

Daisy felt chilled and hugged herself and rocked back and forth on her chair with her legs tucked underneath her. She could not suppress, as she looked at the black stubble on the man's cheeks, the remembrance from some murder story that a dead man's beard continues to grow for several days. Her mind involuntarily travelled out to the wet mound of earth in the cemetery half a mile away behind their house and she shuddered, seeing under the earth.

"Appolinari," she said. "You keep talking about Appolinari. He's not ... the man we ... who looks like you?"

He shook his head.

"You met him in New York when you did that film on the rackets?"

He nodded again.

"Did he ever show up?"

"Twice. The first time he was fooled. Anyway, we thought so. Pinch was down in the basement, in the old lab, soldering some circuit components one night, before we got Fred and Peggy. I was in the kitchen. Pinch said he lifted his eyes from his work and Appolinari was just standing there. I heard them talking and went down. We managed to look confused and defeated over amplifier problems and Pinch got out the fake notes and Appolinari pretended to understand them and then we gave him some coffee and he went away and we thought we were safe for a while.

"Just after I got back to the lab for this last ... after my six months here ... he found out about the second lab. He was going to kill Pinch – he was mad enough. But listen Babe, you've got to wait until that part of the story comes along, because it's connected to everything that happened."

The dripping from the coffee pot had stopped. The man rose and poured, took milk from the refrigerator and held the cup to warm his hands for a while. He sipped and then went on.

"If you're up to it, this is the hard part now."

She pressed her lips and made an effort to focus. She said, "All right. You had those six months at home. You took a course in transcendental meditation. You did all the housekeeping. You produced a series of four damn good short films for the network. You ate a lot and you exercised. You played tennis again. You started swimming again."

"It was a training program."

"I know it. I'm just trying to show you that I'm with you ... that I'm understanding this, all of it. So far. You were getting ready for, for a trip. Weren't you?"

He nodded.

"You had to be the first man in the world, didn't you?"

"It couldn't be Pinch."

"I don't see why the hell not!" They stared at each other for a moment.

Daisy said, "You were doing all the old familiar things in your life, to strengthen all the patterns in your mind that were, well, that were *you*. Is that right?"

He nodded again.

"A lot of things you used to do when you were just a kid. I wondered about the paper cuttings. Now I understand it."

"And playing solitaire," the man reminded her. "And reading my old science fiction magazines out loud to you at night."

"Stuff to reinforce your identity. Was that Pinch's idea?"

"We worked it out together," he said. "I did all the training in the simulation chamber first. It was easy enough. Then we agreed I should go home and be me for a good long time before the actual trip."

"The chimps made the trips because they were so trainable, but you both knew that the human imagination might cause a lot of trouble. Is that right?"

He smiled at her with admiration. "You're great, Babe," he said. He meant it, and she knew he meant it.

"But there was trouble after all, wasn't there?"

His face was wet again. A line of wetness streaked down from beneath the eyepatch on the left side and the whole of his cheek on the other was splotched. She sensed his terrible reluctance to continue, and although she knew she was yielding to a weakness that had betrayed her in the past, and even suspected Rob of playing on her vulnerability, she gave in to it and when she spoke this time it was with a welling of tenderness and support.

"Now, Rob. Let's finish it. Let me come all the way with you my darling. You have to."

"I know it." His voice was very constricted. She managed a strong smile to encourage him, and reached her hands across the table and squeezed his hands and whispered again, "Now, Rob."

He cleared his throat a couple of times.

"I went to Montreal. I felt great. You were fantastic those six months; I felt you were really with me; I was sure I'd be home in a few months. I'd make the trip in the lab, then we'd do the patent work and the whole thing could come out in the open. See, Pinch had prepared to hand it over to the people of Canada, as Best and Banting had done with insulin. All he wanted was an annuity for his lifetime, and research facilities. And better than that: the patent was to be ceded to the people of the world at the end of ten years, if the lawyers could work it out. Pinch said he'd be damned if his discovery was going to divide the world the way oil has – and it's far more valuable than oil because it can never be exhausted."

"Rob, bless Pinch and bless you."

Rob had recovered a measure of optimism. He laughed at his

wife in an affectionate way. "Hold tight for the next part, Babe," he said. "We'll both need it."

She pressed his hands again. She felt a warmth, a rush of gratitude for the smile, warmth immediately cut by the spreading growth of that line of fear in her throat that became a network of lines constricting her breathing and swallowing and yet made her need to breathe deeply, swallow frequently.

She said, "I'm trying to be calm and I'm doing pretty well. Somebody wanted me – and the rest of the world – to think you're dead, and if they find out I know the truth they'll try to kill me, or both of us. Is that it?"

"No, not exactly." He looked hard at the wide grey bloodshot eyes. "You really know what I'm going to tell you, don't you?"

She gazed at him calmly.

"You know and you're trying to think it must be something else? Something less ... unthinkable?"

Her nails bit into his palms, but her face was placid and her eyes did not blink. With her heart she offered him all the strength she could. "I'm ready, my beloved," she said in a perfectly steady voice.

He took a deep breath.

9

August 29th. Remember this date, Rob thought, as Haig listened to his stethoscope.

"Your blood pressure's a touch too high and your pulse is fast, and that's normal enough when the adrenalin is pumping. How scared are you?"

Rob watched the scientist put away the blood pressure cuff, and shrugged, and said, "You're tense enough yourself."

Haig said, "It's all right. I wanted you to be normal. Not like some overtrained astronaut without any human feeling left. You don't have to perform anything more complex than pushing the disk on the lock release and you don't have to do any calculations. You just have to keep a grip on yourself, and from what you said you're more sure who Rob Nelson is now than you were six months ago."

"Yes, some." Rob rose from his chair and started to take off his shirt and pants.

"There's no real need to go naked," Haig told him. "Peggy wore her ID tag. The plant went in its pot."

"Something about how I feel about this trip. The 'I' that's making the trip ... I just want to be alone. Do you know what that's about? It's a metaphor."

Haig blinked at him. "I'm not so sure."

"All through this six months, working at the old desk, doing well, turning out good shows, being closer to Daisy than I have for years – except that I couldn't tell her what was really deeply in my guts – retracing the old paths, riding the Kawa over the old Toronto streets like I used to, reading my old magazines, I felt stronger and stronger, and yet I felt more ... alone than I ever felt in my life. And sad about that."

Haig looked sideways at the younger man.

"Alone, eh?"

"Not desperate about it. Just a kind of feeling that something in my life was over."

Haig said, "One of the things we mean when we say a person is strong is that he is able to live with his sense of being alone. But strong people aren't always happy about being strong, that's the paradox. You were preparing yourself for something extraordinary and you know that after it the world will never be the same, so in a way you'll never be the same. That has to do with why you feel something in your life is over."

Rob walked naked toward the red-lined chamber. The lamps were turned down to a comfortable level in the lab. The reflected gleam from the stainless steel outer shell of the two chambers sent fragments of light into some of the darker corners of the room.

Haig said, "Maybe you'd better wear your clothes. Something familiar. An anchor with the outside world."

"No, Pinch. My body is what I know best about the outside world. I've been with it longer than anything else. I don't even want this," he said, remembering the eyepatch and tossing it on the chair with his clothes.

He stepped into the red chamber.

They had spent the whole of the afternoon in tests. All electronic parts with any known risk of failure had been replaced and then Peggy and Fred, so accustomed to being transmitted that they asked for a trip whenever they were brought up to the lab, had each been sent from red to blue three times, and on each occasion Rob had gone over the readings with Haig before and after and had pressed the transmit switch himself. They had taken time for a good supper of cold roast lamb and red wine and fruit, and they had put the chimps to bed. It was not until they had come back up to the lab again that Rob had begun to feel frightened.

But he had it under control. He managed a good strong grin at Haig. "I'm fine Professor. If we didn't know damn well it was going to work we wouldn't be here, would we? Let's do it."

Haig reached into the steel shell and took both Rob's hands

and squeezed hard. He tried to think of something more original to say than "have a good trip," and couldn't, and so said nothing, just smiled, squeezed Rob's hands again, stepped back, swung the door of the chamber to lock it, changed his mind, and opened it up again.

"Listen Robbie: about feeling alone. I don't know why I should take the time to say this now ... it's not even terribly important, but I'll say it anyway. The self inside the skin is a spring, a steel spring, a spring coiled tight in on itself, full of tremendous power for invention, for poetry – to share itself if you like, power for creation, for worship. For love, finally. It's held in place by fear. We're afraid of rebuff. That means we're afraid that we don't really exist. It's an understanding I think you should take with you. It may help to carry you across that gap.

"If the spring uncoils and lets out all the power, and then discovers that there's nothing outside to deliver that power to, no other person – I mean no response, you understand – well, then it'll be spent. Or maybe when it uncoils there'll be no pin in the centre to hold it in place and it won't be able to connect to its power with anything inside. No self. So it coils up again. I guess I mean it stays coiled up in the first place. Out of fear. We call that coil loneliness."

"You said the self was the coil."

"No. There's the difference. The self is the spring. The coil is the shape it takes. Holding itself back. I'm no poet, Rob, but I've seen that connection between strength and loneliness. Between potential and loneliness. So it's not all a bad thing, this coil of ours. That's all."

"I love you, Pinch," Rob said quietly.

"And I you, Robbie," and he shut the door and set the lock.

Haig walked to the mid-point between the two steel chambers. Always before, Rob had been at his side. The video camera was aimed across the first chamber at the second, and was focussed at the second. The red *record* light was on and the spool turning. Haig looked round for a moment at the room that seemed so empty with no other living being moving in it.

He picked up the little control box, extended the antenna for no reason, collapsed it again to its normal three inches, and looked up. "I can't really pray, you know," he said to the ceiling, with something like a smile. Then he decisively pressed the switch.

There was a silence that lasted a heartbeat.

The door of the far chamber opened, and Rob stepped naked from the blue interior. His eyes were gleaming with an intensity that Haig had never seen in them before. Rob shook his head, speechless, several times, and then rushed to Haig and embraced him.

"It ... It was ... Pinch, it's like your first dive into deep water. Scarey as hell and then you know you could do it again. Cold ... terribly cold, and dark too, at the same time. There was ..." He tried to find words for it "There was a kind of negative flash. Do you know what I mean? As if a black flash-bulb went off. Everything was totally dark and cold for a ... dazzling instant. And I thought I was going to be dizzy and then the red wall was gone and the blue wall was there and that was all. Pinch! Pinch! My God, we made it! We ..."

But he couldn't go on. His eyes were wet and he began to laugh extravagantly, with excitement and triumph. He tightened his embrace of the older man's shoulders, and then the laughter changed to sobs of relief, and he sagged against Haig's frame and hung on, shaking and crying. Haig's eyes were moist and blurred too. Over the sob he heard the vidcotape run out and the machine switch itself off. Then, suddenly, his back stiffened and his skin went very cold and on his neck he knew that individual hairs were rising, each in its own little gland of fear. At the edge of his vision Haig saw a gleam of motion ... from the direction of the transmitting chamber – the red-lined chamber.

He wiped his eyes with a cold hand and tried to focus.

The door of the red chamber was opening.

A naked man stepped out.

A man with one opaque eye, and a wry grin on his face and a scar across his hairy belly.

The man said, "What the hell happened, Pinch?" He wore a look of puzzled amusement. "I mean, how long am I supposed to wait? I was going to suffocate in there."

And then he said, as if he had seen the naked body sobbing in Haig's arms for the first time, "And just who the hell is that?"

10

The sobbing naked man heard the voice of the other naked man behind him, and recognized it, and felt very strange even before he turned to face his other self. And then the two naked men simply stared at each other for a long time.

Nothing was said in the subdued light of the lab, but all three remembered afterward the sound of rhythmic, almost explosive exhalation from three pairs of nostrils.

Haig said later that the struggle between the scientist who knows he must quickly and accurately record, and the man, friend, bewildered frightened child who has opened the door of the forbidden room, nearly overwhelmed him: he felt as though he would split in two; he was paralyzed, unable to speak, or reach for notes, or start up the videotape. He could neither function with control, nor yield to the emotions that swept over him.

Yet he could observe and remember.

And, as he watched the two men, each the same, each staring at each other, they began to move. Slowly. As if under water or in a dream, their eyes unblinking, they moved toward each other across the room, their mouths half open, their right hands beginning to rise as if to clasp hands and moments later, as if to point in accusation. Their movements were perfectly matched; their bursting breath in unison; they drew toward each other and then, when half the ground was covered, each began to circle to the right. It was a dance of terrible compulsion, of seeking and fear, Haig saw; and although his mind registered, and knew it was registering and knew he would remember, he still could neither speak nor weep nor yield to a grateful loss of consciousness and escape the unreal ballet. Helplessly rigid, he could only watch and expect his heart to burst with the pressure of it.

The two men circled warily, still to the right. The circle was closing. Their hands were outstretched. Their finger tips were a foot apart. Their eyes were locked on each other, the single eye that saw, and the single opaque eye: each to each: hard-focussed, still unblinking. What was it in their faces?

Haig said, afterward: the urgent need to confirm; the desperate hope to deny.

Now the mirrored men stood with their hands less than an inch from contact, and they stopped moving. Their breath continued in unison and Haig thought that they must not be aware of that unison or they would stop it – it was a bizarre supercharge upon the already impossible duplication. Then he realized: they cannot stop it; they cannot stop anything they do now. Will is suspended until something here is resolved.

The outstretched hands were shaking, yet not touching. The two chests were heaving with the effort to breathe against the shock they both felt. Then for a moment, as though the shock had been overcome and life suspended, there was a total arrest of motion; breath stopped; the trembling in the fingers ceased.

Haig saw a tightening of the features and knew the two had simultaneously made a decision. The flexed arms extended. The hands touched – first just a fingertip, a tentative touch, then an urgent reaching, as though through the glass of a mirror sud denly found penetrable – a firm grasp of two hands, the knuckles of each going white with the intensity of it.

The color drained from the red staring faces, the tension went out of the two bodies, the hands slipped listlessly apart, the legs buckled, and wordless, they both fell unconcious to the floor.

The spell imprisoning Haig was broken by the fall. He opened his throat and roared at the cosmos in protest, "NO! NO! ... NO!"

He clutched his hands to the sides of his head and a long shudder passed through his body. With his eyes closed he said three times, "I must." He forced the last of the shudder out of him. He opened his eyes, quickly scanned both the identical bodies on the floor, noted that their chests were rising and falling – no longer in unison now – in shallow breaths, and that they were not choking or otherwise in physical danger.

Haig shook his arms and upper body as though shaking

off water after swimming. Then he moved decisively to the videotape machine. He was astonished to find his hands steady, sure. He took off the small reel that had recorded the exit from the blue chamber and had run out before the appearance of – whom? – from the red chamber. What shall I call him – them? – he thought as he methodically opened a second box, slipped a larger roll of tape from its vinyl envelope and laced the tape into the machine.

"Which one is real?" he asked himself aloud, moving, still certain and measured in his motions, to the camera, aiming it at the unconscious bodies on his laboratory floor, and checking the focus. He stepped across to the steel sinks and filled a beaker with cold water. Then he walked rapidly back to the videotape, thinking what tests he could devise to see the differences there might be between two men whose experience for thirty-seven years was entirely the same, and who differed now only in that one had travelled, in the space of a microsecond, some fifteen feet in space while the other had not, and that one had momentarily ceased to exist as a physical entity while the other had continued – or had he? Haig had to assume that he had, but he could not prove it since he still did not understand at all what had happened.

He switched on the tape recorder. He knelt by the two men, met with and overcame a momentary squeamishness about touching them, realized as he splashed water on their faces with his fingers and sponged a little on their half-open lips that he was totally incapable of telling, from looking at them now on the floor, who had stepped from which chamber.

The two bodies began to move, and their lips to form words. One said, the eyes still closed, in a faint voice, "Pinch, I've had the most incredible dream," and the other one murmured, "A terrible dream, Pinch."

Then their eyes opened, and when they saw each other they looked back at Haig with supplication, and both began to weep.

"Are you cold?" Haig asked. He felt foolish. He could not think of anything else to say.

The two men nodded.

Haig ran to the daybed and brought the two blankets and

the men sat up and pulled each a blanket around him. Then together they reached toward the beaker on the floor, which was still half full, and stopped in mid-reach with a slow, courteous deference, and the Rob Nelson on Haig's left, spoke first and said, "You go ahead."

The Rob Nelson on Haig's right lifted the beaker and drank all the water in it. Haig looked quickly to the man on his left for a reaction; the man nodded. "That's right," he said, with a kind of wondering approval. "That's what I would have done." The other man's eyes crinkled and he gave a short laugh, which the first man echoed. "Please get ... us ... some more, Pinch," he said.

Haig ran for the water and came back with two beakers this time and knelt by them and spoke firmly, and calmly, as the man on the left drank deeply and the man on the right held the beaker to his lips and sipped.

Haig said, "Now listen you two: it's amazing that any one of us is either conscious or calm. There are some things I've got to get said right away, because I believe we all three risk going mad and I think I know how to deal with it. At least I know how to begin. But you've got to listen and listen hard for a few minutes. Without moving, I think. Before we do anything else. Will you trust my judgment in this for a bit?"

Both men nodded gravely.

"All right," Haig said. "We're faced with something no one has ever faced before and one of the things that could happen very soon if we don't undertake some fundamental politics, is that the two of you are going to be absolutely in competition with each other because you both want the same things, expect the same things – including your identities, y'see – that you'll have to fight. And I'm not going to let you do that if I can help it. I'm going to ask you for the next few hours to completely, totally, take orders from me. Orders. Not suggestions. Incontestable orders."

The two identical men huddled in their blankets on the floor began to stir restlessly and look quickly at each other and back to Haig, and the man on the right opened his mouth to speak but Haig stopped him.

"Don't speak yet." Haig said sharply. "Just listen. There may be a way to make it possible for both of you to live and work together and if that's so then all the talent that one Rob Nelson had half an hour ago is doubly in the world. Better if you both live. You cannot deny that, do y' see. But you may want to deny it later when the conflict's too tough and you start thinking about some things in a few minutes or a few hours. So to give us all time I'm saying take orders. You know it's not like me to do that. You know I don't like taking orders or giving them. I'll find it hard too. But I say ye've got to do it. For survival."

"What conflicts worry you so much?" one of the men said, and the other echoed, "Yes, I was just going to . . ."

Haig interrupted sharply, "Will you accept my orders!"

Both men nodded at him, subdued by the uncharacteristic-ally imperative tone.

"Good," Haig said. "Wait there a minute."

He went to the desk and came back with a broadtipped felt marker pen.

"Hold out both your hands."

They instantly obeyed.

"You've got to have names," he said, uncapping the felt pen. "And never mind protesting that y' have names. I know y' have. But we're going to be in chaos if we can't distinguish one of you from the other, and we start with names. All science begins with names."

He made a big roman R on the backs of the right-hand man's hands. "That's for Robert," Haig said. "Not Robbie or Rob but Robert. You're Robert. And you," turning to the second man who looked anxious, "are Nelson. Robert and Nelson. You will address each other that way, even if you feel foolish doing it." He began to paint a large N on the second man's hands.

"You can start now," Haig said. "What's your name?" he said to the man whose hands he was marking, and stared hard at him as he said it.

"I'm Nelson," in a firm voice.

"Good. And you?"

"I'm Robert."

"All right. Now this next part is going to make you feel

foolish but you'll do it anyway. It's very important because y've got to make contact with each other, not as warring halves of a divided person but as two separate persons with distinct rights. And I think we're off to an amazing good start, because of the way y' handled that drinking water. Stand up."

They did.

"Now you're going to shake hands, and Robert, you're going to say, 'I'm glad to meet you, Nelson.' And then Nelson, you're going to say, 'I'm glad to meet *you*, Robert.' Try to understand why I'm doing this."

If Haig expected protest at this kindergarten ritual he was wrong. He could see that Robert and Nelson understood. He concluded that both, for a while at least, would co-operate. And so he felt a little easier, a little more confident.

"I'm glad to meet you, Nelson," Robert said with a chuckle, slightly forced, slightly theatrical.

"I'm glad to meet you, Robert."

"Good," Haig said. "What's your name?"

"Nelson," the man answered unhesitatingly.

"Nelson what?"

There was a pause. "I think you mean it just to be Nelson, don't you Pinch?"

"That's right. What's your name?"

"Robert," the other man said. "Just Robert. But I think you should know that ..."

"Just a minute! Here's another order. One of you is going to want very badly to establish his claim as the original model. Wait!" He held up his hand to silence the men who both started to speak. "It's going to happen and it may be what Robert was going to say or it may not. I don't know which of you came from which chamber. I don't want to know until we've done some considerable talking together, and maybe made some tests. I'm not sure it matters, but ..." He paused and looked from one to the other.

"But I've been thinking about this possibility." Haig continued. "That's why I never referred to the *Pietra* unless you brought it up. I found it too painful. I never believed that duplication would happen again, but I had to face the possibility that it could. I was expecting it in the first months. Once, just after Peggy had made a trip and while I was watching her walk out of the receiving chamber, Fred walked into the transmitting chamber behind my back. He wanted a trip too. I didn't even know he was in the lab, and when I turned and saw him open the door of the red chamber and walk out again, I thought for a terrible moment it was a duplicate Peggy.

"That's when I forced myself to work out a strategy against the impossible. And all the time I kept saying, 'this is a foolish waste of time.' Then I'd look at my splendid bank balance, and I'd remember where it came from, and I had to tell myself it could happen again, even if I didn't know why. So I've had a rehearsal, so to speak, of the thing that I was more afraid of than ... Lads, that's what I meant that night when we got drunk after Peggy's first trip; when I said I wasn't worried about Peggy, I was worried about you."

He looked at them with grave affection.

"I'm not going to leave you alone with each other. Soon, but not yet. And I'm not going to be alone with either one of you because the other one would become suspicious, jealous, and the one with me would try to tell me things. So Nelson, pick up those clothes and we'll all go down to the guest room and get another set. I can turn this off now."

Robert watched him switch off the videotape and said, "I'd like to play that back." And Nelson said, "Yes."

"Later," Haig said, and motioned them toward the stairs.

When the men were dressed, he fed them hot soup, toast and cheese. He tried to keep them physically active so that they would not start to think too much, too soon. After the meal they went back up to the lab and put on a fresh roll of videotape. In front of the camera, Haig recorded their temperatures and their blood pressure and tested their reflexes; he took their fingerprints and weighed them and drew off blood samples which they all looked at under the microscope, and then they all helped with the chemical tests.

There was no discernible difference between the two. Toward midnight both were beginning to look drawn and pale and anxious, but Haig was at once relieved and puzzled to see that they seemed to accept the fact of each other's existence. With the tape running and the microphone hanging above them he asked, "What is the strongest emotion you feel now? Is it fear?" To save them having to choose, he addressed himself squarely to the Robert.

The man said, "You know I hate those questions, Pinch. I never let an interviewer ask 'What's your favourite color,' or 'What's the most important thing in your life,' but ... I guess a kind of ..." He could not finish.

"I'll try," Nelson said. "I think he wanted to say 'resignation.'"

"Don't tell me what I wanted to say!" the other said sharply.

Haig said, "Easy, lads."

There was a pause.

Then Robert said, "Yes. I'm sorry. Resignation is accurate. And confusion. And a sense that maybe tomorrow will have some ..." He faltered again.

"Answers," the other one finished.

There was silence for a moment.

"Now you two," Haig said at last, still very authoritarian, "we'll go downstairs to the spare room. I'm going to give you a massive sedative because as tired as you are, your fears are going to keep you awake unless you have some help."

"I could use a drink," Nelson said.

Haig said, "Drink could set you quarrelling. I want you sedated, not steamed up. But what I'm giving you will let you dream. And that's important, because you've got a hell of a lot of emotional overload to work off, laddies, as I'm sure you know."

They went to the spare room on the third floor which contained twin beds. Haig made Robert and Nelson carry in a third cot from what used to be a servant's room. They found pillows and bedding. After giving them a hefty injection and talking to them in a calming way, Haig lay down on the cot across the room from them and soon was breathing deeply and regularly.

The two identical men in the twin beds tossed uneasily for a long time. After a while Robert whispered, "Nelson?"

"Yes, Robert," the other man said sleepily.

"We've got to try to follow Pinch's lead, at least for a while."

"Yes, I was thinking that."

"I suppose we'll find ourselves thinking and saying the same things a lot."

"Yes."

Both men yawned. Soon their breathing settled down and the rolling about diminished as the drug fought a slow winning battle with their turmoil. Haig, listening in the dark, gave up his imitation of sleep but still waited a good hour before swinging his legs silently off the cot and padding across the room in his stocking feet, carrying his shoes. At the door he paused, listening to the heavy breathing from the twin beds until he was quite satisfied. Then he slipped out and quietly climbed one flight of stairs to the lab.

The cluttered room had an eerie atmosphere in the subdued glow from a single light left burning on the desk. The doors of the two polished steel chambers hung half-open. Their dark interiors seemed like entrances to another universe. The cold water tap in the steel sink was dripping. Haig turned it off. He gathered up the two rumpled blankets from the floor between the chambers and folded them neatly on the daybed. For a moment more he stood looking at the room, seeing the scene of earlier that evening play itself out in his mind.

Then he crossed to the desk, sat down, pulled out a foolscap pad, opened an old fountain pen, and began to write, in longhand, an account of what had happened.

From time to time he consulted his notes on blood pressure, time, temperature, and copied the figures into his report. Twice he examined the equipment, the chambers, the amplifiers and the beam generators. He pulled out two or three drawer modules of electronic components, scrutinized them, probed here and there with the electrodes of a voltmeter, shook his head, returned to his desk and made more notes.

Had he not been so absorbed in retracing each step of the evening's experiment, so driven to find out what had gone wrong (or was it, he asked himself, what had gone *right*) he would have heard the subtle sounds of movement below him in the house. Somewhere a door closed quietly; an alert ear would easily have heard it; Haig worked on, unaware.

Presently he gathered his notes and a fresh pad of note-paper together and moved over a chair and a small work table beside the videotape machine. He rewound the last tape and put it back in its box. Then he laced up the tape of the trip itself, the tape which ended just before the opening of the red chamber door and the preposterous confrontation which followed.

He sat beside the tape machine and put his elbows on the table and his finger tips together, resting his lips against his index fingers and the end of his nose against his middle fingers.

"What do I have to do to protect myself from corruption now?" he thought. "Have I done a Frankenstein thing? The kind that brings down holy retribution?"

Then he thought, "But these two people are both real, experienced people with their good sides and their bad. And I did not will this duplication."

He wondered if he was looking for excuses. He believed that he risked taking too much satisfaction in what had happened, assuming too much authority in the playing out of its implications; there, he decided, was where the risk of corruption lay: In believing that both of these people, not just one, had, because of their transmutation by his, John Alexander Haig's imaginative power and re-ordering some of the structures of the universe, become his property.

"Yes," he said aloud in the lab. "That's how God punishes the meddler: by letting him think thoughts that can destroy him. Watch out for that, Pinch my boy."

And yet he could not extinguish the thrill of what he had done. The absurdity of it, the risk, the responsibility. All those things acted upon his mind. But the thrill acted at a level he had not, for all his powers of analysis, really come to perceive. Not yet.

He snapped himself back to practical matters and turned to the tape machine. He pressed the *play* switch. The head whined up to speed and the screen flickered and rolled and then came alive with a picture of the same space he could see before him, to his left. In the left foreground of the picture on the monitor, slightly out of focus, was the red chamber with its door open. In the center of the frame Rob was removing the last of his clothes. Haig heard Rob's voice, echoing slightly in the single mike hung from between the two chambers.

"My body is what I know best about the outside world."

Haig saw the hand toss the black eyepatch across the room, out of the frame of the picture. Beside him, the videotape machine whined and partly masked the sound of the small elevator coming to life at the back of the house, and the cage sliding upward within its well-greased rails. Haig only heard his own voice: "... the self inside the skin is a spring ..." and could discern, even in the imperfect focus on Rob in the foreground, half seen through the open door of the red chamber, the way in which Rob's brow had furrowed in response to the words.

"... we're afraid we don't really exist ..."

And then, with heightened power in the intensified framing of experience that the screen created for him.

"I love you, Pinch."

"And I you, Robbie."

The sound of the door closing on the red chamber seemed to echo in the now dark room. Haig felt his skin tingle in anticipation. He could already sense a second presence forming in the air. On the screen he had stepped out of the frame but his hands, holding the control box, were thrust forward so that the picture consisted of the slightly soft-focus red chamber in the left foreground, his hands and the control box in the right edge of the frame, and the closed blue chamber focussed sharp and gleaming in center background, but not at all small in the frame. Haig saw his finger press the button firmly. He relived the heartbeat's pause. He watched the door of the blue chamber being opened, Rob coming out looking confused, the rush of words, the naked man stumbling across the room toward him.

And then he heard the hiss of an indrawn breath in the room behind him, *not on the tape*, a hiss so sharp it penetrated his thought and drew him spinning around in his chair as the flutter of the tape running out rattled beside him and the screen went black.

A figure stood in the shadows. Haig, his heart pounding, said. "Robbie?" There was no answer. "Robert? ... Nelson?" he repeated. Then he caught the scent of carnations and tried to remember what it was he disliked about that smell. He felt afraid. He held his breath. He controlled his voice as well as he could and said, "I can't see who you are."

Neither man moved. The visitor stayed in shadow. After a moment a quiet voice said, "Nobody cheats Appolinari, Haig. I told you that. Nobody cheats Appolinari and lives."

"I know how the chambers work, Appolinari. I'm the only one who does."

Appolinari moved out of the shadows. He fixed his eyes on Haig as if to hypnotize him. He indicated the television screen. "Play it again."

Haig shrugged. He stood up to rewind the tape. Suddenly his elbows were grasped from behind, thumbs digging into the muscle with excruciating pressure. He gritted his teeth and said nothing to the man who had moved in so close behind him that Haig thought he would suffocate in the carnation perfume.

Appolinari released the pressure. "I get secrets out of stronger men than you, Haig." His voice was very low. "Play the tape."

As the spool was rewinding, Appolinari said, "If you wanted to fool me with that phony lab in the basement, you should have dusted it once in a while."

Haig said nothing. He felt trapped. He thought of the two men asleep in the room beneath him and could not decide whether he wished them awake and with him or not. Alone and vulnerable, he was determined Appolinari should know no more than necessary. He mentally gave thanks that he had not been screening the second tape – the awakening of Robert and Nelson – when Appolinari arrived.

He flirted with the idea of pressing the erase switch on the tape machine. Then he dismissed it, partly out of fear for what Appolinari might do, but mostly because he was a scientist.

He started the tape.

Appolinari watched in silence; only his eyes moved. When the tape ran out again they had narrowed so that just the whites shone under the clenched black brows, like the whites of his cuffs in the dark suit.

"You thought you could cut me out," he said in a slow, considering way. He looked around the lab carefully. He walked to the red chamber and opened it. Then to the blue. He looked at the animal cages. A few white rats still ran about in the woodchips and nibbled at grain from a small dispenser. "I'm going to show you something."

He reached inside his coat and withdrew a small revolver. From another pocket he took a leather case, flipped a gunmetal cylinder from it, a silencer, and fitted it to the end of the revolver barrel. He put the gun back in his coat while he drew on a pair of gloves. Then he opened the top of the rats' cage and with his left hand grabbed one rat tightly by the back of the neck. The rat struggled and tried to twist its head around to get its teeth into its captor, but Appolinari was accurate in his grip and unafraid of the darting head and grasping yellow teeth.

Appolinari glanced around the room, selected the daybed as a backstop, held the struggling rat firmly down on a cushion, pulled out the silenced revolver, pressed the barrel against the base of the rat's tail, and pulled the trigger.

There was a noise like a sharp thump. Then the rat began to scream. Appolinari advanced on Haig, holding the rat at arm's length. The screams pierced the air of the room. Droplets of blood formed and fell from the severed stump of the tail. The hind legs hung immobile although the rest of the body twitched and struggled more fiercely than before and the head slashed back and forth in a vain attempt to fix the teeth in this terrible enemy.

"The rat is telling me something, Haig. He is talking very freely. He will tell me anything I want to know."

"Kill it, for God's sake. You've made your point."

Appolinari smiled, nodded, put the end of the silencer to the back of the rat's head and turned towards the daybed again.

Then he stopped and turned back. "You're really quite squeamish, aren't you Haig," he said softly.

"Kill it ... please!"

Suddenly Appolinari danced over to the red chamber. He flung the bloody, squirming rat on the floor of the cylinder, slammed the door, and set the lock.

"Send the rat," he said.

The rat's screams echoed faintly through the steel.

"Send it, Haig. Then I will end its agony. I want to see." He pointed the long, silenced barrel straight at Haig's knees. "Send it, Haig."

"You are truly a very terrible man Appolinari," Haig said. "Rob warned me. I wouldn't listen."

Haig went to the blue chamber, and as he closed it, he saw that his hands were trembling badly. He thought, "I have never really wanted to kill before. I hate killing." He turned and looked back to the man in the dark suit with the tight smile and the gleaming cuffs. "I hated killing," he mentally corrected himself.

Quickly he brought the voltage up to the mark, ran through his checklist, and without a pause pressed the switch on the control box. Instantly the faint screams of the rat were heard now to come from the second chamber.

Appolinari shook his head once in satisfied amazement. He flung open the door of the blue chamber and pulled out the bleeding rat with his left hand. Less deftly this time. The rat sank its teeth into the end of Appolinari's thumb. Appolinari did not flinch or cry out. He walked coolly to the daybed, held the rat against the pillow again, took out his pistol, and calmly blew its head away, a half inch from his hand. Then he pried the still gripping jaws from his thumb and turned once more to Haig.

"You're going to send me, Haig. I'm going to make the trip." His eyes shone with the desire of it.

Haig tried not to let his tormentor see the wave of calm that passed over him just then. He forced his hands to continue to shake. He thought, "I am going to remove something evil from the world."

But then his heart sank because Appolinari – had he sensed Haig's sudden tranquility? – said, "But you're going first, Haig. You're going to show me how to set up the machine, and I'm going to set it up for you, so we both know it's safe, and then you'll go, and then I'll tie you to the desk and I'll set it up for me, exactly the same way, and then all you'll have to do is press the little button."

Haig fought for control. He said, "I don't think you need to do that: Nelson has made the trip, that's enough demonstration for one ..."

But Appolinari brought his gun up so that it pointed at Haig's groin, then dropped it a few degrees. "I'll save something for the interview," he said coldly. "Perhaps we could just start with a big toe. I am told it is incredibly painful. Now show me the checklist."

Haig held the list and read it out while Appolinari followed with his eyes and then, under Haig's directions checked each gauge and set each switch.

"Remember, it's you that's travelling," he said when Haig faltered for a moment.

Haig's mind raced ahead of what they were doing. He eyed the distance from the desk to the panel. He chewed his moustache. Several times Appolinari had to snap his attention back with a brusque command. Finally it was done. Then Appolinari did it all over again, to see that he had it memorized, while Haig followed his eyes.

"Step in!" Appolinari said, gesturing at the red chamber.

Haig now had to be an actor, to act as he had never acted before. He forced his powerful will to suppress the terror that he felt at the prospect of the void, of disintegration, of all that they had spent so long preparing Rob for. He fought back the vertigo of a picture in his mind of two more identical men stepping from the chambers, two Haigs. And then he thought (and could not tell whether it was insight or simply the projection of his own will) that the duplication of the stone and the duplication of Rob Nelson were some form of cosmic irony, unique, remote from this reality, however near in time. Finally – and all this mental struggle consumed no more time than a reasonable pause in moving across the room might take – he told himself firmly that Rob's trip had demonstrated all he had to know and in a giant silent sigh of resignation found he could accept that. He showed Appolinari nothing more than a shrug which said, "Why not. Nothing to it," handed over the little box with its antenna protruding three inches and closed the red-lined door behind him.

There was a pause then a sort of vanishing of all sensation followed by a deep, deep cold as the world went from red to black, intense black, black of the void, and then to blue. His heart was pounding but he found some saliva and worked it over his tongue and whispered a few words to himself to prove that he could speak and then pressed the disk and stepped out of the receiving chamber.

Appolinari's eyes were gleaming with excitement. He ripped off his white silk tie and motioned to Haig to approach the desk. Wordlessly he made an excruciatingly tight knot around the scientist's left thumb with the thin end of the tie and secured the other end to the heavy desk, jamming the knot so tightly that it would take an age to loosen it.

Haig shrugged again, as if this was all of no importance.

Appolinari ran the checklist, confident, quick, his eyes dancing. Then he stepped into the red cylinder, his gun pointing at the scientist.

"I'm going to give you five seconds, Haig. I'll count them out loud so you can hear. Five seconds, and then if I haven't made the trip yet, you lose flesh and we try again. Got it?"

Haig, still acting, said casually, "Probably work better if I have the control box."

Appolinari tossed his head impatiently, ran across to the panel where he had left the box, handed it to Pinch and stepped back into the chamber.

"Five seconds then. You ready?"

Haig tried not to look at the switches on the panel ten feet away. I'm ready," he replied indifferently.

But even as the door began to move shut, the instant its steel mass eclipsed Appolinari's eyes, Haig had begun to move toward the panel, stretching his left hand out and pulling hard, painfully, against the strong unyielding silk. Holding the control box in his free right hand, he grasped the end of the shortened antenna with his teeth and, pulling the box away from his head, extended the slim chromed telescope to its full length. By the time the lock had set on the door of the transmitting chamber and Appolinari had called out "One!", the tip of the antenna had engaged a toggle switch on the panel. As Appolinari called out "Two!", Haig poised his thumb over the button, and pressed down on the toggle switch with the end of the supple antenna which arched discouragingly while the toggle did not move.

"Three!"

Stretched as far as he could, Haig tried to shorten the distance from him to the toggle switch. He tugged so hard against the inhibiting necktie that he felt his left thumb tear at the ligament holding it into its socket, but the desk moved, perhaps six inches, enough to send the tip of the antenna that far beyond the toggle switch and bring the second tube of the telescoping metal onto the switch. The arch was less now. He pressed as hard as he could with his outstretched, aching fingers; the toggle went down against its spring and the red alarm light above it winked on as Appolinari's angry voice called "Four!"

"There's no other way," Haig said silently. Straining, he pressed the control button and thought he felt it go all the way down before the antenna slipped off the toggle switch, whose spring sent it back up into the ON position.

And almost with no delay at all, the lock of the receiving chamber was sprung. The door opened a fraction of an inch and stopped. A sickening smell of carnation flooded the room, overpowering, hot. The crack of the door widened more and then a hand emerged, part of a dark-suited arm followed, and then the door flung suddenly full open and with a lurch Appolinari sprawled face-down on the floor of the lab.

Haig turned to the desk. Quietly he put down the control box. Opening the desk drawer, he groped around for something to cut the silk, finally found a small pair of scissors, slipped one blade between the noose of silk and the numb discolored skin of his right thumb and carefully cut through the cloth. He turned back toward the chambers and the slumped figure on the floor. He rose decisively, pushed the chair aside, grasped the ankles of the body on the floor, swung it around and dragged it across the room. With no trace of squeamishness, he dragged the dead weight onto the daybed and covered it with a blanket. He put the mangled carcass of the rat into a plastic garbage bag. He wet a sponge and cleaned the floor of the room and the floors of the two chambers until no trace of the rat's blood could be seen. He rinsed the sponge and wrung it out. He walked to the videotape machine and rewound and repacked the tape that was on it. Then he started to take the second recording of that evening's work out of the box, and stopped, and put it back again.

"No," he said, aloud but very softly. "I'd better return to them."

But he did not move to leave the lab. "Something is wrong," he told himself. "I'm not behaving normally," he thought, "but it doesn't seem to matter."

He looked a long moment at the shrouded figure on the day-bed, walked to the head of the stairs, paused with his finger on the light switch, left the light on, turned from the stairs and headed instead for the little lift, stepped into it, and pulled down the starting handle.

He went to the ground floor and opened the liquor cabinet. Finding the wine bottle he wanted, he decanted a large glass.

Just enough, he thought, to ease me through the night. He carried it back up to the bedroom. He sat in a deep chair and watched the sleeping figures. He sipped the wine slowly and waited for the dawn.

II

Daisy Nelson's struggle with disbelief produced in her an over-powering desire to sleep. There was no thought in her mind that she really could sleep. But her eyes were closing involuntarily, inexorably. To fight against this, she stood up and walked to the back door of the kitchen, which opened onto a small yard and an unkempt yew hedge that hid the cemetery's high link fence. She opened the door and drew in the fog-laden air through her mouth, filling her lungs and forcing it out, and then sucked in the cold again two or three times. Soon she began to shiver. She closed the door and leaned against it and wished that the world would vanish. She had no interest in coming to grips with the wrenching, preposterous things she had just been told. She wanted it all to stop.

But there was a natural toughness in Daisy that fought back against the heaviness in her eyelids, the urge to black everything out. There was a stubbornness to her mind; it kept demanding of her. She was irritated at its persistence; she wanted to let go for a while, to give up, but her brain would not concede. It kept noticing, as this man talked, subtleties of emotional tone, the particular sounds of words, the smell of him.

Now he had stopped to give her time to respond. Aware that he was patiently silent as she struggled, she expected him to do what he always did when she did not quickly respond to something new and wonderful that he told her: to *demand* a response. She waited for him to say, "What are you thinking? What are you feeling? Can't you say something?"

But he remained silent. She felt this showed either a new generosity, or something else, something dark. If it's madness, she thought, and his madness is that he believes it, then maybe his patience now is part of some deep psychotic logic. He's waiting, like an obsessive.

Then another possibility entered her mind. Dully she formed the words without speaking them. "He seems a different man."

She opened her eyes and dared looking at him again. What she saw was physically Rob. There could be no doubt about that; his face was regarding her slowly, with a gentle anxiety. She said hollowly, "Which one are you?"

He sighed. "I never took the trip."

"And the one I buried?"

"My ... duplicate."

"Prove it."

"I can't. I know you have to doubt me, because you think he ... the other one would've made the same claim. Pinch might know something that would prove it, but I don't."

She did not pursue that. Instead she said, "You've changed, after all."

"Of course I've changed. I've been through ..." He stopped, feeling pretentious.

"I don't know where the strength to do this is coming from," she told him. "But I've got to know about what happened between ... between you and ... and the other one. Nelson?"

"I'm Nelson. He was Robert. That was arbitrary on Pinch's part. He made a mistake using our own names, my name, whatever you want to call it. Robert and I came to speak of the past as 'us' and 'we.' It was the only way we could make sense of the relationship."

"I don't understand that."

"I'll tell you how it was. But before I go on I want to know how you think I've changed. I've got to have some feedback. I can't just tell and not hear back. I need a response. I'm sorry about the pain you're having, but there's no other way."

"No," she said wearily, "there's no other way."

She came back to the table and sat down. She said, "I think what's keeping me from losing my grip on reality is ... or have I lost my grip?"

"No," he said firmly. "You have not."

"No, I don't think I have. That's what's distracting me, Rob. I'm watching myself not go under and trying to understand why. A minute ago I wanted to go all the way under. I would have welcomed dying. But at the same time, I wasn't afraid of you. I should have been. I've been dealing with the idea that only a madman could say what you've said and believe it. And I know you believe it."

She paused to give him an opening. He waited for her. She said, "And I've never seen you so patient with me. You've never given me the courtesy of my own silences before."

He nodded agreement.

She said, "I told myself you must be mad to believe your own story, but there's this: when I have time to think, I know it's a crazy story, but when I listen to you, I believe it. I saw how pained and frightened you were while you were telling me. You know I might scream and run out of the house. Or just reject it all, you, everything. And you've been in the same fix before – admitting to me about some woman. Only then you weren't frightened; you were cocksure. You took it for granted I'd stick with you, and if I didn't, it didn't matter. *I* didn't matter. If I ran out on you, that was the lumps you had to take."

He nodded. He seemed very calm.

"And now it's different?"

"Yes." Very solidly.

"You always said you never wanted to depend on anybody. Now you're acting as if a whole lot depends on what I do next."

"Everything." He said it undramatically, with neither restraint nor emotion: a simple statement.

"Rob, when you came home with the Flaherty Prize and the Gold Medal from Cannes and firsts at San Francisco and wherever else it was, you were intolerable for months. You went around screwing every woman you could find, treated me like dirt. And the only times you went the other way and pleaded with me and hung on to me were when things went sour – when you couldn't finish a show and had to let them take it away from you and turn it over to someone else; or when you totalled the Aston-Martin; when you burned your eye. Then you needed me.

"So you see, Rob, when you started tonight I thought, 'Something's gone wrong. Rob needs his momma.' But now I'm confused because I do think you've changed, and I'm willing to listen about that. But I'm still not close to you. I partly believe you and I partly trust you, but I'm holding back because I've been burned a lot. You want me to tell you something rough? When I was standing in the living room tonight, before you came in, and thinking ... about the funeral, I was saying to myself, 'To hell with him. He was a faithless bastard and I've got all my life ahead of me.' "

"Daisy, I know that."

"And you still want me to come with you?"

"We're getting straightened out. But a lot had to happen to me before we could do that. And a lot has. Try to imagine getting to know yourself the way I did."

Daisy felt the sweeping wave of sleep wash down over her again. "I was trying to forget about that," she said plaintively. "I can't imagine it. And you understand that I don't believe it: not with my rational mind."

"But you said you had to know what happened between me and my duplicate?"

"I know you're changed. I can't help being afraid that you're not you. Why shouldn't I think that? This afternoon I buried my husband, for God's sake. Now he wants me to go away with him. And he tells me he was copied, somehow, cloned maybe. And I see a man who's different – importantly different. And I know somebody got killed. And I'm not going to make any more decisions until I know a whole lot more. But I don't know how much I can stand! For the last half-hour I've been almost overcome by the need to sleep."

"You mustn't go to sleep."

"Don't worry, I can't. I'm just telling you how I'm reacting. We've got to do it, get through it. But if they think you're dead now, why do we have to decide so fast. I don't want to understand too fast. You shouldn't want that either."

"I don't. But I've been tricked by Appolinari's people once. I'm not sure they'll stop looking; I'm not sure they won't come here."

She shivered.

"I've reserved plane tickets for this morning and I'm ..." He broke off, looking rueful. "The old me," he said. "I really was about to say, 'I'm going, even if you're not.' I even thought that when I came in here tonight. But I don't think it any more. I think you'll come with me. I'm counting on it."

"Why are they doing this? Because of Appolinari? Do they know that Pinch ... ?"

"We split up. Robert and I agreed we'd go underground together. We figured the contract was out for me. I'll get to that in a minute. They wanted Pinch alive but ... I'm getting ahead of the story."

"But what happened about Appolinari, the body? It's hard to think of Pinch killing anyone!"

A hint of the old, familiar irritability from him now, but controlled: "What's easier to think of? Pinch getting killed? Or slowly shot to bits until he told them what they wanted to know? And then killed?"

"I know. I know. I just ... there's too much happening. I can't help it. I have to know, just some ... housekeeping things – to help my mind with a little orderliness. I have to know about Pinch's reactions to that terrible thing. I have to know what you did with the body."

He sighed. "It's still at Pine Avenue," he said.

"Where, for God's sake?"

Reluctantly he told her. "There was an abandoned coal bin in the basement. There was a coal shute coming in from the back alley. We used the boards from the coal bin to build forms for a short false wall and then we ordered five yards of ready-mix concrete and had the truck pour it in through the coal chute."

Daisy looked less shocked than he had expected. Her practicality responded first. "They'll find him. They'll come looking for him and they'll search that house and when they find new concrete they'll knock it down and when they do they'll never rest until they've got Pinch and you and me."

He shrugged. "It was safer than trying to get the body out of the house."

After a while Daisy said. "You and Pinch and ... Robert? You really did that? I'm trying to see the three of you together. What you did with the body seems remote. It's so disgusting. But it still makes me want to know more about you and this, this other one. Have we got time for that?"

"Yes. That's the point. Until you hear the rest of Robert's story ..."

She looked at him keenly. "Something ... something vast happened between you and ... him. Didn't it?"

"Yes."

"So I have to know about that now."

"Yes Babe. Yes, you do."

12

In the third floor bedroom on Pine Avenue in Montreal, direct sunlight began to leak through the south windows at about eight o'clock those late summer mornings For several days the two men in twin beds awakened almost simultaneously and lay watching each other without expression for many minutes before speaking or moving – studying each other, reading the fine texture lines in the skin, the crowsfeet at the corners of the eyes, searching the opaque eye, the good eye.

On the first morning they had both wept silently upon seeing each other. Haig waited for realization to settle on them, and then told them what had happened in the night and said that he welcomed the crisis of Appolinari's death; it would force them all into an intensity of activity that would leave little room for speculation or introspection or even for verbal exchange about anything but the business at hand. He demanded that a workable plan for disposing the body be reached in half an hour. After a hasty breakfast they started to carry it out.

They sawed and hammered urgently in the dusty back end of the basement, preparing the traditional underworld sarcophagus, and several times the two identical men darted puzzled glances at each other because, over the buzz and clatter of their work, from the other end of the room where Haig was sawing the boards to length, there came the loud cheerful sound of whistling.

By mid-afternoon Haig clapped his hands in satisfaction, picked a ready-mix concrete company from the yellow pages and phoned in his order. Then the three of them climbed the stairs – the lift was uncomfortably crowded with more than two in it – to gather up their carnation-scented burden and send it back down to the basement in the lift. Haig dealt with the body as if it were a sack of old rubbish, and hummed under his breath as they put it into the boarded-up area and held it in place, away from the boards and tightly against the original basement wall, with a dozen bricks.

Forty minutes later the ready-mix was running down the chute and the forms were filled. Nothing remained to do but knock the boards down a day later when the concrete was set.

The identical men wanted to call it quits once the grisly job was finished. But Haig would not let them rest. He thought it was important that their minds be constantly occupied. He immediately started them on a program of work in the lab, playing and re-playing the videotapes, including the cue track which had frame-by-frame recordings of temperature and weight indications from the two chambers. They found that the weight in the red chamber, at the moment in which the mysterious duplication took place, showed no discernible fluctuation; whatever had happened to the original Rob, as he stood there waiting to be transmitted to the second chamber, had not changed his physical mass.

In every other way the records of the transmission appeared completely normal except for some irrational voltage fluctuations. Haig could conceive of no reason for them and no connection except coincidence in time with the improbable thing that had happened.

Late that night they sat in the kitchen for an hour reviewing their day's labor. Haig drank cocoa and the two shared a bottle of wine which Haig had agreed to with some reluctance.

"We'd better start moving toward a normal existence," one of them had said wryly, and Haig had liked the humor of it, the bravado, thought it was a good sign, and gave in.

Haig guessed questions were brewing that might be premature. By now he had quelled any uneasiness that might have accompanied his speculations about himself, hours ago in the early pre-dawn. His strongest feeling was an optimistic one of being in control; of knowing exactly what should be done. He relished the sense of timing with which he had moved the day along from one episode to the next and the efficiency with which he had handled what he now thought of as the garbage disposal problem.

He had not slept; his eyes were very tired and his breath was short, yet he thought himself alert, unassailable. He listened for the silent preparation of challenging words to be spoken in the dark kitchen, and he turned his eyes back to the two men who were as he knew they would be, already looking at him, preparing to ask something difficult. Quicker than they he said, "There'll be another visit from New York. Any day now. We've got to decide what to do about that. What are your suggestions?"

So once again Haig forced the current back into channels of the urgent, the practical, and postponed what he knew he had not thought out, what he did not yet admit to himself he was avoiding.

Before they went wearily up to bed, he had led the two to propose what he had already decided: that the upstairs lab be dismantled and its key components moved into secure storage until the time when work could safely be resumed, and that the dummy basement lab be re-activated against the inevitable visitors from New York.

When they settled at last, long past midnight, their bodies all aching with the day's efforts and their minds numbed, Haig was able to fall into an uneasy sleep.

The next morning, as the two lay silently and studied each other before rising, Nelson said after a while, "Did you dream it was all a dream?"

Robert, startled for a moment, recovered, and nodded, Yes.

The days passed in an atmosphere of intense physical and mental work, and the fact of the existence of two precisely identical persons began, as Haig had intended it should, to shade from the nightmare into the normal. Haig's optimism and sense of control still radiated strongly. But in the upstairs lab, as the dismantling procedures got under way, the two men noticed that from time to time Haig became totally immobile, staring at the panel on the receiving amplifier, so lost in thought that they felt they could have left the room or set fire to the lab notes and he would not have noticed. Once they caught him looking furtively at the two of them after studying the amplifier and walking in this same preoccupied posture from the transmitting chamber to the receiving chamber and back again. But he told them nothing.

There came another evening, over cocoa and wine in the kitchen. The computer terminal had been returned to the basement and patched in to the computer proper. The videotape equipment was crated for shipment. In the lab upstairs all that remained were the chambers and amplifiers, still hooked up and functional except that the monitoring devices had been removed and packed in preparation for storage. The task for the following day would be to move all the items of heavy equipment to the basement where crates were built and ready for them, and to ship them off to a bonded warehouse.

According to arrangements made earlier in the week, a truck from the Toronto zoo was due to arrive midmorning for the chimpanzees Peggy and Fred who had been herded, grumbling, into travelling cages.

The day had been very productive. Haig had driven them all hard, with the result that they had reached their day's objective early and were having their evening drinks at eight o'clock instead of what had become their standard quitting time of eleven p.m.

Haig noticed the two glancing at him surreptitiously from time to time. "So there's something on their minds that has to do with me," he thought. "Probably wondering where we go next once the dismantling of the lab is finished. Well, that's all right." He said to them easily, "Now that we're having a bit of a breather, is there anything you'd like to ask?"

When Robert and Nelson turned to each other before replying, Haig, oblivious to the reproach they were preparing for him, felt only satisfaction in seeing that his control had produced results, in that they now assumed a habit of collaboration instead of the natural competitiveness that might have led them, had it not been, Haig thought, for his careful planning and direction, to try to outdo each other, each one jostling to speak first, to dominate.

So he was complacent and taken by surprise when Nelson drove his left fist hard into his right hand a couple of times and burst out, "You said the other night you hate giving orders. Well goddam it, the fact is you've been having a good time these last few days. You've been really up on top, giving us one-two-three-sir, yessir-nossir. You liked it when we were pouring the concrete on ..." he broke off and licked his lips. "Now what the hell is going on in your head!"

"Because you're not reacting to what you did, Pinch," Robert put in. "You killed a man the other night and you go around whistling the next day. What the hell?"

But Haig suddenly stood up. His eyes were shining with excitement. "These are good questions you're raising and we'll deal with them when there's more time," he said in an unconvincing, mollifying tone. "But I need your help with something practical right now. No, no ..." dismissing their protests with a wave, "there's no time now, and I warned you about the dangers of introspection. We'll talk when the work's done. Come up to the lab with me, and bring Peggy and Fred. There's something we have to try before everything's broken down tomorrow."

But it was slowly and reluctantly that they got up from the kitchen table and followed him. The two minds, formed in the same genetic mold, shaped with the same thirty-seven years of experience, made different only by one inexplicable spatial shift and by a few days' seeing the self from without, perceived events with such congruence that each knew the other's hesitation without its being spoken.

Yet they followed obediently; they had agreed to be obedient.

In the almost empty lab, the two chimpanzees, gleeful at being let out of their cages, sensed adventure and pranced around the austere-looking chambers, the apparatus now stripped of everything except the hulking transmitter and receiver and the bare control panel. The apes chattered and searched the men's pockets for bananas, begging for a trip. They seemed pleased, not at all puzzled to find two "Robs" to play with. Haig patted them eagerly as they jostled him while he turned on the power in the amplifiers. He chuckled excitedly under his breath and pointedly ignored the sullen looks of Robert and Nelson who watched the meager preparations without speaking, until the amplifiers were warmed up and humming and Haig had begun to explain to Fred and Peggy that Fred was going to make one more trip, a farewell trip, a last little adventure on his last night in Pine Avenue, and Peggy held onto the scientist's hand trustingly as if she understood the words, and at that point the other two men simultaneously said, quite sharply, "No, Pinch!"

Haig looked up quizzically. Robert and Nelson exchanged their now habitual consulting looks. Robert deferred and Nelson said, "Why don't you tell us what's going on? You can't send Fred on a trip; there's no heat monitoring, there's no weight monitor, the VTR's gone, the checklists are packed away – there are too many risks. What's the hurry?"

Haig cocked his head to one side. "Of course!" he said brightly, too brightly, "Of course I'm going to tell ye. It's a great moment lads, and nothing's going to stop it. Nobody says 'can't' to me in this lab, by the way, but certainly I'll tell ye. I've decided that the one way the duplication could work, the only way, was for a freak RF feedback loop, which might conceivably have been generated if the voltage was just so, and if there was a bit of crystallization in the circuits on both sides. I've got a glimmering of understanding of how it might work, but it's got to be tried! I'm going to try it! I've got to know about this!"

He took a patch cord from the control panel and plugged the jacks on each end into adjacent receptacles. "That will simulate the feedback. Do you understand? By rerouting the main amplifying circuit once on itself, the same parallel double impulse could be produced. Just *could* be, mind; that's what we have to verify!"

Nelson said, "No. I don't get it at all, Pinch. Why use Fred to do this crazy thing? Use a book, a diamond, anything that doesn't risk someone getting hurt."

The scientist waved all their objections aside. He was proceeding now on pure will; nothing could stop him. Fred seemed bent on collaborating too, and hopped excitedly around the door of the red chamber chattering without pause at Haig as if to say, "Let's get started!" Peggy still held Haig's hand; happy to be there, to be involved with her friends, to see her mate having a good time.

Rob said afterward, recounting it to Daisy, that he could not tell just then whether it was the accumulation of fatigue from overwork, or an emotional warp at the prospect of there being yet another element of unreality thrust upon his life, another impossible duplication, or whether it was the subtle tone of mania in Haig's behaviour, but both the men who watched felt then, and later shared with each other, that time itself was distorted. There was an impression of long arrests when nothing seemed to move except the mind seizing upon something real, searching for some way to get life back to normal. There were lurches in which bodies appeared to be several feet away without having crossed the intervening distance: Haig at the control panel suddenly became Haig by the receiving chamber, closing and locking the door. Then another suspension of time in which Peggy, with her eyes confidently following Haig's every move, was frozen there, the room gone silent while the two watchers tried to understand what was happening, grasp a way to stop it, and yet were paralyzed by the force of Haig's overpowering will and, they afterward admitted to each other, never even thought of physical intervention.

And then there was a moment when Haig was opening the red chamber door for Fred, and Fred was about to step in and Peggy was still hanging on to Haig's hand when both men called out, "Please!" But it was as if no sound could move across the room because Haig appeared not to hear at all. He closed the door of the chamber and set the lock. He picked up the control box and gave a cursory glance at the panel. He held the box up as a kind of beacon, showing it to them. Peggy jumped up and kissed the scientist and ran to wait at the door of the receiving chamber.

Haig drew himself up tall. His hand held the control box still thrust toward the ceiling: "Watch now!" he cried as if they were not already rivetted. He paused a dramatic instant, then his thumb tightened on the switch.

There was a deafening BANG from the receiving amplifier and a filament of blue light raced along the antenna turning all their faces livid until it spread into a halo and died, and they realized that the lights had gone out and there was a terribly hot smell in the room.

There was a moment of dreadful silence. Peggy began to

whimper; then Pinch's faint, frightened voice in the darkness, said, "Oh, God."

The spell broke. Robert and Nelson rushed together toward the circuit-breaker box at the back of the room and Nelson, as he passed by the receiving chamber brushed for a moment against the searing metal of its outer wall and pulled his arm away with a hiss of pain.

Robert groped, found the box and opened it. He ran his fingers over the circuit-breakers and found the one that had popped and reset it. The lights came on.

Haig was on his knees halfway between the chambers. His hands were over his eyes and he was shaking his head as if half-stunned. "Get him out!" he croaked and Nelson was already at the lock, ripping his shirt to give him something to protect his hands from burning.

The door swung open. Inside there was a dark, inert, huddled form. Nelson dragged the warm body out and sadly laid it on the floor.

The female chimpanzee came and stood by her mate's body and called to him to get up. She stamped her feet angrily and chattered. She knelt beside him and pulled the fur on his chest; she sniffed his face, rubbing her nose around his head. Then she pulled back, a low cooing sound coming from deep in her throat. She took the left hand of the dead male in her right hand and turned to look at Haig who was still kneeling in the center of the room with his back to the chimpanzees. Slowly, but with little effort, still cooing a long sustained note, she drew the body of her mate along the floor with her until she was directly in front of the kneeling man, where she let the animal's lifeless hand slip softly back onto the floor, and then put her own hand on Haig's shoulder and turned him around to face the body of Fred.

When he turned it was to find Peggy's eyes inches from his own. The expression of reproach was profound, unmistakable.

Haig's face was stricken. He drew the grieving ape to him and held her in his arms like a child. For the first and last time in their acquaintance, Robert and Nelson saw their friend, seemingly very, very old just then, break down and sob without control.

13

They comforted him the best they could. For a long time he had stayed on his knees hugging the bereaved Peggy, weeping harshly. When he could speak he thanked them for trying to warn him, for seeing what was happening to him and doing what they could. He asked them to take a sleeping pill with him, and gave a double sedative to Peggy, and kept the sleeping ape with him in his bed through the night.

The next morning his face was drawn and there were dark circles etched beneath his eyes, but he worked hard to take down the chambers and the amplifiers and get them into their crates. He forced himself to stay with Peggy until the truck arrived and arrangements were made to take care of Fred's body. But Haig turned his back and stepped quickly into the kitchen when it was time to say goodbye to the chimpanzee. Robert and Nelson found him cowering at the table with his hands over his ears to drown out her crying as her cage was carried to the truck.

He told them then, halting and clearing his throat often as he spoke, what an intoxication it had been to be seized with the illusion that one could make life and assume the right to take it away.

They had not eaten since a hasty breakfast hours before. Haig said he was not hungry, but when Robert got lamb chops and french fries out of the freezer and began to fill the kitchen with savory smells, he brightened up somewhat.

The night brought a September north wind. As the younger men prepared supper and the sun lowering west of the mountain left the house in shadow, the hard, clear air had an unseasonal nip to it. They made a fire in the dining room fireplace and opened some wine and finished off with a big bowl of fresh fruit and cream and brandy. During the meal Haig did not talk except to say please and thanks for things passed or offered and the others did not talk either, but the sharing of the meal was good communication and there was forgiveness and reconciliation in the room as the fire crackled and the street outside fell deeper into shade.

"You're bloody good friends, you two," Haig said at last, slowly, looking from one to the other. "I don't mind admitting that what happened came just in time."

He shook his head as if bothered by a mosquito. "Listen, both of you. If you're perfectly honest with yourself, which I've not been these last days, then you'll admit that from time to time in your life you've had dreams of killing, sometimes real dreams, sometimes waking dreams, daytime fantasies. There's a satisfaction in those dreams. You kill and you get away with it. You feel powerful. You feel invulnerable. Am I right? I know I'm right, lads. It's a universal experience but a lot of people can't admit they've had it so they forget it. Suppress it, really.

"And what's been happening to me since the other night is that I've been living that power. It was magic. I felt I could do anything I wanted! Do you realize what a fantastic thing it was to think of a way to destroy an evil man and then do it? Just like that! I had power. And I was using it on you, and you were letting me do it, and I might have gone on and on. It's hard to say."

He got up from his chair. His eyes were distant now. "Poor Peggy," he said softly.

"Where are you going, Pinch?" Robert asked.

The older man stopped at the door of the kitchen. "Don't worry now," he said calmly. "I have to work for a while at something that uses my brain good and hard. I want to re-run those temperature tables through the computer now that we've got the terminal set up again downstairs. I'll work a couple of hours, be myself again. No illusions this time. I want to let you have some time together without me tonight anyway. You're ready for that, aren't you?"

He stepped through the kitchen door and in a moment they heard his footsteps going down to the basement.

They were alone together for the first time.

Robert said, "Maybe we should go down and just sit there with him."

"What the hell! You heard what he said. He needs his goddam work to get him back on the rails."

"I know," the other man said dubiously, "But all the same . . ."

"No, listen," Nelson said. "That's dealt with now. He says he'll be all right, and he'll be all right. But there's something else that hasn't been discussed around here and it's time to deal with it, so leave bloody Pinch alone and let's get on with what *we* have to do."

"Just because he says he's all right," Robert began, but the other man held up an accusative finger and looked sideways at him.

"I get it," Nelson said bitterly. "You're sorry Pinch went, aren't you." It was a flat, ironic statement, not a question.

"What do you mean?" Robert said a little hotly, sensing a threat in the words.

"Because as long as Pinch plays the chaperone he won't hear any discussion about which one of us was transmitted and which one was not."

"So what?"

"So this: you don't want to face the fact that I'm Rob Nelson and you're something else."

The two men stared hard at each other. Their mouths were drawn tight, each with a hand on the arm of his chair, the elbow up, the other hand on the knee. The identification R's and N's were faded and needed renewing. From a distance they would have appeared like a pair of wax sculptures struck from the same mold, artfully arranged in chairs in a lifelike pose and expressions of alert anger.

Presently the man with the letter R on his hands said, "You know that's bullshit."

"I don't know it! Do you want to know what I think? You're really worried about just who the hell you are."

"I know damn well who I am! I was primed for that trip for six months. I was ready for it. I'm the first man in the world who ever took such a trip and I'm pleased with . . ."

Nelson interrupted him. "Wait a minute! You can't say *you*

were primed for that trip, not in some kind of bloody exclusive way. I was primed for it too, don't forget."

"But I'm the one who took it."

They glared at each other. Both were breathing hard through their nostrils. "It didn't take long, did it?" Robert said.

"What didn't take long?"

"As soon as Pinch leaves the room we're at each other's throats."

Nelson said loudly, "I'm glad we're off that polite crap we've been keeping up for Pinch's benefit. I was sick of it."

"I wasn't doing it for Pinch," Robert said slowly. "I was doing it for the reasons Pinch suggested."

Nelson's eyes narrowed as he considered this.

Robert went on. "For survival."

Nelson jumped on this. "Because you were afraid you'd be the one to lose if it came to a showdown."

"I don't know what you're talking about."

"Sure you do. Would you admit to Pinch it was you that took the trip?"

"Look," Robert said, "I know what you're driving at. If I took the trip, which I damn well did, then I'm changed and you're not and that has implications. I understand that. But you better remember I'm the one who did what we came here for. That's no small matter."

"You talk as if you did it alone," Nelson said bitterly.

Robert got up and reached his foot into the fireplace and kicked a log into a better place, sending a spattering of sparks up the chimney. He drummed his fingers on the mantelpiece.

Nelson said impatiently, sarcastically, "Well?"

Robert turned around and looked at him out of the corner of his eyes, as if he were determined to get on with it but fearful of how it might go. Determination won. He said firmly, "All right. *We* were trained for it. *We* made it happen."

Nelson said, as though he had won a point, "That's right."

"But I was the one who travelled."

"That's right."

"You stayed behind."

"Yes."

Robert said slowly, "That was a mistake. That was because something went wrong. What I did was according to plan. I was intended to travel. You were not intended to stay behind."

There was a measured pause. The tone of the conversation had become lower in pitch, and yet in the air there was something of the quality of lives at stake. They had the sense of moving around each other like boxers looking for an opening.

Nelson said, "You are saying ... that I am a mistake. But you were the one who stopped existing for a moment in time. Not me."

"How do I know that?"

"That I didn't stop being? You saw the recordings. There was no weight change in the red chamber. Nothing happened to me. Nothing at all. Take my word for it."

"Is this a game where the players trust each other's word?"

"Don't you think we'd know if the other one was lying?"

"We were always pretty good at lying. And listen, you say that nothing happened to you. Well goddam it, *I* happened to you. Would you say nothing had happened to you if Daisy had a baby? You've been copied. Now there's two of us. Whatever happened in our lives, what's a bigger happening than that? For both of us?"

Nelson relaxed his expression a little. He said, "But you said it happened to *us*. To both of us, then."

"What else is there to say?"

"A minute ago you were talking about how *you* were trained for the trip. You. Not me."

"Okay, I was wrong. And we're learning something about what's happened. We're learning how to talk about it. When something completely new happens in the universe you ..."

"... almost have to invent a new language to talk about it."

They both laughed a bit uncomfortably at the congruence of their sentences. The peace had been restored somewhat, but there was still a tangible anxiety in the air. Finally Robert opened the subject that they had been carefully avoiding. "We're both married to Daisy."

Nelson, much less hostile than before, but edgy still said,

"That proves there's a difference between us. Otherwise you'd have raised that long ago."

Robert gave a short laugh and said without rancor, almost affectionately, "Go to hell. I thought of it the same time you did – the first time Pinch said he was afraid we might fight. Right?"

"Yes."

"We're not so different, you and I."

There was a pause, then Nelson spoke carefully and firmly. "We are. We're different because you travelled. That's the difference. That means I'm responsible for what we did in the past. The law would say that. The law ..."

"The law! The law couldn't open its mouth, Nelson! The law never saw anything like this. And anyway, what you're trying to tell me is you own what we owned in the past. Isn't that it? Isn't that what you're after?"

Nelson did not answer

"Daisy? The house? The indivisible things? Credit for the films? Would you say the intelligence that made those films is mine as well as yours? I've had the same experiences you have."

Still no answer.

"Be back in a minute," Robert said. He stepped down the hall to the small toilet by the front door. He urinated. He washed his hands, watching his face in the mirror. He practiced his benevolent look, preparing to convince the other man when he returned to the dining room of the generosity of his motives. He raised an eyebrow and worked on a sincerely bewildered expression. Then he thought, "Christ, what a marvellous hypocrite I can be, and for whose benefit?"

"I've been thinking about it some more and I think I know how we can work this out," he said, as soon as he was back in his chair at the table.

Nelson looked guarded. "Well?" he said suspiciously.

"If you're responsible for what we had in the past, does that include ..."

"... all the mistakes? Sure. Has to."

"So I'm off the hook then? I'm clean? I don't have to pay those bills? Answer to any paternity suits that might crop up?"

He looked into the fire for a moment. He said, "If you mean that, I agree. As long as you're not going to say 'we' in the liabilities department and hold ..."

Nelson spoke over him, finishing the thought, "hold onto the 'I' in the assets department? No. If you concede that I'm the original and you're the copy, then you're clean. You can't cash a ..."

"... cash a copy," Robert finished. "You can't cash a Xeroxed dollar bill."

"That's amazing. I was going to say the same thing."

"It's amazing it doesn't happen more. Anyway, we agree."

Nelson rocked back and forth a few times in his chair and clenched and unclenched his fists and said, "Well? Are we going to talk about it or not?"

"Daisy?"

"You know that's what I meant!"

"We settled that," Robert said easily. "I agreed. You're the original. Why are you looking so goddam glum? That's what you wanted, and I say you're right and I really am satisfied. So relax. That's it."

But Nelson pounded his fist on the table and stood up, looking furious. He rushed around the table and grabbed the other man by the shirt, his face deep red with anger. "Why the hell are you being so bloody nice!" he yelled. "What the hell's in it for you? What've you got going with Pinch that I don't know about? Nobody gives up his wife and his bank account and everything else just like that. Snap! It's done! 'I agree.' I don't trust you. Something's going on here and I want to know what it is!"

The room was silent except for their heavy breathing. Then Robert slowly reached up and took hold of the hand gripping his shirtfront. "We never used to react very well to threats, did we?" he said.

Nelson released his grip but stayed leaning over the chair, almost nose to nose, and said, "So there is something. All right. I withdraw the ultimatum. But you've got to tell me. You said yourself, survival; we've got to share things or one of us will go under. Tell me!"

"Please sit down," Robert said.

Nelson stayed leaning over his counterpart for a long five seconds, and then went back to his own chair, still red-faced and breathing heavily.

"I was prepared to fight you," Robert said. "Fight you or con you. From the beginning. Over Daisy or anything else. I knew I was Rob Nelson and those things belonged to me. I think I was still prepared to fight you tonight when Pinch left us. I was afraid, frankly. I felt if we ever did fight it wouldn't end easily. I could imagine killing you then. It's that cosmic, the 'you' versus the 'me', isn't it?"

Nelson nodded guardedly, and Robert continued.

"But here's what happened, and it happened fast. First of all, I always knew that if there was anything to be argued, you had to be the original. Not any better than me, not any worse. You said that you were responsible for what happened in the past. I knew that was right, and I saw it would only work if you took all the debits and all the credits, and you agreed to that. I remembered all the times we used to say, 'If only I could start over again!' About a lot of things: Daisy, the films that got screwed up ... we could talk all night. I've got that chance now. If we can survive all this, if we can work it out with the world, with the law, with – I don't know who – well, I may not have anything, but I know a lot and I've got no attachments. It's a fair bargain. I'm prepared to take my chances.'"

Nelson had scrutinized Robert's face intensely during every second of this declaration. Now he said, somewhat reluctantly, "I believe you."

Then he got up and came around the table again and took Robert's hands in his.

"Nelson, it's the only way." Robert said. "It's survival. And it's a good deal."

"If you ever need money ..."

"I'll get it from Pinch. He's got plenty and he bears a lot of the responsibility, and you know what he's like. He'll offer it long before I have to ask. There are more important things to deal with than money."

The logs in the fireplace lurched and settled and Robert

went to put on a fresh one. He stirred the coals with a poker and wondered if the brief exposure to absolute blackness that he had known and nearly been vertiginous in, between the red chamber and the blue, had been a gift, an epiphany in which he might find himself ... he did not know how to think about it, how to articulate it yet, but it teased at him and he wanted to share it, as a way of getting at the understanding that might be found in the moment of pure blackness, pure non-experience. He turned back to Nelson. "About being different, after the trip. We knew there would be some sense of difference, but I have a feeling, it sounds pretentious but ..."

"No it doesn't," Nelson said, fascinated. "You have a feeling about touching eternity."

"Yes," Robert said, and a sweet calm spread through his limbs, a calm he could not remember feeling since he was a child listening to his mother read to him stories by Rudyard Kipling, and smelling her skin, a calm that had its origins in the depth of need that lies in every person to be known by another person; now this – he looked keenly at his mirror image sitting across the table, his twin, and felt strangely moved – this other person had known something about his thoughts, something so remote from his usual avenues of thought and from his usual language that he had been uncertain about expressing it at all, and there had come within this recognition, perhaps intensified by the storms between them that had risen and passed so quickly, an amazing calm.

And he said, "Yes. Touching eternity. That's exactly it."

14

It was deeply quiet in the tall grey house. In the basement a troubled and sobered man was forcing his mind to wrestle with masses of numbers and reticent lines on graphs. In the fireplace in the dining room the wood was burning silently, all the early explosions and hisses now cooked away, sending a steady roseate heat across the room. The street outside was unusually still.

Conversation at the table had come to a pause as both men sat and dreamed into the firelight.

Then Nelson said, "Some things matter less and some things matter more now."

"That's right."

"We can talk about Daisy if you want. The war's over."

"I know. But it all turned around that. A lot of it anyway. Christ, Nelson, all those women. All that searching for something you never ..."

"Something you never found? But sometimes it seemed to be there. What does that look like to you now? Was it there and I ... we couldn't handle it? Were we kidding ourselves? All the time?"

"Really want to take a look at that?"

Nelson moved forward in his chair. He seemed to be confronting the other man, not in hostility, but demanding something. He said crisply, "Look at this: I ... we were terrifically popular. Invitations were always coming in. Everything we put our hands to came up roses; if it didn't, we were good at covering our tracks, even after some turkey, right?"

Robert acknowledged with a nod, and looked as if he would pick it up, go on with the catalogue himself but changed his mind and waved to Nelson to continue.

"Women chased us. We had notable men calling us up to have lunch, talk about things that ought to be filmed, talk about ideas, about going into politics or ... Lots of work. Interesting work. Applause. And we'd look in the mirror and we'd know we were lonely. Incomplete. Then down here, working with Pinch, that's when we began to think it might have something to do with the whole issue of excellence, that we were empty because we were just flittering around the edge of things, never getting right into the center. That's probably part of it ..."

Robert was inattentive. Because he knew where Nelson was going. He waited for the voice to stop, not listening, starting into something of his own about separateness and brotherhood.

"... All the same," Nelson was saying, "it felt like loneliness. And we'd call it lonely and go out on the prowl again. I'm wondering if the trip did anything for us in that department?"

Robert was aware that the voice had stopped. He said "Sorry, what was the question?"

"I said I wonder if the trip did anything for us in that department?" Nelson said irritably.

Robert laughed and said in his best Bogart voice, "We've got each other, sweetheart!"

And Nelson laughed in return, a laugh too loud, then broke it off and turned away and closed his eyes and felt profoundly depressed as if there were a physical weight hanging around his shoulders, compressing his chest.

Robert said calmly, "I meant that as more than a joke."

Nelson said to the wall, "Only if we can share whatever it is you know and I don't."

"No it's not like that. It's being able to deal with it. You're still puzzled about looking in the mirror and finding a lonely man, right? That seems absurd to you. You hate it. You feel, why is this happening to me? No different from the last five years we've been feeling that way."

"And it's different for you?"

"Not because I know anything you don't know, but because I've been able to think about it differently." He hesitated. "Want me to tell you something you already know?"

"I ... I'm not sure."

"Try," Robert said encouragingly.

"Okay. Go ahead."

"What was the Aston-Martin for?"

Nelson frowned skeptically. "Are you lecturing me on the ethics of conspicuous consumption? The Aston-Martin was the best damn piece of iron ever made, that's what it was for. Don't give me any of that status-symbol stuff Daisy used to bitch about either. It was a piece of joy. Flowing across the country like a goddam river. Remember when we drove all night from Montreal to the lake. Left Pinch's place at one in the morning. Hundred and ten all the way the minute we hit the auto-route. Four hours. Beautiful. Pure bloody existential joy. Life. Flight!"

"That's right. Terrific. For who?"

"For who? What do you mean for who? For me! For us! You know. We were alive in that car."

Robert held his hands out in a gesture meaning, 'Be patient.' He said, "Daisy hated it."

Nelson shot back impatiently, "And Thérèse loved it. So did Erica Douglas. And so did Lindy. What the hell has this got to do with anything?"

Robert sighed. "Don't get angry. Let me have some time to work this up. I've only started wondering about it."

Nelson shrugged and sat back.

Robert said, "We had a three-week love affair with Thérèse. Three short weeks. Erica Douglas we screwed. Once. Lindy we see if we go to Vancouver or she comes east. Terrific woman. But we don't live with her. No commitment."

Nelson grunted, but Robert went on. "Now think about the big loves – the great people; the great interludes; Jenny in Paris; the ..."

"That was trying to fill up the empty spaces. Trying to find something. That didn't make the spaces. You eat because you're hungry. You don't get hungry because you eat."

"Are you sure? I'm not any more. For one thing, it forced a lot of secrecy on us ... protecting us from Daisy. Or we said sometimes, protecting Daisy. It meant carrying a lot of secrets. Secrecy's a lonely craft. The spy in the cold."

Nelson shook his fists in the air in frustration. "Whenever we went to Boston or Chicago or London there was love there. Somebody tremendous to be with!"

"For a short time."

"Well?"

"With no commitment."

Nelson stood up, walked over to the china cabinet, brought out a forty of Johnny Walker and then went to the kitchen for ice and glasses. When he returned he poured whisky over ice – no need to ask – passed Robert the glass, filled his own and quickly drained it. He opened the bottle again and poured. He fooled with the ice, puddling it with his finger. He smelled at the glass and drew a little of the cold amber liquid through his teeth. He put it down again and looked at it instead of across the table and said with a bitter edge, "I don't remember that we used to be much in the line of preaching. Is that what you get out of a J.A. Haig electric trip? If it is, the hell with it. I'm glad I didn't go."

Robert studied the petulant face across the table staring into the whisky glass. He said, "Do you think I'm trying to punish us? I'm just trying to figure out this loneliness thing."

Nelson sat back again and sighed and said, "Perhaps I know where you're going and I think it's crap. Or perhaps I can't handle it. Can you?"

"I think it might be easier for me because I'm starting over."

Nelson was once more slouched in his chair sucking at the edge of the glass.

"We have a pact now," Robert reminded him. "You wanted the past, I agreed to give it up. I'm a poor man. But I don't have to deal with the old visions or the old illusions any more. Because everything I might have worried about is yours now. Are you sorry, by the way?"

"No. I've got Daisy." He said it without gloating.

"Let me tell you what else I might be prepared to give up, because I think some of the things we were so stuck on were the things that made us lonely. We were really a prideful man, Nelson. Everything we did we said we would be responsible for. We would take all the credit for the good and take all the flak for the bad. I've just begun to see that as one of the dozens of ways we set ourselves apart from other people. And not just by being prideful and stubborn and tough ... because we weren't even sincere about it. It was just another way we manipulated people."

"Cut it out, Robert! That's bullshit."

Robert leaned back in his chair and pulled the curtain aside and gazed at the September sky a while and then down into Pine Avenue. He remembered looking down at the street years ago, and Daisy coming to pick them up and take Haig to the airport to go to Rome. Then he thought about another more distant September in Paris with Jenny, looking out of the window in her tiny flat in the Rue du Pélican and smelling the bread and coffee from the café on the corner, and Jenny, still naked in the bed saying, "What do you mean? Why would you be afraid of manipulating?" And how her asking the question had saddened him because he had been so certain she would know why he was afraid of it and would tell him why and what to do about it, as she had told him so many things about himself, with her distressing, endearing clarity. And how that sadness had struck so deep because he had been counting on Jenny and she had never let him down. Why did he make such absolute demands on people, he asked himself now.

Not realizing that the other man might not be sharing the same memory, he said, "We never went into that with Daisy – our feel of manipulating people. We could have. She's tough. But we wouldn't do it because we'd sold ourselves to Daisy as a kind of myth which we didn't have the courage to kill. We couldn't admit to her how much we'd been manipulating her. The man she married didn't believe his own story."

Nelson rose with his drink and went to the fireplace, feeling cold and depressed, but no longer reluctant to pursue this investigation. He said, "You've really got it in for the old Rob Nelson, haven't you? You're angry at what we were."

"Maybe. We lost our nerve when it came to the manipulation issue. That's why we were lonely with Daisy. We tried bringing it up with Jenny, hoping she would turn out to be the really big love we had been searching for all the time, and we hadn't invested any bullshit there. But by then we'd gone too far alone. We didn't always know when we were acting; whether we were telling the truth about how we felt or whether we were in love or manipulating or whatever it was. Double knots. House of mirrors. That was part of the price of always insisting on doing it our way."

Nelson poured a few drops of scotch on the polished mantle top and sentimentally traced out a heart with an R and a D in it, in the liquid.

Robert said, "You're going to have to think about that when you get back to Daisy."

"That's my problem," Nelson said shortly.

"But you see what I'm talking about, don't you? How we brought our loneliness on ourselves?"

Nelson just stared gloomily into the fire.

"Look, Nelson. It doesn't have to be so tragic. Feeling alone may be good, it may be real. A lot of people kid themselves that they're close to somebody, and then get hurt by that illusion. We used to be puzzled because we felt cut off, but if you come to terms with how we lived, we wanted it that way. We set up our lives that way."

Nelson said with some resignation, "We set it up so everything we did made us different. Apart. On top of the heap if we could pull it off, but top or bottom we were never part of the heap. Never part of something else. But I'm not sure I'd want to change it. Maybe you're right ... the sense of isolation shouldn't be so puzzling and perhaps that's better. I understand what you were saying about the car. And we build a cabin in the woods and fight like hell to keep anybody else from building close by and then wonder why nobody comes to visit, right?"

Robert smiled. "Played records with the headphones on. Tore around back roads on a bike with a big helmet and a blank blue face mask. Jesus, Nelson, a million things we did. We're not stupid. We wanted to be alone. Now why not accept that instead of moaning about it."

The phone rang in the kitchen. Nelson put his drink down and started toward the door.

"Leave it," Robert said. "Let Pinch get it. He can pick up

in the lab. We have to talk some more about Daisy." The phone stopped after the third ring.

"But we settled that, didn't we? When you agreed I was the original and you'd have to start fresh. You said that was okay."

"But it hurts. I'm asking you to help me. I don't know what that means, even, but nobody else in the world ..." He stopped at the sound of footsteps hurrying up the stairs from the basement.

Haig came through the kitchen door fast. "Who's Pete Brady?" he said.

"What?" they both said at once. They came to their feet looking alarmed. "Was that him on the phone?" Nelson asked.

Pinch sat down heavily in front of the fire studying the fright in their faces. He said, "Here's what happened. When I answered the phone, the operator said, 'I've got a collect call for Rob Nelson from Pete Brady in New York. Will you accept the charges?' I said, 'Just a minute, I'll go and get him.'

"Now then, a man's voice said, 'Tell him Pete Brady.' Very distinctly. I mean he was speaking in a forced way, to make sure I heard the name. I was a bit fashed. I said, 'Operator, tell Mr. Brady I heard him perfectly well,' and then the man's voice said 'Good!' and there was a click. And the operator said, 'He hung up. I'll have to get him back for you sir.' And that was it. I said, 'Never mind,' and hung up myself. Who's Pete Brady?"

Robert took a deep breath and let it out again. He looked at Nelson, who nodded, and Robert said, "It's a signal, Pinch. Brady's a hit man. He's a lean brown guy with beautiful white hair and white eyebrows and a very steady hand. He did a lot of work for Appolinari. I ... we did him a favor once."

Pinch did not understand. "What's the melodrama, lads? You're telling me he's returning a favor, is that it?"

"You could say that."

"So?"

Nelson said, "I never thought this could happen. It's like fooling around with dynamite. I once asked Brady, privately, if he'd ever take a contract on a friend."

"What does that mean?" Pinch asked.

"A contract to kill. So much in advance, so much when the contract's been made."

Pinch sensed the drift of this and stiffened. "What did he say?"

Robert answered. "Brady laughed. He said 'That's part of the game, kid. You don't have friends in this game. You're a pro or you're not. I'm a pro.'"

"I ... we knew him," Nelson said, "how to get him talking, telling stories. He enjoyed leaving a trail. If you were cool he lost interest telling stories. He liked to shock. So I let on I was horrified – to keep the stories coming. Then he said ..."

Nelson closed his eyes. He felt unsteady and he wished he hadn't taken so much scotch. Robert finished it for him: "Brady said, 'Don't worry kid. If I ever get a contract on you, I'll phone you first – give you a running chance. But if I find you, I'll still make the contract. I've never lost one yet.'"

15

"Pete Brady killed the man called Robert, and I identified him, and this afternoon we buried him. And you have come back to me to ask me to believe all this, and to run away from here and start our life ... afresh." Daisy spoke the words like a litany, like a statement of realities unseen but desired to be held as truth. She stared straight ahead of her, into a space that had no focus, a line of sight that had no terminus.

The man across the kitchen table from her waited, and drank his coffee. He did not confirm or disagree with what she had said. He was tired of talking, his throat was sore from it, and there was more to come, but the bulk of it was over now and he would rest before he finished it and then plunge on to try to show her that out of all the horror and confusion still flourished a kind of hope they had never before had reason to grasp.

She continued, still without looking at him and still with an inward and recitative tone, although the words were even more poignantly meant for him now. "I first had to decide whether or not it really was you, since I knew you were dead. Then I had to decide whether you were telling the truth, and that has always been very hard to determine in the past. Now, when I decided you were telling the truth ..." She turned and looked full at him at last, and said in a thin, slightly strained voice, but not without sympathy and warmth, "When I decided you were telling the truth, I also decided that you were crazy. You understand that? Why I would think that?"

"Of course," he answered softly. "But I'm not crazy. It all happened. They thought Galileo was lying at first, and then they probably thought he was crazy, because what he said couldn't be." He looked at her with a curious, half-quizzical, half-challenging look and when he spoke again it was with an almost questioning inflection. "Finally they decided he was telling the truth and they made him shut up. They chose not to know."

"And you want to know what I'm going to choose."

"Were you able to believe what happened to the *Pietra della Reconciliazione?*"

"It's only a stone."

"I had a hard time believing Pinch at first, but Pinch doesn't lie. You know that."

"Can I talk to Pinch?"

"If you can get him. There's a recording on his phone, an answering machine. I've no idea where he is. He might call back. You'd have to find a way to make it private. We can't risk anyone listening in. Would you believe Pinch before you'd believe me?"

"Rob, that was a shabby thing to say."

"I know it. I'm tired and I'm anxious and I'm not above saying and doing shabby things even though I'm trying to avoid them. You wanted some verification and Pinch is the best person. I understand that."

"I don't think you're crazy anymore," Daisy said.

She got up shakily and went upstairs to the toilet and sat on it for a while with her eyes closed. She wondered if anyone had ever been given such a perplexing challenge as she now faced. Then she thought that, of course, if Rob's preposterous story was true, he had been in a position of utter perplexity and must still be. She felt a rush of sympathy for him, and tears came to her eyes. She stood up and ran cold water and bathed her wrists and her face for several minutes before going downstairs.

"I'm not dependent on what he says, Rob, but I'm going to call Pinch anyway. If he's there, I'll say that a man claiming to be a relative of yours, who looks a lot like you, has been in touch with me and says he knows you. I'll ask for a character reference. Do you think that would be safe enough? Does Pinch know what happened to ... to Robert?"

"I've no way of knowing. I could never get him. Only the recording. Anyway I ... we'd just not been using the phone.

Too dangerous. I wish you wouldn't, but I guess you'd better. I'd really like you to talk to him. *I'd* like to talk to him. I wish to hell he was here. Sure. Let's give it a try."

But they reached an intercept recording in Montreal *"Nous regrettons, Il n'y a pas de service* ... There is No Service To The Number You Have Dialled. Please Check Your Listings."

They tried dialling it once more, to be sure. The same result.

"He said he'd get in touch when he could. He was going to hide out, but when we left Pine Avenue he still hadn't decided where. Pinch hasn't got close friends any more – besides us."

"When was that?"

"About two months ago."

"Where have you been for two months?"

"I was coming to that. The most important things that happened were in those last two months. Up until now, everything I've told you is really explanation. I don't know if you're ready to believe any of it. But if you do at all, or if you think you might be able to believe it, or believe in me, you've got to know what happened over those two months. Then you'll know whether or not you want to come with me. Obviously I'm betting you will. But I'm still scared you may not."

Daisy had her second wind now. She thought that if Rob had really changed in these last few months it must be because of his encounter with this other self, this unbegotten 'Robert.' She decided that she was ready to deal with Robert as a real person. Even if the whole story were only a metaphor for something that could not be told in any other way, the more she heard of it the more normal it appeared. Credibility had grown with the telling. She had become sharply tuned, from the private examination of witnesses and the interviewing of doubtful clients, to those subtle hesitations of eye and voice, the flicker of a dropped lid, the catalogue of micro-movements that reflect uncertainty or betray a lie. And although Rob had often skillfully hidden things from her in the past and sometimes successfully lied to her, she knew his manner too well to be misled at length. In this strange night, throughout his narrative, what Daisy had seen was the Rob she knew, trying as hard as he could to communicate something that mattered.

And the substance of what he had said about that first un-supervised conversation with the other Rob rang true. Daisy recognized the things they said to each other; all those struggles had taken place before. Some had surfaced when Rob was drunk and so he soon forgot them. Some had been only half-articulated. Some she heard obliquely, listening to him in conversation with other people – particularly when he was quizzing someone hard about that person's attitudes or behavior – she had been able to sort out which were the issues that really meant something to Rob, which were the ones he could not deal with in terms of himself.

She had known for years that he was anxious about the readiness with which he manipulated people, although he had never discussed this as a characteristic of himself. It made Daisy angry to learn that he had broached the issue with the fabled Jenny, but she was not surprised. She had long understood that what went on in all those other beds was not simply a matter of sex, and not a rejection of her either. She knew he was looking for echoes and reflections from different mirrors, for things about himself, for confirmation of his own existence. She believed that she could have helped him if he had not been so impatient at being led (by anyone but bloody Pinch! she thought wryly) so intolerant when tough issues about himself were raised by anyone except himself.

She had spent so much time in her long months of solitude punishing herself for not having found ways to carry him past the point of intolerance, to force some of the issues into the open. Now that he was so explicit about his hunger for that kind of investigation she felt resentful.

Why hadn't she been stronger? If he was too weak to handle it, why hadn't she known? Well she *had* known; so why had she let it pass?

Fear, of course, that she might ignite one of his rages, and send him away for good. But she should have taken the chance.

But now! Now he had lived a nightmare, a spectral en-counter that she finally saw she had to accept as real; there was no other way to deal with it. The more she thought it over the more she began to feel optimistic. Not an hour ago she had been wishing for the world to close down, had been almost overpowered by the weight of her eyelids, starving for sleep and oblivion, and now she felt – not alert and lively, but tentatively ... positive.

Having survived the shock and confusion of Rob's revelations, she was buoyed by the renewal of her curiosity about what had gone on between Rob and his duplicate. She wished, nostalgically, that she had met the other one. She was anxious to hear more about him. The idea of "negotiating for the future" fascinated her and she wanted to believe Rob when he suggested that there was a new hope for them as a partnership: she could accept that he had no hidden reason for suggesting it.

Something else that he had said struck her, and she asked him about it. "Did the subject of excellence come up between you and Robert?"

"Yes."

"You see I can call him Robert now, just as if I knew him. I feel odd about it and maybe in the morning I'll think I was silly and credulous but ..." She looked at the clock, "It is the morning. It's five o'clock!"

"Why did you ask about the excellence thing?"

"Because you said that was why what you were doing with Pinch was so important. And then you bridled at Robert when he was making his list of all the things you used to do that were really shabby, and you both seemed to think there wasn't much excellence in what you had done. But you're wrong. You never gave yourself enough credit. That's one of the reasons you were always lonely. You took public credit, but privately you gave yourself a hard time. I knew that. You should have asked me."

"You should have told me."

"I should have. I know that now. I've gone through despair, and I found some strength in my own loneliness that I didn't know I had, and just now I'm feeling optimistic, but you better know I'm still watchful."

He smiled his familiar half-smile.

She said, "I've wanted to say things like, 'Oh my darling!' I still do, but I have to hold them back, not trust my optimism too much. Can't."

"Give yourself credit, Daisy. Like what you said to me."

"Oh I am. I am! I'm not being hard on myself. But I'm still being very hard on you. Only I think you can take it; that's why I'm optimistic. I'm assuming you'll stand up to scrutiny."

"All right then. Let me tell you what happened at the lake."

"You were at the lake? I sent the police to the lake."

"When?"

"Two or so weeks ago."

"We must've just left. It never occurred to me you'd have the cops looking for me."

"Mac told them he hadn't seen you this year."

"Mac's a good liar; I wouldn't be here if he wasn't."

16

Less than an hour after Pete Brady's call, Robert, Nelson and Haig were in the alley behind the house, packing a few belongings into Haig's old rusty Volkswagen, an inconspicuous green and corrosion-streaked car of indeterminate years which concealed a carefully rebuilt and smooth-running engine: one of Pinch's few indulgences.

When the car was packed, the two looked uncomfortably at Haig, uncertain what to say and wishing that he was coming with them.

"Don't worry about me, lads, will you now? I've got money and I've got my wits and I'll be in touch with you as soon as ever I can. But we're much better off splitting up for the while. You're agreed to that, now?"

The two men nodded.

Haig said, "I've grown older and wiser in these last days. I think you have, too. Did you ever read any Shakespeare? *The Tempest?* Do you remember Prospero said at the end he was through with magic? He said, 'I'll drown my book.' Well ..."

"You can't, Pinch." Nelson said. "You've come too far, you –"

"No, no lad. I don't mean I will. I considered it ... after Fred, but then I thought, no, the only thing that got me into trouble was trying to rush into the part I didn't understand – the duplication. I'm torn now between the scientist wanting to know how to do it and the human being who fears it will violate something sacred. I've made a hard decision. If we get through this next bit all right, I'm going to give it to the world. The Faust element only happens when you've got a secret. If everybody knows the secret, then people will watch each other. It's risky, but it's not as risky as keeping it to yourself."

"Then you don't know how the duplication happened."

"No. I'm even prepared to believe it's essentially mysterious. And that's a scientist talking. But if I suppress the process, it will surface again. Things are always in the wind. Someone's working on this problem somewhere, bound to be. None of us can even envision the implications of making the duplicate ... if we ever do."

He embraced them. He handed to Nelson a packet containing two hundred and fifty twenty-dollar bills. Robert started the engine. Nelson climbed in. They both gave him a thumbs-up sign through the windscreen. Robert backed the little car in a tight turn, then straightened again and slipped quietly down the alley and away.

Haig hugged himself and shivered. He looked at the stars for a moment. He went back into the dark house.

Robert and Nelson drove all night to the lake, southwest of Algonquin Park in northern Ontario. They found the experience exhilarating because of the extraordinary sense of partnership and the trust that had blossomed in their earlier exchange.

For the time being they eschewed further talk about Daisy or about anything else that might divide them: they concentrated on developing a strategy for escaping Pete Brady. The head-lights of the car played fantastically on the bottom layers of mist that hung a few feet above the deserted highway up the Ottawa valley, and then, as they left the valley and rattled westward into the Madawaska Highlands, the air cleared and the road was black beneath the stars. As they pressed deeper into the wood-lands, they began to live an ecstatic collaborative pattern. Both minds would seize upon the same goal, not redundantly, but with the swiftness of comprehension that was, they both re-flected, like the satisfaction of writing a piece on the typewriter and seeing, as you re-read each line, how it could be better, your own words talking back to you, only in this case the paper was not a passive receptacle, but human and gifted with imagination. Their sentences soon grew shorter, until a third person would have had difficulty following much of what was said.

"Phone Daisy?"

"First place they'd."

"She'll be desperately."

"Yes, but first we have to."

"Foolproof, right. Better she worry."

"Old Mac?"

"Gossips. Shop in Mactier."

"Too small. Huntsville."

"Port Carling. Nobody we know."

"A month?"

"Pinch gave us five thousand."

"Lots of time."

At dawn, still forty miles from their destination, they passed a public campsite by the edge of a usually busy lake near the road. The only vehicle in it, frosted with dew, was a rusted, battered half-ton pickup truck with a camper in the box.

"Good God!" Nelson said from the passenger seat where he could read the inscription on the door of the truck and the faded patched cotton banner on the side of the camper, "Lucas Rankin, Preacher of Petitcodiac, New Brunswick." And then he said "Ooh," with a groan, remembering another weekend, when Daisy had hoped the preacher would not come knocking at their door. He glanced across at Robert, knowing he was remembering as well, and both of them were too perplexed about their feelings to speak further.

The sun was casting long morning shadows across the still dew-darkened road as they pulled up at Canopy Lake. There would be people coming up on weekends from Toronto, but on this Tuesday morning it was deserted at the north end, nearly five miles from Old Mac's store on the road that led to nowhere else. Rob's pursuit of privacy, his near bankrupting himself to buy up as much surrounding land as possible on the newly opened lake ten years earlier, paid off well now in protection.

For three weeks nobody knew they were there. Weekends, when the lake was busy, they stayed indoors during the day and used no lights at night. They kept the car out of sight in a shed next to the boathouse. They shopped only at night, limiting their diet to what could be bought in the resort town of Port Carling, in a dawn-to-midnight store that carried canned goods but nothing fresh except bread and milk, bacon and cheese.

Robert let his beard and moustache grow, and when they went out at night he wore dark glasses. Nelson cut his hair very short with a razor, and kept clean shaven. This gave them mobility of a sort; they could go into a strange town together without exciting the curiosity that identical twins would draw.

After a while, bored by their isolation and emboldened by the completion of their scheme for dealing with Brady, by the peacefulness of their retreat so far and by the lack of notice taken of them when they did go out to shop, they became less cautious. Daring the exposure of a sortie on a Friday evening when the road around the lake might be travelled by neighbors even this late in the fall, they drove one night into Huntsville. Nelson went alone into the Hudson's Bay store and bought identical suits of work clothes so that when the time came, with a shave for Robert and matching eyepatches cut from an old piece of denim, they could again be indistinguishable one from the other.

The strategy, now refined and agreed upon, evolved a physical trap for Brady. They would rent an old house in Toronto and booby trap it and, when it was ready, find a way to tip off Brady that they were there, lure him into the trap, immobilize him and then ... ? They had not been able to resolve the 'then.' Failure of the nerve? In any case, they recognized that their opponent was experienced and might well be wily enough to avoid traps, however carefully planned. So to add to their chances of survival, they had decided that once Brady had been tipped and they could expect him imminently they would dress as perfect doubles. This would spread the odds should the trap fail. Brady would have two targets to confuse him. They could split up and divide the pursuit.

Rob was to reflect later that the real impulse to resume identities may have been something deeper, touching the question of self and sharing which would be particularly acute as the hunter closed in upon the hunted.

But now, relaxed and tanned and cheerful and looking quite dissimilar in their different clothes, one cleanshaven and with an eyepatch, the other bearded and wearing sunglasses, their enemy seemed distant, and their mood, if not carefree, was lighter than it had been since leaving Montreal.

"Christ I'd like to eat something somebody else cooked," Nelson said. "And some fresh meat!"

They drove by a restaurant on the Huntsville street; "Home-made Blueberry Pie!" a handlettered poster in the window advertized, and underneath in a big scrawl "Fresh Today!"

There were few people in the restaurant. They turned the car at the next corner and drove slowly by again, scanning for familiar faces and finding none. They parked, crossed the road and stopped outside again long enough for a scrutiny of the few customers bending over vegetable soup or hot gravied sandwiches – and one with a fat slice of blueberry pie, clearly enjoying himself. Nelson nudged Robert who was looking at a smaller cardboard poster propped against a vase of dried cattails on the shelf below the window.

"That guy dogs our footsteps. We should go and see what he's all about. Might be a film in it," Robert said teasingly. The poster announced a tent meeting with Lucas Rankin, Preacher.

The vegetable soup was homemade, the steaks tender and tasty, and the pie so good they had seconds. After the waitress brought their second cup of coffee and retreated again, Robert said, "I wasn't joking about going to the meeting ... not entirely."

Nelson thought for a minute. Then he said, "It'd be a break. Too bad we haven't got a camera."

"An agrarian Billy Graham?"

"A pastoral pastor?"

"A rural revivalist?"

"A bucolic ..."

They were both laughing.

"Did it say where?"

"Attrey's Corners. I noticed the turn off on the way up."

They found it somewhat north and east of Canopy Lake, on an uninviting backroad, often noticed and ignored. Nelson slowed the car to a crawl while they read a big banner stretched between two poles over an open gate in the rail fence. They looked at each other hesitantly less sure now that this was a good idea.

The banner announced: "Lucas Rankin, Preacher of Petitcodiac, New Brunswick. Prayer Meetings Friday and Saturday. Healing Sunday. Renew Your Faith! Discover Your Savior! Everyone Welcome."

The tent was in a sprawling pasture and the meeting was in full swing. They could hear the hefty vibrato of an electric organ and the voices of the crowd – raw voices, cheerful voices, singing an old familiar hymn:

> *The Church's One Foundation*
> *Is Jesus Christ Arr L-o-o-ord*

The flaps of the tent opened and closed slowly in the light evening breeze like the fronds of a coral-dwelling undersea plant. Lights twinkled through seams and holes in the faded canvas, and a single electric line looped over a few makeshift poles trailed across from the little country corner store which was lighted too, but looked deserted.

> *She is His new creation*
> *By water and the Word.*

"Why not?" Robert asked.

"Just ... feeling cautious."

"We could stay at the back. Look it over carefully. Slip out early."

Nelson eased the car a few yards around the corner onto the crossroad that justified the village name, a poor dirt road even less substantial than the one they had been following. He shut off the engine and they climbed out and walked slowly through the long grass behind the store. A new song had begun, a powerful jazz-like rhythm this time, with explosive hand-claps on the off-beat and soaring young voices belting out the words as the two threaded their way among the forty or fifty cars parked between the store and the opening of the tent.

> Oh there's a
> New (clap) *light* (clap)
> *Shinin' in the* (beat – clap)
> *Sky tonight!*

> *Oh there's a*
> *New* (clap) *light* (clap)
> *Shinin' in the* (beat – clap)
> *Sky tonight!*

The tent throbbed with music. On the makeshift platform at the front, a gaunt woman, whose bony elbows made wild points in the sleeves of a worn winter coat, worked over the electric organ like a hawk walking a branch. Her long claws dipped into the keyboard and came out with clutches of pulsing chords whose fat rhythm seemed no part of this beaked and stern-eyed Ontario-granite dame until you looked at her feet. Strong calves above half-rolled black socks and bright new black and white high-school basketball shoes pumped feet limber as otters, the right foot caressing the swell pedal independently to make the music soar and sink with the melody, the left foot kicking hell out of the pedal keyboard with a stride that would beat the Devil, pounding out the rhythm of a God-loving song of praise.

> *Yes there's a*
> *New* (clap) *light* (clap)
> *Shinin' in the*
> *Sky! To! Night!*
> *And it's the smile*
> *(Oh Yeah!)*
> *On the face of God!*

Any anxiety Robert and Nelson had felt about being recognized disappeared. The singing faces of the crowd were all drawn to the front of the tent and no one turned as the two men entered and stood in the shadows at the back. But it was not the spectacle of the wild-winged bird of prey at her organ that held the crowd, nor the contrastingly gentle conducting of a young, heavily bearded man in his late twenties who stood in a wrinkled grey suit in the centre of the stage and led the singing with a soft smile on his lips and long, easy waves of his hands. What the crowd was watching as it belted out this hymn with increasing confidence and power was a group of dancers.

On the packed earth between the front row of folding grey metal seats and the edge of the stage were a dozen people, some in their teens, some twenty or so, some middle aged and one proud, athletic man of sixty or more with a full white beard and a brilliant grin who stood roughly in the center of the group and stared out at the singing congregation, holding his hands high and clapping steadily with the music. The dancers swayed and bent and moved almost as one. Their hands shot skyward to clap like lightning between the words. A floodlight on a stand at the edge of the stage rimlit the darting fingers with a hard edge of light casting a surreal pattern of shadows on the tent wall opposite, and Nelson could not resist holding his hands up to frame a shot and pan across from left to right, from the dancers' hands to their shadows, and automatically began to plan a visual sequence in his head as they danced.

The bodies moved in undulant synchrony; limbs and faces and hands radiated a joy approaching ecstasy, not so much with the hymn, Nelson thought, as with themselves, with each other rather, with something secret they were sharing, something he thought he recognized but could not name.

He leaned against Robert. "What is it about them?" he whispered.

Robert shook his head. "They're the only ones not singing. Look! Look at her."

Dancing at the edge of the group farthest from the organist, her head thrown away back, her eyes half closed and a smile of transcendent happiness on her wide mouth, a girl in her early twenties, wide cheekbones, long dark braided hair and a face of utter innocence seemed to draw the energy of the whole group of silent dancers into her own swaying body. She wore a black crocheted stole wrapped around her flat torso. Presently she began to unwind it and pass the ends out to the dancers nearest her, who took it and threaded it under their arms and around the backs of their heads and their waists until it united the whole group and soon they really were one organism, united in the music and the movement and the band of long black wool. Suddenly Robert knew, and he gripped Nelson's arm and whispered fiercely, "They're all deaf mutes!"

"But how . . . ?" And then Nelson saw how the music reached them. The girl, he guessed, could hear well enough to pick up the beat; perhaps one or two others could as well; the rest watched every movement of her hands, every bend of her body, and danced to a visual beat, now taken up by pulsations through the wool, winding against it, bending and swaying, their skin glistening, their eyes gleaming, their expressions transfigured.

The music stopped.

There was an embarrassed flurry of applause and several robust "Amen's" from the crowd as the last echoes of the organ died away. The bearded man on the stage held up his hand and bowed his head.

The group of deaf mutes closed into a circle like a flower folding, and bowed their bodies and heads together, the black band of wool still wreathed over and under arm and torso, neck and hip. They bent lower into the center of the inward convolving circle until their heads were below their shoulders. Arms and hands circled sweating backs, fingers spread, comforting and touching and kneading gently, and the group came closer together in its attitude of prayer and its physical metaphor of love.

Except the girl. She leaned back against the pull of her stole, now completely intricated in the group, turned her face toward the man on the stage, her eyes still half closed, her expression full of love and peaceful waiting as she gazed at Lucas Rankin, Preacher, for that is who he must be Robert and Nelson thought when the bearded man spoke a soft short prayer, held his hand still in the air and said, after a pause, "I am seeking, and we are all seeking," paused again and then said "Amen." He looked at the girl with a comfortable, complicit smile, and then nodded at the whole congregation as though something now would begin that was more formal, official. The dancers melted away from each other, loosening the stole which the girl wrapped around herself again in a few easy motions, and moved away from the stage.

The spell broke. Robert and Nelson realized that the girl with the stole was striding straight toward them, and that they were the only visitors who were still standing. The audience was shuffling and coughing and settling into chairs. Nelson put his hand on Robert's arm.

"Perhaps we better go?"

But Robert was not paying attention; his eyes were fixed on the girl. She approached them quickly, with one hand stretched forward in a sign of welcome. Then a strange thing happened: her large dreamy eyes swept back and forth from one to the other, not searching their faces but as if she were somehow balancing their bodies. With a look of recognition, she smiled broadly and motioned them into two empty chairs, right at the back, with such an air of quiet authority that they went along and sat down.

Robert glanced again at her as she took up her post by the tent door, then turned to Nelson and said softly, "She knows. She knows we're ... twins."

"How?"

"Isn't that what you saw?"

Nelson nodded, feeling vaguely uneasy at the perception, yet certain as Robert was, that the girl's eyes had scarcely bothered with their different faces – one in dark glasses, the other bearded – but had somehow seen congruency of pattern in their bodies and had smiled in secret realization of their unity. What they did not know was that she had also, in the deep intuitive pools of her silent mind, sensed in them a unique anguish, and a thought had formed, a thought, which, if she had been able to put words to it, would have been something like: "These men need Lucas. They need my brother."

Several people turned curiously and the two were glad it was so dark. They made a stagey business of searching the crowded tent as if they were looking for someone they knew.

Then the bearded young man began to speak, in a clear, light, country voice, and they knew from his first word that he certainly was Lucas Rankin, Preacher of Petitcodiac N.B.

"People, it's four years I been coming up to Ontario in the fall to preach. Some of you have been with me before, some of you are new. I see familiar faces and strangers. Martha, my sister there," – he gestured toward the girl at the back of the tent – "has been happy to be with her good friends from the

Deaf People's School and we all had joy again in their worship-
ful dancing, didn't we?"

Sounds of assent in the crowd.

"They are seeking too," he said. "I believe it. And it's good
to see both friend and stranger here, and we have to say as well
that some dear faces are gone. And that's the way life is. And
I've come this time partly to say goodbye to you all."

There was a murmur of mild consternation at this.

"Oh don't worry, people. We'll have our preaching and we'll
have our healing on the sabbath, and all the good talks we always
had. But then after this weekend I'm turning in the old pickup
truck and I'm going to school!"

This time there was more than a murmur; people clucked
and whispered their surprise. Some, who had clearly been to
his meetings before, wondered aloud why Lucas the preacher
would ever need any more learning than he already had; others,
the newcomers, seemed to be intrigued with such an unorthodox
beginning and sat with looks of curiosity to hear why this announcement should be a matter of such unusual import to the
old timers.

Rankin was a country boy who had the Gift (they could hear
the capital 'G' as he spoke the word). He was not ordained; he
had never studied theology, but from the age of sixteen he had
been driven by a powerful call to tell people about the strength
and the comfort his own faith and his love of the Bible had
brought him. So all through the long damp New Brunswick
winters he had travelled the back roads of his home province,
staying in farm houses and talking with folks about Jesus and the
world today. Late in August, the hay safely in his father's barn
and the potato crop sold and ready for the contracted digging
machines, he would come back to the house for a quiet day to
sit with his voiceless sister and read the Bible to her for an
afternoon while she watched his lips with her wide eyes. From
time to time she would touch his arm and stop him in the middle
of a phrase or a verse and look at him long and gravely, and
when he re-read the verse she wanted to hear again, she would
indicate her satisfaction, always watching his lips, and he came
to know that she was directing him with these choices, sending

him an insight that came somehow into her almost silent brain, an insight not accessible to him without her. Once, as he read from Ecclesiastes, "In the morning sow thy seed, and in the evening withhold not thine hand," and she stopped him there and made him read it again, he did not understand at all what she meant, until finally she pointed at the evening sun hanging over the western hills and made him understand that while he had labored in the fields and preached in the houses, he had withheld himself from the lands stretching west. And so it was that he had begun to move his mission into Maine and Vermont, and later to Quebec and Ontario.

He had learned over the years that he had the power not only to move hearts and revive the flame of religious fervor, he also could make people feel better physically. Headaches and rheumatism, insomnia and tremors seemed to drift away when he touched people as they prayed together.

"Not miracles, people," Lucas Rankin was saying, "Not any more than life itself is a miracle. It's just that healing simply means people getting back together in themselves, which is what coming to the Lord is all about, because he's always inside all of us waiting to be recognized.

"Or waiting to call us," he said weightily after a pause, and then went on. "And it's a sore trial for the human body when the spirit is refusing to take account of what a power of love there is coiled up inside waiting to be led out! That's why we get sick, people. And it's not me that heals, it's your love striking free at last and touching the love of Jesus lying there within you!"

At the phrase "coiled up" Robert and Nelson turned and looked at each other with an odd expression. They had already begun to feel impatient with the preacher's quiet, low-key story; here was none of the vibrant country revival melodrama they had expected. But in those last words there was such a striking concordance with Haig's observations about loneliness on that transfiguring night in late August, that their attitude changed in the moment. They leaned forward intently, listening to the voice as it told how a group of people in the Maritimes – not followers, just people who wanted to see him, armed with the best traditional credentials, take on the country's religious establishment – had put up the fees and expenses and persuaded him (not easily, he declared) to go to college, to get ordained at last.

His story finished, Lucas Rankin called to his sister and waved her toward him. "Martha guides me, people. Just before we start I'll ask her, like I always do, to show me a text or two." He held up a small worn Bible.

The girl moved toward the front of the tent; as she passed the back row of chairs she turned and let her soft eyes rest again on the two identical men, swinging her gaze from one to the other for just a moment and then giving them a little half nod, sideways, before continuing on to the platform. The preacher handed her the book. She opened it, her face warmed by a wide smile and her eyes still soft, looking out over the crowd. Then her fingers moved across a page, and she looked down at it, nodded slowly and passed it up to her brother.

Lucas Rankin looked at the page and turned again as his sister signalled approval, watching his lips. "These stories here, Martha? These ideas from Saint Luke? All right then."

Martha moved smoothly to her place at the back of the tent, not looking at Robert and Nelson this time. And now the preaching began in earnest and the mood changed dramatically. The two men were astonished, they agreed later, at how quickly they caught the spirit of this lean Maritimer who had, with his other gifts, a considerable intellect. It would be interesting to see what happened to him at divinity school, they thought, and more interesting to see what happened to the divinity school.

His theme was despair and rootlessness in a world so crazy after owning things that people had lost sight of people. And his remedy was to see, through the Savior's eyes, that human life is the one, unique and precious manifestation of God in all the universe, and that the glory of knowing the Lord would bring mankind back to love and thus to health and to salvation.

Robert was thinking, "Six months ago I'd have thought this all crap!" And Nelson was half saying to himself, "What the hell am I doing here putting up with this shit?" But they were both listening closely.

Lucas Rankin said, "People, even in those times in Galilee

and Jerusalem there were those who thought they understood life. Learnt men from Rome and Athens. The kind of people I'm going to have to meet and deal with in the university. These were learnt people, who understood life. *And they wanted to spit on it*. That's how they understood it! To be done with it. Noble men and women who said the noblest thing to do with your life was to end it.

"And then, people, along comes Jesus. And He takes life up in his sweet hands! Smelling of the earth and sunshine and growing things, and the love of God. And He makes men want an eternity of it, don't you see?"

Now there was a hush of rapt attention in the tent so that the few slow crickets in the October grass could be heard, their rhythm brought almost to a halt by the descending chill outside.

"But life's coming to an end, people."

An electric silence gripped the watching tent, "I don't mean next month or next year. I'm not one of those end-of-the-world preachers; you know that! I'm just a seeker, like the rest of you. Only some of you haven't realized that when you feel that awful hunger to know ... to know what life means, that's when you're really seeking after Jesus Christ. The earth will run out of oil one day, and it's just as certain that the sky will run out of sun and the ground will cool and crack, frozen and wasted. And life will come to an end on it. All our bones and our books will be under the ice. And then ... what? Nothing? Meaningless nothing? You don't believe that, people. You *can't* believe that!"

An easing of held breath now; clearly many had believed it.

"Man is very special to God. After all the decades of probing the stars and the galaxies with powerful telescopes man found nothing smarter than himself. Why should he? Statistics? Statistics say there's more stars out there than hairs on all the heads of all the human beings ever born. So there ought to be some wisdom out there too, some creatures more advanced than us.

"But what if there isn't? What if life on earth is a unique miracle, people. Would that surprise you? Our sweet Lord Jesus Christ wasn't surprised. He said we are children of the Highest. The elect of God. Chosen and beloved. And we have a special life to look forward to. And one said to Him, 'Bring back somebody from the dead then, to tell us about it.'

"But He said that wouldn't persuade anybody; if they wouldn't listen to Moses and the prophets they wouldn't be persuaded by somebody back from the grave. Now! You might think you'd be persuaded. Am I right?"

Puzzled looks in the tent. What's he getting at?

"But what would you really do if He came to us tonight? 'Here I am. You may touch me.'

"So. 'Lord, it's wonderful to see you. Thanks for everything. Thanks for all your blessings, you bet! Come again some time when you're not too busy looking after all the sheep.'

"He says, 'Well, no. You misunderstand. I intend to dwell among you and be your teacher and your savior right here every day.'

"Well! 'Did he say right here? In Attrey's Corners! In the poaching season? Could you wait till after the poaching season, Lord?'"

No outright chuckles, but many eyes gleaming with the seriousness of the humor.

Nelson whispered close in Robert's ear, "Lenny Bruce."

Robert held his hand up, irritated at the interruption.

A very serious voice now from the preacher. "But why call ye me Lord, Lord, and do not the things which I say?"

A long silence.

"But He *is* here, people. In Attrey's Corners!"

Almost a shiver in the tent. Nelson half-expected people to turn around and scan the seats for Jesus.

"He's among us. Can't you feel His presence?"

The atmosphere was like the edge of a storm.

"He'll call us soon, people! Listen for His voice in the night. Don't put Him off. Don't go on with that busyness of life, never catching up with anything. Make Him your business. Because He'll call us in the night. Listen for His voice in the night."

And then, looking straight at Robert and Nelson, although he could not possibly have discerned their faces in the dim light at the back of the tent, he intoned, "In that night there shall be two men in one bed; the one shall be taken and the other left. Which one will you be!"

Robert grabbed Nelson's arm. He held tight during a short moment of indecision, but he felt profoundly uncomfortable; then he tugged at the other man.

"Let's get out of here," he whispered.

"What's bothering you?" Nelson hissed back.

"Come on!"

Together they slipped unnoticed out of the spellbound tent.

17

"That was just coincidence. You shouldn't have let it hit you like that. You were going to put your thumb right through my biceps!" Nelson was driving too fast, trying to find a short way back to Canopy Lake. They skirted half a dozen lakes with winding shorelines and shore roads to match. Twice they came into unmarked dead-ends and had to backtrack. Nelson soon wore pretty thin. He called "Damn, Damn, Damn!" in a strained voice at every cul-de-sac and unmarked turn. He scolded the County Road Commissioner and thundered against the signpainters. Spinning the wheel harder and wilder with each curse and using the brakes violently and sliding through turns as if it were the Aston-Martin and not some old loose-arsed Vee-Double-Yew, he consigned the Minister of Highways to eternal immersion in a lake of cold shit and for good measure he excommunicated the Premier of the province.

But Robert sat silent in his side of the car, muffled up in his thoughts, his head against the jolting window, his eyes locked on the quarter moon that rode with them, as it dipped behind the occasional scud of thin luminous cloud or became eclipsed by trees or a hill and then glided free again if they hit a stretch of straight road.

Nelson left him to his reverie which was not so much formed and lucid, as a nostalgia, somewhat wan and self-pitying he admitted to himself, a homesickness for the time when he was one person.

"There shall be two men ... one shall be taken ... Which one will you be?" The bizarre prophecy of the evangelist had unnerved him and led to a chain of dark reflections on the difficulty of escaping from this twindom that had taken over his life.

Suddenly he remembered something: the text had been

picked by the girl, Martha. She had seen them as two identical men and probably something came into her mind about that two-men verse, and if so, it was not such a spooky coincidence. He opened his mouth to say this to Nelson and then closed it again because coincidence or not, the words still had an uneasy power and he wanted to ponder them more, privately, and the ways in which it seemed he had so few choices, now, as an individual.

What he did each night and each day was done within the pair and for the survival and safety of the pair. They talked casually about the relief that would come once the Brady business was over and done with, but they had no picture of what they would do when the threat to their lives was eliminated.

"If it ever is," he said under his breath.

Nelson heard. "What's that?"

"Nothing."

There were lights in several of the cottages they passed on the road down Canopy Lake, but the last half mile was dark since it all belonged to ... Nelson, now, Robert reflected, feeling the nostalgia again. It had been so important, building up that parcel of land, his freehold, his seigneury and retreat; now he had given it up ... in exchange for a future that seemed an endless obligation to his old self anyway, in the guise of the original Rob Nelson known in this pair as Nelson, pure and simple.

But then he thought, "No. Why am I bound to him? Only because of sentiment and because I can't really get it into my head that Daisy is no longer part of my life."

He felt morose and looked it when they pulled up and put the car next to the boathouse and turned out the lights and got out the scotch. He was grateful that Nelson had stayed off his back during the tortuous drive but he knew what he himself would have done in the past, whatever "himself" meant now, and he was braced for it when Nelson shortly demanded to know what was bothering him.

He had some answers ready, diversionary answers: honest in their substance, but not really what he had been thinking about. He did not feel sufficiently robust to take the inevitable recrimination and hair-splitting argument that would ensue.

"It's not still that damn fool preacher and his two men in a bed, is it?" Nelson asked a bit sardonically. "His sister did that."

"But he's *not* a damn fool. You saw him the same as I did. You know he's got power, and I think a lot to say."

"Yes," Nelson admitted. "But that line was a quotation she remembered when she looked at us and decided we were twins. It had nothing to do with us, I mean the actual us. What's really bugging you?"

"I had a train of thought from that sermon ... some of the gloomy reflections about death and meaninglessness. And then ... I found myself wondering about how we became so different so soon."

"Yes."

There was a silence. Nelson hadn't been prepared for the bluntness. He knew Robert had touched on something important and that perhaps they should talk about it, but all he said was, "Want some more scotch?"

"No." Then, "I think I'll crash."

"We have to think about leaving here. Getting started with it."

"I know."

"We're ready. We're putting it off."

"I was thinking it would be nice to have ... a kind of reprieve for a week. We know what we're going to do about Brady. We know it's dangerous. We know we might never be here again. We're going to stick to our pact about who owns what, and I'm going to have to go off on my own. Maybe I'll go back with Pinch, if you'd agree to that. But this place is yours and it would be easier for me ..."

He did not need to finish. Nelson said, "We could stay another week."

"Thanks."

The moon was down but the sky was alive with stars. Nelson looked at the profile of the other man silhouetted against the window. He chuckled and said, "Cheer up, kid. I used to think I was the most interesting person I knew. Now I think you are."

Robert acknowledged the joke with a perfunctory laugh but said, "The truth is, we never really thought we were all that interesting."

"Let's not start in on that now."

"We ought to talk about it. I think I've got some ideas."

"For Christ's sake, Robert!"

"All right."

"I meant what I said about how interesting you are. I don't know whether I find that depressing or cheering. But enough's enough!"

Robert could not see the other man in the gloom of the little house. From the dark kitchen an edge of a whisky glass reflected a minute gleam of light. Robert thought there was a genuine warmth flowing between them then, welcome after the sense of alienation earlier, in the car. He sighed, a quick optimistic sigh, and rose and headed for the daybed.

"It's your turn for the double bed," Nelson reminded him.

"I know. I feel like the daybed. It's by the window. I ... I want the sun to wake me up."

That was only partly true; the daybed was hard and uneven. Robert had chosen it in order to give Nelson something. It was a private gesture in response to the flow of warmth. He felt grateful but thought it foolish to say so.

"You're feeling better." Nelson said.

"Yes. Yes, I really am."

Robert snored softly on the daybed. Nelson lay on his back in the dark cabin and thought of Daisy. He recognized a familiar and unwelcome cycle that had dogged him in the past and led, when it appeared, to an implacable insomnia: he would tell himself that everything was calm and quiet and there were no demands on him that he could not easily meet, and the effort of so persuading himself would make him wonder what subconscious worry must be teasing him. Then he would be wide awake and staring. It was happening now.

He arose quietly, shuffled into the kitchen and opened the scotch again and poured half a glass over some ice. The placid body on the daybed did not stir. Nelson stared morosely at the dark form of the other man and felt resentment growing in his belly.

"Jesus Christ, thank God this is coming to an end," he whispered, half hoping the other would hear, but not wanting to be caught in a deliberately disloyal utterance. If Robert should overhear a spontaneous virulent whisper, then he, Nelson, could apologize and say he didn't really mean it, and the message would be accomplished without the hassle that would result if he said it directly to Robert's face.

But Robert seemed to sleep undisturbed.

Nelson glared across the dark space and poured again. As he drank he became more angry. He thought, "Who is this moralistic bastard anyway, telling me what to think about Daisy and Jenny and the cars. He's stealing from me. He's stealing *me*. He knows things nobody has a right to know. He's using them to put me down. That's why he's so peaceful! He thinks he's winning something. He thinks he's on top now."

The relationship was intolerable. It had to be maintained for now, he told himself, until they had dealt with Brady. After that, all obligations were over; he would find a way to rid himself of this moral monitor, this interloper, this ... this fraud! The thought nourished his anger in a deep satisfying way. If this other person was a fraud then he had no rights; or he was jeopardizing what few rights he might claim, with this insistent pursuit of self examination. In which he had no right.

Then he remembered Robert's startled response to the preacher and the Two-Men-In-One-Bed theme, and laughed sardonically and quietly at that discomfiture.

The laugh penetrated Robert's consciousness and he woke, without moving, and in the faint light from outside saw Nelson sitting at the table with a twisted, bitter expression of hatred on his face. Robert was in shadow. He put his hand over his face and felt tears running down his cheeks because he believed he had never known such hatred before and intuitively he knew at whom it was directed.

Nelson stumbled over the double bed and fell asleep in his fumes of whiskey and self-righteousness.

When Nelson awoke he rolled over and looked at the daybed and saw it was empty. He felt vaguely uneasy. He remembered that he had drunk a bit too much but could not recall what it was he had said to himself that had made him feel self-righteous, so angry, and yet free of some burden. He rolled over to go back to sleep but soon knew that he would not drift off so he got up to make the coffee. He put water on the stove to boil. Then he went to the window, yawning and rubbing his eyes, and looked out at the lake.

Robert was out there, in the water which was so cold that neither of them had been in it for two weeks. The bearded man was naked, standing on the bottom, the water almost to his hips. As Nelson watched he saw the muscles in the back tense with an effort of will as legs bent steadily into a crouch. Nelson shivered thinking about it. He saw the other man hesitate a moment and then bend his head and slip out of sight beneath the surface.

Nelson turned back to the coffee pot and settled down groggily with an old magazine. Suddenly he realized he had been reading for ten minutes and Robert had not come back.

He stood up, alarmed. He ran out to the beach. There was no sign of the other man. He felt his stomach muscles clench into an acid knot. He sprinted to the boathouse, yanked the canoe down from the rack and carried it out and put it in the water. He hesitated, thinking perhaps he should get some rope, and glanced up toward the house. Robert was sitting inside the kitchen drinking coffee.

Nelson pulled the canoe violently back up on the beach and ran to the house.

"Where have you been, you stupid son of a bitch? You gave me bloody heart failure ..."

But when Robert looked up, Nelson stopped his tirade. The face under the beard was pale and the expression bleak. The uncovered opaque eye stared sorrowfully.

"What's the matter?"

Robert said slowly, "I'm all right. I know I look terrible. For some reason I couldn't sleep. Not much, anyway. I went for a swim and then I went for a walk. I'm sorry. I didn't think about you worrying. I shouldn't have done it. Please don't worry now."

The tone of voice was not convincing. The face was one of moral desolation. Partly from sympathy and partly to avoid conflict, Nelson decided not to make an issue. He started to prepare breakfast. From time to time he watched the other man and saw him gazing vacantly into space. He thought, "I've been like that when I haven't slept." But he still felt doubtful.

Wondering uneasily if it was his fault, he said, "Listen. We're giving ourselves this week off. I know I was against it, but not any more. I was thinking, let's take the canoe and portage up into Ranger Lake, take the tent and stay out a couple of days, catch some trout. Soon as the crowd goes down Monday."

Robert looked around slowly. Then his features relaxed a little. He said softly, "Nelson, I would really like that. I would like that a lot."

But it was not to happen. Because it was that Monday, two mornings later, that they lost their cover.

18

Nelson was in the outdoor toilet when he heard someone drive in the lane and stop. His first thought was, "He won't look here first," and with his stomach tightening in fear, he pulled up his pants and stood to peer through a crack in the door. He could not see anyone. A motor turned off some feet away to his left. He heard a door bang shut, decided from the noise that it was a light truck and thought with relief, "Whoever it is doesn't want to surprise us." Simultaneously, he saw a curtain on the porch window of the cabin move and knew that Robert had been watching from concealment. Next the door opened and Robert came out with a strained smile and waved at the footsteps. The back of a man came into view through the crack in the out- house door, a red checked wool coat and an old felt hat. Nelson heard Robert call out, "Hi, Mac."

"Cut yourself shaving?" the storekeeper called back.

Robert rubbed his beard and laughed a fair imitation of an easy laugh. "Just trying to keep warm," he said. They shook hands.

Then Robert said, "Listen, Mac, I'd ask you in but ... there's a lady in there who would be very embarrassed."

"Guess that explains it, then," Mac answered. "But you maybe better get your tail out of here."

"Explains what, Mac?"

"She's got a husband?" he asked, tilting his head at the cabin.

Nelson sensed the hesitation before Robert replied, but he thought that Mac would not perceive it, and he guessed what Robert would say. "Could be," Robert said, on cue. "What's up?"

"A fellow in a green Dodge around the store just now, asking if you was here. I told him no. Only I knew you was. I seen a light a couple of nights when I was setting nightlines by the island. Up a couple of weeks now, ain't it? I never come bothering. I figured you're up here and never come around the store to chew the fat after all this time, you must want to be alone so that's the way I left you. Fellow had white hair and white eyebrows. Looked kind of mean. Asked how to find your place. I told him. Only by the time he gets where I sent him, he'll be dead-ending round by the swamp other side of the lake. Figured that would give me time to get over here and give you the latest weather report, if you know what I mean."

At the mention of white hair and eyebrows, Robert felt a taut anguish in his bowels. But he held his fear submerged, as much as possible, showing Mac only an appropriate edge of concern, a terseness, a decisiveness. And remembering his camouflage of the fictitious, hidden woman, he said, "Thanks, Mac. You better beat it now. He'll be here and we're getting out. I don't want anyone to see her. Even you."

"We're old enough friends I can keep a lid on it, but you should never tell anybody you don't want them to know something unless you really want them *to* know."

"Thanks, Mac. And Mac, that's a very mean man in that green Dodge. If he finds out you gave him a bum steer, you'd better close up the store for the day, take Nelly up the lake somewhere."

"Thanks for the caution, Rob. But I'll be okay. If that guy does find his way out here, you'll be gone?"

"We'll be gone."

"Omer and I'll come and sweep the road, soon as you leave," Mac said. "Nobody'll know you were here."

"Mac, you're —"

But the old man waved away the gratitude. He stumped back to his decrepit half-ton and slammed the door and rattled off under the canopy of red and yellow leaves that hung over the narrow road.

Despite the chill that had spread from his scalp down the line of his spine and across his back when he learned that Pete Brady had tracked him down, a chill whose fingers still were lambent on his skin, Robert welcomed the need to act. The last few days had been too flat, too reflective, too conducive to self-pity. He could not escape a brooding sense of the hatred he had seen that night on Nelson's face.

On Sunday night he had taken the canoe a hundred yards off shore and practised with the spinning reel in the moonlight, using the action of the rod and the plop of the plug into the water as a forgetful rhythm, a wordless, physical chant to bring him into a wholesome, simple relationship with the physical world, so that for the space of half an hour a deep peace overcame him. Cast out rhythmically and reel in, plop, wind, snap the rod, plop, wind it in. And he felt transported into a clarity and tranquillity that he had never known. He did not reflect on it. His old habits of watching himself from without did not intrude. There were no words racing through his mind. There was just the moonlight and the water and the crisp air and the whir and the plop.

Then it had passed. He picked up the paddle and began to think again. He wished for the morning and the slugging, long hike into Ranger Lake – he would carry the canoe the whole way himself and maybe there would be an absorption in that too – and, as his mind started talking to him again, he felt the return of his sense of defeat, but it was tempered somewhat.

And so he was not as disappointed as he had thought at first he would be, when he heard Mac's sinister news. He welcomed the emergency.

As the sun sank and the sky faded, shadows deepening in the tire tracks of the departed Volkswagen, the old truck, appeared again. Two men climbed out carrying cedar branches. An observer not familiar with the ways of poachers would have wondered at the two men bent over the dirt road, gently sweeping with the boughs.

Then it was night, and silence. The truck had gone. The moon was not yet up. Car lights approached, cutting the blackness under the trees. A green Dodge pulled up quietly where the road petered out by a lane with a small faded sign in red paint: NELSON. A white-haired man climbed out quietly with a drawn pistol pointing ahead of him. He shone a flashlight at the yard behind the cottage and was disappointed to see no tire marks, just soft, smooth, apparently windblown sand and a scattering of fallen autumn leaves. At the house he saw that there was sand blown into little heaps at the corners of the wooden steps. He flicked his light towards the beach; it was smooth and flat – no footprints. Had he been a country man who uses his nose as well as his eyes, the cool night breeze flowing down from the hills and through the shallow cleft in the rock where the outdoor toilet stood would have told him something; so would the acrid trace of wet woodash and the faint sour smell from the garbage pit on the other side of the cabin. But Pete Brady was a city man and the country made him tense. At the rustling of an animal in the undergrowth nearby, he spun around with his gun pointed, and then he caught himself and said, "You crazy bastard, Brady, there hasn't been anybody here all summer."

And he climbed back in his car and headed for Toronto.

19

They had found a semi-detached house in Toronto's Cabbage-town district, an area perfect for their purposes. Its other half was an empty shell partly damaged by fire. The whole building was scheduled for demolition in the spring. The owner had said that he didn't much care what they did with it, had cheerfully pocketed five hundred dollars in cash for two months in advance and implied that if they burned the house down in the mean-time he would not lose any sleep.

They set about to furnish it from the Army-Navy and the second-hand appliance stores on nearby Queen street. After hanging some cheap curtains to disguise their activities, they ripped down the wooden fence surrounding the small back yard and used the boards to barricade the downstairs windows. The yard faced onto a lane running along the backs of the houses between their street, and the next street over. They agreed to stay awake at night – their most dangerous time – and do their construction work then, and sleep from early morning to early afternoon.

When they went out shopping, to buy a second-hand stove or refrigerator, or a power handsaw to use on the tricky con-struction of the trapdoor in the little front hall of the house, Nelson would stay in the car, and Robert, disguised in his beard and sunglasses, would go into the store to buy what they wanted. Nelson would watch through the window as Robert made his purchases with a kind of gravity that seemed alien to Nelson, a courtesy that appeared wasteful and time-consuming in this emergency.

But he held his counsel, and was mollified and irritated in turn by the same courtesy and consideration as it was offered to him while they worked.

Robert, handing up the Skilsaw from the basement as they cut away the floor of the front hall and reinforced the surrounding joists would say, "Thank you" and "Please" in a way that was natural but unfamiliar. He seemed always to be at Nelson's elbow, helpfully holding a bolt ready for insertion or a piece of wood to be nailed. His expression was usually friendly, sometimes remote as if lost in meditation, but increasingly attentive as the time passed. Robert insisted on preparing the meals which allowed Nelson to work on his own for a while to escape the oppressive closeness.

In the middle of the day, when the street was quiet and deserted, the children not yet back from school, the mailman finished his rounds, people dozing in back rooms and the city beyond busy with the high activity of the momentous afternoon and forgetful of small back streets, they would walk down to Dundas Street after they got out of bed, and have thick black coffee and fresh hot rolls in *Innocencio's*, a Portuguese snack bar. Walking through the piles of fallen leaves gathered in the curbs waiting for the garbage men, smelling the deep fall smells, looking at the gleam of sunshine on the two brilliantly painted, green and orange brick houses that the owner of the snack bar had bought, almost like gate houses at the foot of the street, they would sense an easy cameraderie returning. The gaiety of the colors on those two houses held a vitality of contrast for them after the drab enclosure of their lives in the derelict in which they prepared their trap; often they would just stop in front of the gleaming bricks and blink in the sunshine, smile generously at each other, enjoy a temporary benevolence.

Some thirty blocks from the house on Ontario Street is the handsome grey stone building of Emmanuel College, a theological center and training ground for protestant clergy in the University of Toronto, a breeder of ministerial candidates – men and women in the new enlightenment – for the United Church of Canada.

Lucas Rankin, the preacher from Petitcodiac, had come to Emmanuel on sufferance as a "mature student," which meant that while he lacked the normal academic requirements, he had age and an unusual amount and quality of experience on his side.

He was strong of character and sure-footed on his own ground. But that ground was country ground. Now he felt as unsteady in the city as a streetwise kid who suddenly found himself for the first time in the bush. Lucas looked at this bright, lively confident group of theology students and saw that while they were sincere enough, they were remote from his life. The teachers puzzled and dismayed him. With neither group was he in harmony. He was far from home and in a strange land, and he began to doubt himself. Was he strong enough? Were there hidden threads of hypocrisy and misplaced intention that would surface in the same kind of subtle cynicism he noticed among too many of his teachers?

Never very patient with fools – though he always regretted his irascibility later and could turn it into humor in a disarming way – Lucas tried some of his old tricks of scoring points with scripture. But it did not work in this company of Biblical scholars. They knew their text as well as he did and had a devastating extra advantage: they could cite the original Hebrew or Greek. When Lucas lashed out irritably in class with a verse that would have silenced all the elders of his home parish, here were teachers who had no compunction about humiliating the ungrammatical country boy with their unctuous smiles and a few lines of an incomprehensible language followed by a gloss that reversed the meaning he had always felt was solidly entrenched in the old English words he loved so much.

His confidence began to erode badly. Doubt worked on him and homesickness fought with his sense of duty to his sponsors so that at times his usually buoyant spirit sank to a level near despair.

Had it not been for his silent, mystical sister, he would have packed his bag. Martha had agreed to stay with him through the rush of registration, and when she saw how troubled he was she made no move to return to New Brunswick, and the days stretched to a week and then two.

The sponsors had provided a pleasant second floor apartment in an old house on a quiet street near the University; modest enough, but to Lucas and Martha it seemed grand indeed. And there, after the fourth night of deep, prayerful anguish, Lucas decided to share his trouble, and poured it all out to Martha, and she, listening, knew she could not leave at all until he had found his balance again.

All the rest of that evening, as he worked over the stubborn books, she tended him. A cup of tea would appear at his elbow. If he looked up to relieve his eyes from the strain of the crowded print, she was patiently there. When he settled down to sleep, close to midnight, he called into her room, "Martha? Can you hear?"

She tapped an acknowledgment on the side of the bed.

"Martha, you being here makes this place near home for me. God bless you Martha!"

Her heart swelled with joy and gratitude. If only she could give him something more!

In the morning after he had gone to the college and she was cleaning the appartment, she began to straighten his closet and to sort out the clothes that needed washing. She saw his old, worn football shoes, stained and forlorn on the closet floor, and all at once she thought how she might cheer her brother up, if only a little. She dug into her purse for her small, secret savings, ran out to Bloor Street and returned home with a pair of flashy white and blue sport shoes, running shoes, not football shoes, but she did not know the difference.

Lucas loved the shoes. The other students smiled behind their hands, but Lucas wore them to class, proudly, every day. Martha, however, was not satisfied. She tried to think of something much more significant she could offer her brother, something that would please him deeply, that would express her joy in being with him and serving him in this time of struggle and confusion.

When they had free time they rode buses and streetcars and visited the Science Center, the Planetarium, the Zoo and the Island. Often they just climbed on a streetcar and rode it to the end of the line and back again, to look at the spreading city with its unending variety of colors and streets and people, its spectrum of riches-to-poverty ranging from the huge Royal Bank

Tower with its windows dusted with real gold, to the grime of east Queen Street.

One afternoon their streetcar was stopped for a moment at a red light on Dundas Street. While Lucas daydreamed in the hazy sunshine and wondered if he should take the train back to New Brunswick with Martha, Martha's eyes, always caught more by the movement of people than scenery and buildings, were arrested by a familiar pattern in the bodies of two men – one bearded, one clean shaven – who came out of a coffee shop and turned up a side street at the corner. Martha had seen those men before. She knew that there was something strange and important about the symmetry of their stance and body movements. Suddenly she remembered. Remembered where she had seen them. Remembered that she had decided they needed her brother somehow, needed healing in a way so strange she could not begin to guess at it. She remembered something else, too. They had run from the tent. When Lucas had spoken the words from the Bible she had meant them to hear, not knowing quite why those words had been important for them, but hoping perhaps the words would draw them to Lucas, they had run in fear.

Now there they were; perhaps it was not too late. She grasped her brother's arm and drew him from his reverie to the window, making the one weak *ah-ah-ah* sound she was capable of, her face eager and smiling and trusting that he would see and understand and know what to do about this mysterious thing, this wonderful pair of exact people.

"What is it Martha? What're you showing me? Those beautiful colored houses?"

But Martha was cross that he should have missed what was really important. She shook her head sharply and pulled his shoulder to the window, which she stabbed at again and again with her finger.

He was puzzled. He knew that Martha would not make a fuss over something trivial, but he could not divine what it was, and when the light changed and they began to move again, Martha shrugged in disgust and shook her head meaning "Never mind." But Lucas continued to stare back at the brilliantly colored houses that flanked the entrance to the sidestreet and did not see the two men kicking leaves along the gutter as they headed north away from the restaurant.

Each evening when he returned from the college, Lucas recounted his day to Martha. As evening followed evening she saw the hurt growing behind his eyes. She would listen in her own careful way, only her eyes and the soft inclination of her head eloquent of attention. Sometimes she would put a hand gently on his arm, meaning "Say that again, please," because occasionally her mind would leave her for a while. But if the events that caused her brother's anguish might lose her sometimes in their complexity, his suffering was daily clearer and she began to feel that it was up to her to find him a way either to escape it or bear it. She hoped for a dream to guide her. She waited for a dream. Whenever such a dream had come in the past, clear enough to her but so painful as it bruised against the barrier of her manacled tongue, as it rushed to be told to her adored brother, Lucas would stop whatever he was doing to draw it out by questioning her like a player in a game of charades. The process finally became so conversational that Lucas, telling someone else of Martha's dream would forget how silently it had been brought to him, with nods and shakes of the head and a cautioning hand on the arm.

When Martha went to bed, she would open the door of her room enough so that she could see Lucas bent over his work should she wake, and then she would turn eagerly to sleep, praying for guidance. For several nights it did not come. And when at last she had the dream she had been waiting for, its meaning nearly escaped her.

She woke suddenly from a vision of the Crucifixion, a dream she had often had before, not a frightening or alien dream, but a familiar part of the reassuring pattern of the Bible. The picture that lingered in her mind as she sat up in bed, feeling alert and optimistic, was the picture of the three crosses; but the face of her brother Lucas was the face of Christ.

She slowly deduced that she had slept only a short while; Lucas was still at his desk in the sitting room and his small desk lamp cast a thin shaft of light onto her face through the half-shut bedroom door. She remembered that she had prayed hard before going to sleep, and she felt that the reason she was sitting up now, wide awake, had to do with her prayer, and that the dream must have been an answer. But it was an old dream, nothing new to it. She tried to see into the dream as if she were searching a picture and as she scanned this canvas in her memory and saw, mirrored perhaps from a Sunday School lithograph, the Roman Soldiers and the weeping women and the lowering clouds her inner eye came finally to the figures on the other two crosses; and then she knew.

For one of the crucified thieves in her dream was bearded and the other was not, but in all aspects they were the same men. And each had one good eye. Martha knew then that Lucas was going to help these men. She had not forgotten her quick disconcerting perception of their need of healing, and now if Lucas had a mission, something real instead of that awful college where they talked so much and did so little, he would be whole again too.

She was about to leap from her bed and pass her hand over her forehead for Lucas to see, so that he would ask her about the dream, when she had another, a better vision. *She would find the men first*. And bring Lucas to them! It would be her surprise gift. Like a birthday. She remembered a street, a streetcar, colored houses. Her wordless visual mind traced the path of that streetcar, from the moment she had spotted the two similar men walking up the street. Now she saw that all unroll again, like a film in slow motion; saw the streets go by; saw herself and Lucas change from the streetcar to a bus, then get off the bus and walk some blocks; began to visualize familiar streets approaching the house; and knew she could find her way back to the corner with the colored houses.

She was determined that she would do that. Tomorrow! She would find those men who drew her so strongly, who were suffering mysteriously. She would learn something about their pain. Perhaps she would show herself to them. Images of them in the tent meeting regarding her furtively – yes, they were *interested* in her – came to her mind now. For a long while her heart beat with a sense of adventure, and the light of Lucas's desk had been dark for hours when she finally fell asleep.

In the morning she was up early, and when Lucas stirred she was dancing quietly in the sunlight by the tall east window of his room, her eyes half-closed and her face calm and radiant. Breakfast was already on the little table; the teapot was steaming.

Martha danced in slow, grave movements as he watched from the bed. She seemed much happier than she had been since coming to this difficult city. He had begun to worry that he was burdening her too cruelly with his anxiety and complaints; now he felt reassured. She glowed and he sensed the warmth coming from within her.

20

The two besieged men on Ontario street took a break from their almost-completed work, put down their tools shortly after three a.m., came up from the basement and went out on the back porch to drink a beer and look at the stars which, that night, were unusually clear for a Toronto sky. Nelson was more amiable now, replenishing Robert's drink, and making an effort to recapture the pleasure and excitement of the best moments they had known together, the moments of exhilarating, lucid, cryptic conversation, the synchrony of feeling and ideas.

"I still think sometimes," he offered as a token of goodwill, "about that first conversation; how I knew with such certainty that you had been thinking about touching eternity. A totally improbable idea for either of us to have in our heads, and yet I had hardly any hesitation about saying it. You had more hesitation than I did."

Still hot from his exertions in the cellar, despite the cool night air, he pulled his eyepatch away from his face and wiped the sweaty ring under it, waiting to hear what Robert would reply. Robert tilted his chair back against the wooden railing around the little porch and, looking up toward the north, said, "Speaking of eternity!" He gestured with his chin at the sky. It was beginning to take up the pale fire of a coil of Northern Lights. Nelson swung his chair around, tight beside Robert's, and watched wordlessly as the first spiral that had caught Robert's eye now began to move out from its epicenter in a series of slow radial shocks that added, each one, another larger ring of light to the first spiral. Soon rays were lancing out with some speed and climbing toward the zenith over their heads.

"That's amazing for Toronto!" Nelson was surprised at the depth of emotion which this display, so unusually clear for the heart of the city, produced in him. He said softly, " 'So excellent a thing I have not seen!' Do you remember? We never knew where those words came from? Pinch said it once, at the microscope. But we'd heard it before. Where?"

"We never knew," Robert confirmed.

They were silent again as the light continued to spread until it filled all the sky within their horizons, limited somewhat as those horizons were by the tops of houses and cut here and there by the etched blackness of the branches of naked trees. Presently a ribbon of green light, harder-edged and more defined than the darting radial pulses that had spread the original spiral out so wide, detached itself and seemed to hang under the surface of the larger auroral canopy, writhing slowly so that its river course changed imperceptibly, but changed, and then, in minutes faded and was gone, and the rest of the aurora was much paler. Soon there were only a few indistinct streaks angling sharply toward the northern limit of their view.

They had finished cutting away a section of the floor in the entrance hall between the front door and the inner door. After reinforcing the surrounding joists, they had taken the excised portion and cut it in two again, lengthwise, converting it into a two-panel trap door, hinged to the joists beneath, and held up firmly by a well-greased set of bolts at the edges. It was a replica of a gallows drop that Rob had studied closely ten years earlier for a documentary on capital punishment. In this case, the springing lever was the inner door itself, which opened from the tiny box-like entrance hall into the narrow side hall. This door was fitted with a simple mortise lock. They knew Brady to carry a set of picks and skeleton keys and that he would find the lock easy to open. They assumed that, preoccupied with picking the lock, he would not be inclined to scrutinize the floor. Even so they had cut the edges of their trap close to the walls and the interior edge was concealed under the foot of the inner door. The center seam fitted tightly enough to be invisible in a dark night unless there was a light on in the basement.

The inner door then was fastened on the other side to a slide that worked the release bolts. When a firm pull was applied it stuck at first, as an old door might, then suddenly gave as the bolts slammed free to plummet anyone standing there down into the cellar.

Below the trap they had slung a helicopter cargo net, from the Army-Navy, with a simple arrangement of loops at the four corners that would draw the neck of the pouch-shaped net tightly shut as soon as a weight fell in it.

Fifteen feet away in the front room where they slept they had cut another, much smaller, hole in the floor and constructed a simple periscope from plywood and two bathroom mirrors. This would allow them to view the hanging net without being seen or shot at. Two photoflood lamps in the basement, on the opposite side of a brick pillar from the net itself, could be switched on from upstairs to cast plenty of light back from the whitewashed wall and brightly illuminate a trapped gunman, while providing protection from any attempt he might make to shoot them out. Watching Brady through the periscope, they could order him to throw down his weapons before going down to deal with him.

On this night of the Northern Lights, ten days after moving into Ontario Street, the trap was ready for testing. They had broken for beer in anticipation of the test; so Robert assumed that, the show over in the northern sky, his partner would be anxious to get on with it.

But Nelson said thoughtfully, his head still back on the porch railing, "In a few minutes," and continued to stare upward. Those spectral flickering sheets across the sky had not lost their power to fascinate him. When he was a child it was while watching the aurora that he had first said to himself some words about seeking to know, had first sensed the thrill of that hunger. Now he thought perhaps that it had been a pure kind of desire, one which had degraded itself, as ambition and sexual adventure and journalism had taken over his life, into curiosity about the immediate; and for the moment he nourished a tolerance for the other man's preoccupation with profounder matters.

We never really thought we were all that interesting. That was what Robert had said and Nelson had been annoyed by it, had been preparing defences and derailments against the time when the subject might come up again, as Robert had said that it should. Now he knew that his annoyance had not been against a piece of trivial self-deprecation, but an important observation that he would have preferred to reject.

He considered re-opening the subject to see what he might learn from the other, his other, his second perception silent there beside him, squeezed almost unnervingly close in the tiny space. Robert moved then, easing away. And Nelson knew that the appreciation of excessive closeness had been simultaneously shared.

Robert rose and said, "I'll get us a beer, then," as if answering Nelson's word of five minutes earlier.

The marvellous lights in the sky had produced in Nelson a yearning, swelling sensation at the base of his throat, an aching for something so far outside the self that any idea of what it might be was not possible; only the hunger for it was clear. When this crazy business was all over, he thought, if only he could plumb the reaches of his mind to discover what's there, what's truly possible! But the desire was still imprisoned by his overall perception of himself as someone poised on the rim of mediocrity, just enough emerged to catch a glimpse of glory in the brilliance beyond that rim. No more than that.

So much had swept by on the edges of the viewfinder that he knew was more important than the fashionable things he focussed on. People and ideas had shimmered with vitality just outside the range of his vision, and yet he knew if only he took the time to learn, to sit at someone's feet for a while, perhaps, admitting he did not know ... Loving and dying, that was all there was in the end ... and being alone or not.

Going with Haig had been a gamble, an easy one due to the way in which Haig had responded to his gibes and his insults and enticed him with the flattery of confessing that he had much to learn from him ... Haig to learn from *him*! And so he had attached himself to the scientist, partly because touching excellence had become something close to an imperative, partly because Haig really had seduced his mind, but mostly, he thought now, because *I have to be in something that's unquestionably first-rate before it's too late.*

Then in the next moment he was so startled that his chair tipped sideways, because Robert came quickly on to the porch spilling beer out of the glasses and said with tremendous excitement, "But that's just it! It's never too late! If you really mean it, it's never too late!"

For a moment they just gaped at each other. Robert's hands were shaking, but Nelson felt a stab of anger. "How long has this been going on!" he said accusingly. "You can hear what I think!"

"No! No! It's never happened before, Nelson. God! Don't get angry. This is too magnificent! I heard the words. But inside! And I knew nobody had spoken them out loud; that they had come from you, and before I could even think what that meant I had to answer you, because I've been thinking through that issue myself, and it's a tough one. But you have to believe me that it's the first time. I'd've told you!"

Nelson shook his head. "It makes me feel like I'm in ... in your power. It's weird. It's ... It's not ..."

But Robert said, "Look. It never happened before. If it does again I'll tell you every time, I swear. We can learn something enormous from it. But the important thing is, it happened and we both know it happened and it means something about the way ..." He stopped and looked at the other man keenly. He said, "Do you know what I'm going to say?"

"No."

"It sounds pretentious Nelson, but it's true nevertheless. I was going to say it means something about the way man is in the universe. The Northern Lights: they're one bit of the key to the universe. How many times do you have to see them to know there's an unimaginable expression of energy out there? Once is enough. Now you and I know another bit. We've seen another kind of Northern Lights. Now we know some of those stories people tell aren't bullshit. Even if it never happens again!"

Nelson felt very edgy. The argument was good, and he understood it, but the experience had triggered his anger again and resentment made his stomach feel hot and contracted. "Get hold of yourself," he thought guiltily. The guilt made him feel even worse – alienated, jealous, culled, discriminated against, suspicious. Was this really happening? He had to know more. Trying to sound amiable he said, "Let's test the trap tomorrow instead. Let's talk 'till it gets light, until bedtime."

It was becoming too cold to sit outside. They closed and barred their heavy homemade kitchen door and turned on the light at the folding table in the kitchen. Robert put a can of beans on the stove and cut some wieners into it.

"I'm jealous," Nelson conceded finally, feeling better at the admission. "I wish it would happen to me. Anyway, what did you mean about it never being too late?"

Robert brought the pot to the table and spooned the steaming lumps into dishes. He opened another beer and then said, "I've had to ask myself if I exist at all." He looked at the other man sorrowfully. "I suppose that sounds melodramatic, self-pitying, and maybe it is. But we used to wonder that. Before. It only came to me when I wondered where I was before August 29th. I've come to terms with that since. I was where you were. I'm a copy of all that you've been through and all that you saw and heard and felt, and as far as we can tell the copy's just as good as the original, right?"

"Yes."

"I told myself the reason we made our pact about the future and the past was not because there was any important difference between us so much as because the rest of the world just couldn't ... All the same, I wasn't sure if I ever existed. And I thought the reason people pour themselves into the kind of work we do is that we all have this dark unspeakable doubt, something we hate to acknowledge, and so we're always producing things to smother that doubt – films, tapes, books – anything to prove we were there. Like leaving fingerprints."

Nelson shrugged.

"Then I thought that nothing I ever did, and that means nothing *we* ever did, was really original. We had a knack for putting films together in a fresh way, and we broke some new ground in technique. But I began to feel that I would only be sure I existed if I could look at something I had done and say, 'Yes, that's unique in the world.' "

"Everything every person does is unique." Nelson said, regretting now that he had agreed to talk instead of test the trap. "Even you and me. Much as we're alike. We talked about that the other night at the lake. About the sources of difference, about ..."

"But if you really mean it, about excellence," Robert broke in excitedly, "or if I really mean it about doing something original; if you're really committed, then you're going to start living in a way that puts you in touch with the possibility, and that may be as far as you get, but that's good enough, because if you're doing it all the time, you're there. That's what the preacher was talking about – 'the voice in the night.' If you're living it, Nelson! If you're *living* it, it doesn't matter when the voice comes. Trouble with us, we were always saying, 'When there's time,' or 'Some day.'"

Nelson yawned, got up and stretched. "I'm going to bed. It's getting light. We'll test the trap tonight."

But Robert was lost in speculation, arranging a few spilled beans on the table and admiring the pattern, noticing their tangential relationships, and tasting his beer and thinking about how fine Nelson's clean-shaven face looked as he tackled a problem with the drop and the net, and thinking about so many lost opportunities with Daisy that would never be retrieved.

And yet, perhaps that did not matter, because from now on he would let nothing slip by – no chance to plunge as deep and ask as much and stay as silent and give as much as would suit the moment and the space and the light of day.

He realized that he had come to terms with the necessity of parting from Nelson, and even with the existence, somewhere in Nelson's perception of him, of hatred. He chose to let that strengthen him. To that hatred he would return all the love he could, as long as they lasted together, and then part cleanly, having given what he could give as long as he was allowed to give it. When he crawled into his sleeping bag, he felt again the approach of that peace he had touched on the water in the moonlight.

21

Having talked past their usual bedtime of seven a.m., they slept late and when they woke up, shortly after three-thirty in the afternoon, they stayed in bed, reading a stack of old paperbacks and sipping coffee which Robert replenished from time to time.

Then at dusk they had baths and cleaned up some of the construction mess from the day before. Dark settled and the street was lively for a while with people coming home from work, and then quiet again as dinners were cooked and television sets came on.

It was time to test the trap. They tossed a coin and Nelson lost. They unbarred the thick homemade kitchen fortress door and turned out the kitchen light. Robert waited inside. Nelson opened the door a crack and peered through it; then he slipped silently onto the porch and waited for his eyes to adjust. From inside, Robert watched his silhouette and saw it stiffen as Nelson stepped suddenly back toward the half-open door.

"What?" Robert whispered.

"Not sure."

Nelson put his face to the opening. "It could be a trick of the light, but I think there's somebody in the passageway between the two houses across the lane. Somebody watching."

Robert felt a chill. "Could he see you?"

"Don't know. It's completely dark on this side. I don't think anyone could see."

Nelson turned back and peered across the dark alley, then pressed through the half-open door back into the kitchen and silently closed the door until only a half-inch crack of opening was left. He was breathing hard. He said, "Sorry. I just had the idea of Brady putting somebody on to us, watching us there. But that's impossible, isn't it?"

Robert thought for a moment. "Let me look," he whispered. He pressed his face to the crack in the door.

"Just to the right," Nelson murmured. "At the opening of the breezeway."

Robert squinted. "Nothing" he said finally.

"I could have imagined it."

"But you don't think you did."

"No."

They sat in the dark, waiting until their hearts stopped pounding. Feeling his way, Robert heated water and made instant coffee. They sipped it silently. About nine o'clock Nelson said, "Let's go." He looked out again. "Clear," he said, and stepped out decisively and shut the door quietly behind him. He walked cautiously up the narrow walkway that separated their house from the next one. He paused before leaving the sheltered dark between the houses, assured himself that the street was deserted, listened for a moment to the sounds of traffic from Dundas Street, looked at the heaps of fallen leaves where they had been swept into mounds in the gutters, and found himself suddenly overwhelmed with homesickness and a clear compelling vision in his mind of his house on Moore Avenue. It dawned on him that this was one of the few times that he and Robert had been physically apart.

"I could turn around now," he thought. Behind him, in the lane, they had rented a garage for the Volkswagen. He had the keys in his pocket. He saw himself racing through the empty streets, north to Moore Avenue, rousing Daisy, heading off, west, anywhere, away, changing identities, leaving the country. Robert was waiting patiently in the basement for the trial burglary to begin. Nelson could be half-way to Moore Avenue before Robert gave up and came looking for him.

"That man in the basement isn't real," he thought. "I know he isn't real, because I know there can't be two of us."

He shook his head. "But he knows the same thing. He knows *I* can't be real. This is a dream that will end, so why not end it by acting, now?"

He paused with his hand on the rail of the sagging old porch, and felt flakes of loose paint under his fingers. "He admitted he was the copy and I was the original. A copy's not the real thing."

But then he pictured the faithful bearded man waiting for him, not fifteen feet away, out of sight, behind brick, below ground. He put a hand on the rail and leaped over it onto the creaking front porch. A cat scuttled off the porch, startling him for a moment before he slipped in through the unlocked outer door.

"Robert!" He called in as loud a voice as he dared.

"What kept you?" Half muffled, from beneath the trap.

"Tell you later." He would, too. "Mattress in place?"

"Go ahead."

Nelson crouched into a ball so that he would not risk falling back and striking his head on the edge of the trap. He felt an exaggerated thrill of fear, even though it was only eight feet to the basement floor and a springy net between and a mattress underneath. His hand closed on the doorknob and pulled hard against the initial resistance. The floor fell away beneath him with a terrific bang. His heart seemed to stop for an instant, and then he was swinging loose in the net.

"Shit," Robert said. The drawstrings had caught on the corners of the trap doors and the net had not closed around the body within. Nelson had no difficulty clambering back up into the little entrance hall. He went through the house and down into the basement and together they loosened and lowered the drawstrings supporting the neck of the net so that they would hang clear of the edge of the trap doors.

"No point my going back outside," Nelson said. "Come up and close the door on me and we'll try again."

This time it worked perfectly. His flexed knees took a slight jar as he bottomed on the mattress, and, in the same instant, the neck of the net gathered like a fist around him and he was immobilized, suspended an inch above the mattress and swinging in a very small arc to the sound of the drawstrings creaking in their shackles like a ship at sea.

"Dynamite!" he grunted. "Get me out of here. It's terrible."

"Not so fast," Robert said. "See if you can move your arms first. Try to get into a pocket."

"Can't. He might already have his gun out, though."

"See if you can lift your weight at all. Pull on the net with your left hand where it's highest."

Nelson struggled and grunted and tried his hardest to loosen the grip of the net pulling himself up. It only tightened on him all the more.

"If you had a gun in your hand and you hadn't lost it in the fall, could you aim it, twist it around and shoot out?"

"A little. Not much."

"We could tell him to empty the magazine onto the floor, leaving him hanging till he did it."

"I can tell you he'd do it fast. Get me the hell out of here!"

"Right!"

But Robert hesitated, and suddenly sat down hard on the edge of the mattress, holding his head.

"What's the matter?" Nelson said anxiously.

"Dizzy. It . . . It's passing. Just a minute."

He bent his head down and pressed his hands against his temple and sucked in lungfuls of air. He had suddenly been swept with a dizzying confusion of thoughts, a wave of perceptions, some his own, some from another source, all contending for space with sounds, words, fleeting distorted pictures: someone running hard; a deep chilling fear, an insistent, guilt-laden, amazing image of himself turning away now and leaving Nelson in the net, this treacherous image permeating the others like a theme; something about Nelson gazing at him with a look full of repentance and affection and trust; the face of Daisy weeping; again the image of himself running away from Nelson, from the house, almost screaming with the wrongness of it. He felt terribly weak for the space of a few seconds and then it was gone. He looked up at Nelson's anxious face.

"I don't know what the hell that was!"

Then he yanked the mattress out from beneath the net, sprawled where the mattress had been, lifted himself on his hands and knees and heaved at the body above, with the intention of loosening the tension on the drawstrings by relieving them of their weight. But it was too unstable. The net shifted sideways and remained tightly closed. Robert was puffing from the exertion. "I'll have to go up," he gasped. "Pull you from above."

In the little foyer, however, its floor almost entirely consumed by the trapdoor, there was nothing to hold on to. Lying on the floor in the hall beyond the inner door, Robert could lean over and grab the neck of the net but there was no leverage. He would have had to both lift the net and spread the neck at the same time. He stood up and surveyed the situation from above. Below him the curled body of Nelson was silent, resigned to impotence and waiting. Robert sensed the resignation; the panic that had been edging in around the muscles of his throat subsided. Glancing into the front room as he started back toward the basement, he saw a glint of light from the periscope and remembered that he had not checked the view. He lay down on the floor and put his face to the opening. In the reflected light from the whitewashed walls he could see the trussed body hanging immobile, see the blinking, frustrated right eye and the denim eyepatch pulled away from the left eye and crossed by a strand of netting. He could see the clenched, imprisoned hands, every detail he would need to have to know his prisoner was secure.

He pushed himself up and sprinted for the stairs.

"Only one way," he said. "I'll have to unfasten the shackles." Nelson didn't answer.

Robert found a wrench and slacked off the bolts on one side. The right-hand drawstring pulled free and the net suddenly swung to the right and down and Nelson gave a hefty grunt as he thumped against the floor.

"Sorry," the other said, and brought the mattress over and wedged it against the still partly hanging body so that when the other drawstring let go and the rest of the weight came down it would roll onto the padding. Robert looked at Nelson's face, and was surprised and relieved to find an amused smile on it. For a moment he thought he saw a hint of affection: could that be? His heart began to pound.

"Won't be long," he promised as he climbed up, loosened the bolts on the left side, jumped as the trussed form rolled sideways

onto the mattress, tugged the drawstrings loose and finally released the panting, red-faced man within.

"Sorry," he said again. "Sorry I was so long."

Nelson stretched his limbs and said with a grimace, "That's
a terrific punishment. Christ, we'll get him to promise anything."

"What do you mean, 'promise?' Think Pete Brady ever kept
a promise he wasn't paid for?"

"I worked it out as I was hanging there. Here's what we
do. We wire the phone for a long extension, and we bring it
down and make him talk to New York."

"To tell them the contract's been made?"

"That's the first thing."

"What's the next?"

"We get a sworn statement. There's attempted murder on
Rob Nelson. We tell him we'll let him out of the net to make
a sworn confession and then we bring in ... no *I* bring in – only
one of us can show his face – Morley Stone, or any one of
Daisy's partners, and have him take the affidavit."

"In the net?"

"Can't. Statement under duress. No good. We'll tie him
up; that's legitimate. Sworn statement of a prisoner under
citizen arrest, and he knows he goes back in the net if we
don't get it."

"I think he'd rather be in the net."

"You haven't been in the net. Besides, you know what Brady's
like. I'll tell him the statement goes in a safety deposit box to be
opened only in case of my death. He's a dealer. He knows a deal
when he sees one. And he'll do anything to get out of that damn
net."

"Stone?"

"He'll do it."

"But he'll tell Daisy about us."

"That's why you've got to keep out of sight. Anyway, we've
got some things to talk about there. Daisy, I mean."

Robert bit his lip. "Okay. I think it works."

"Let's go upstairs and talk to Pinch's tape machine."

*

"We're assuming Brady has someone checking that tape in Pinch's machine," Robert said.

"We've got to give it a try."

"But not be too obvious. No point saying, 'Here I am; come and get me.'"

"I know. He's got to think ..."

"We're throwing him off, not trying to suck him in."

"Listen, Brady wouldn't know Daisy's voice."

"We're not bringing Daisy into this!"

"No. I mean do our woman's voice. Say it's Daisy. Ask Pinch to contact her here. At this number."

"So when Brady phones here ..."

"We answer and he hangs up."

"And buys an address for this number from a mob contact here in town."

"Worth a try."

Nelson direct dialled Montreal.

"J.A. Haig speaking. This is an answering machine. You may leave your message at the sound of the tone. Thank you."

The beep flared in the receiver and then there was a silence. Nelson, constricting his throat, sounded not exactly like Daisy but very much like an anxious woman and not at all like Rob Nelson. "Pinch, dear. This is Daisy. Phone me as soon as you can." He gave the number. "Please, Pinch!" And he hung up.

Robert said, "Brady has phoned Daisy before this; must have."

"He wouldn't have talked to her enough to know her voice."

"It may work and it may not. We've got to give it a few days."

It was just after midnight.

Robert said, "Let's have a beer and something to eat and go to bed early for a change."

They settled in the kitchen, opened some beers and made salami sandwiches. They chewed and sipped in silence for a while and then Nelson said, "This sounds corny, but do you have anything you'd like to confess?"

Robert nodded ruefully. "I could deny it. But I figure you might have had some ideas about running off too – that's what was going through my head when I felt so dizzy. Is that what took you so long, outside? Did you think about leaving?"

"I had the car keys."

"Did you think, 'He's not real?'"

Nelson, wondering if he'd been overheard and feeling tough, wanting to test it and confront the other man, decided to lie. "No, you're real enough."

"I felt unreal a few minutes ago. Sitting down on the mattress. "But," he wanted now to offer something of his feeling overtly, to look for a response, "having the thought about running out and leaving you in the net made me feel incredibly guilty. I could never have done that."

When Nelson made no reply, Robert asked, "So why didn't you?"

Nelson looked over the rim of his beer glass. "Why didn't I what? Take the car and bugger off? And leave you wondering in the basement? I don't know."

Robert felt a pang of sadness in his belly. "Is that the truth?" he asked softly.

"I just don't know. I could make something up about all we've gone through, needing your support. Those things are true. I can think of reasons now; at the time it was just one impulse against another. That's all I can tell you."

Robert rose from the table heavily. "Going to shave now," he said dully.

"There's time," Nelson said, and yawned. "Do it in the morning."

"You never know. Brady could be at Pine Avenue, waiting and listening. He might be on his way right now."

Robert paused at the kitchen door. He started to slide the heavy wooden bolt into place, then stopped.

"Nelson?"

"What is it?"

"Do you really think you saw someone in the alley?"

"I saw someone."

Robert turned off the light, opened the door and peered out

again. Nothing but shadows. He stared into the darkness, thinking more about the pain in his heart than about the supposed
watcher across the alley. How could he have come to care so
deeply while Nelson could say only that he had contained his
impulse to run off by nothing more than a countering impulse,
simple practical considerations of strategy and survival?

"For what?" Robert thought. He closed and bolted the door
and checked the curtains, then turned the kitchen light on again
and went upstairs to the bathroom.

While the sink was filling with hot water, Robert stared at
himself moodily in the mirror.

Nelson stretched out on one of the foam mattresses on the
floor of the front room and pulled the sleeping bag around his
shoulders. Robert came in wiping his now-naked face with a
towel and Nelson found the sight of him disconcerting.

"I'd gotten used to your beaver," he said.

"I can always put on a false one if it'll make you feel better."

"I'm just letting you know it's a shock. It's different for
you; you've been looking at your own familiar face on me for
the whole time. Now I realize how much I was letting the beard
turn you into another person."

"I am another person."

Robert zipped himself into his bag and lay on his back, staring
at the filthy ceiling. "Do you feel any less lonely than we used
to?" he asked.

"Sexually I'm terribly lonely," Nelson answered. "I find
myself reaching out, as if my whole skin was yearning. I can
feel it responding in waves along my chest. It's almost as if the
skin was independently inviting a breast to press against it. It
must be the same for you?"

Robert nodded.

Nelson said, "The muscles in my back seem to imagine
hands holding, caressing. My scalp senses it. It's not visual, not
the imagined body of a woman. I feel it more in my skin than
I do in my cock."

"There's nothing we can do about that now," Robert sighed.
"Go to sleep."

"You too. Sleep well."

But neither did. They rolled back and forth in their confining sleeping bags, listening irritably to each other's restlessness.

Finally Nelson sat up in bed. "Scotch," he said, glowering at Robert.

"We said we'd save that for a celebration. Better not get drunk until this is all over."

They continued to glare at each other. Nelson understood that he was not going to get drunk without Robert, and knew that Robert understood this as well, and was trying to make up his mind whether to outwait the other man or say out loud what was going on, when Robert said with a self-recriminatory laugh, "Okay."

They went back to the kitchen and put a full twenty-six and a tray of ice between them.

The whisky began to work half-way down the first refill. They did not talk much; just nodded at each other with a grim look of admission that, after all, it was a tough game they were playing and nobody in the world had ever played it before so there was nothing to guide them. They slowed the pace of the drinking somewhat. An hour went by. They began to give each other knowing winks and more extravagant grimaces. Grimaces yielded to half-lidded smiles. After the second refill the bottle was empty.

"Drunk yet?" Nelson asked.

"Noo noo, not drunk. Just feeling fine. Good idea after all."

"I was just thinking of something," Nelson said. "I always used to wake up with a hangover and ask myself why I didn't tell myself the night before to stop before it was too late, because I always had such terrible hangovers."

"We."

"What?"

"*We* always had such terrible hangovers."

"You did too?"

Robert whooped and coughed because his whoop caused some whisky to get into his windpipe. He pounded the table, and laughter and coughs shook his body, the table, the chair, the floor, the whole house. Slowly Nelson's bewildered face cleared and he guessed he got the joke too and soon they were both rocking back and forth pounding the table and láughing, tears welling up in their eyes, and both feeling perfectly marvellous with the release of such a mighty explosion.

Presently Nelson stood up, still chuckling and wiping the tears from his eyes, and opened the kitchen door for a breath of air. He was too drunk to even remember that he had seen, or thought he had seen, someone watching the house from the breezeway opposite. Robert walked over to stand beside him and stretched and breathed deeply, blinking in the early sunlight and looking at the sky. Then they closed and bolted the door again and found their way back to their makeshift beds.

They wound themselves into their sleeping bags.

"Did you take the key from the door so he can pick the lock?" Robert asked.

"Do it in the morning."

"This is the morning."

"When we get up then. Ready for tonight."

Dimly Robert felt that was not quite right. He groped for the zipper of his sleeping bag, thinking "Just to be extra safe." He rolled on his side and looked at the huddled form opposite, the eyepatch flung on the floor, one arm half out of the bag and the hand draped with exquisite negligence over the edge of the yellow foam. Robert felt a rush of yearning. He whispered across the room, "I love you."

A snore answered him.

He yawned hugely, rolled on his back and shut his eyes.

It was half-past eight in the morning. Children were loping off to school and a garbage truck had started up from Dundas. In the barricaded house the two men slept.

In the alley behind the house the woman, pressed against the brick wall in a breezeway between two houses, stared silently at the shabby back door. After a while she turned, and went back down the breezeway into the neighboring street and disappeared.

22

It is a few hours before dawn. From the basement of the grey house on Pine Avenue in Montreal there comes a steady clinking sound which continues rhythmically, about one blow a second, and then stops. After a minute it resumes again. A black cat prowling the alleyway behind the house, senses a human presence in the sound and stops at the wooden basement door and leans her head against it. The door resonates dully. What has penetrated to the outside as a dim metallic tapping, now thuds substantially in the cat's thin skull and she presses her head against the door, taking a kind of caress from the pulsing sound. The sound stops. The cat rubs her head and her ears against the wood inviting the sound to begin again, but she is impatient and hungry and moves on down the alley; when, a minute later, the faint clink-clink once more pursues her, she does not pause or even look around.

Beyond the wooden door, down the steps and a dozen feet to the left, against what appears to be some concrete work newer than the old, dirty brick and grime of the rest of the room, a figure is kneeling, a small, heavy lump hammer in one hand, a mason's chisel in the other. He is working at the concrete near the floor where some edges of brick can be seen. There is an electric light on the floor beside him, its bulb almost completely shielded with aluminum foil. A narrow beam from the lamp illuminates the work, but most of the basement is in deep shadow.

From time to time the man pauses, lays down the hammer and the chisel, and listens carefully. Once, he gets to his feet and crosses the floor quietly to the head of the stairs leading up into the house. He has heard the telephone, but it stops after the first ring. For a moment, he hesitates, his hand on the doorknob of the kitchen door. He turns and goes back to the wall of concrete, kneels and picks up his hammer and chisel and begins again.

Presently there is a break in the concrete shell as he drives the chisel against it, and a popping sound followed by a sigh of escaping gas. A hideous smell fills the room. The figure holding the chisel hisses an indrawn breath. His stomach heaves. With an effort he controls the impulse to retch and goes on with his work. On the floor beside him is a large square of heavy black plastic, like a tarpaulin. In the alley outside is a black car with a large trunk. The kneeling figure grunts and works harder than before. It will be light in an hour.

23

They had slept late and were awakened by the ringing of the phone, which had been silent since they moved in. Nelson sprang up and tried feverishly to disengage his feet and ended up hopping to the kitchen where Robert was just replacing the handset.

"I said hello," he said gravely. "And there was a pause and then whoever it was hung up."

"It's underway, then," Nelson said quietly.

The rest of the night they sat in chairs, tense, fear gnawing badly at their resources and their stamina.

And this went on for a week. Repeatedly Nelson found his temper snapping over little things: the light left on in the bathroom, a dripping tap, the sound of the radio. Robert tried to say calming things, hopeful things, to suggest that it was the tension of waiting, that there was no erosion of their essential relationship. But he knew from Nelson's eyes that the hope was thin. He wanted to understand what Nelson was thinking. He tried, at first by a deliberate effort of concentration, and when that didn't work, by emptying his mind, to recapture the wavelength, to hear the other man's thoughts again.

Nelson regarded him coldly, waiting for the end. "I hope we can hold out emotionally," he said once, surprising Robert, and yet Robert suspected that it was said strategically.

So Robert revived his determination to offer as much of himself as he could, for as long as he could, and to seek moral strength and emotional stability in that service. Nelson hated Robert's calm; it made him feel weak, victimized. He did not understand it. It seemed inappropriate.

Once he burst out, "Goddam it! We might be dead tomorrow! Don't you bloody care?" And then stormed upstairs to the bathroom and took a cold shower. When he came down again, he offered a surly apology and buried himself in a paperback thriller, but could scarcely see the words for anger.

On Monday night, at nine o'clock, the phone rang again, sounding like a fire alarm in the empty house.

Nelson said, "Let me handle it this time. I'm going to bring this to a head!"

Robert's eyes looked an imperative warning at the other man but it was too late. Nelson nearly pulled the phone off the wall and yelled into it without waiting, "All right Brady, for Christ's sake, come and get me."

Robert watched in horror, and then saw the other man's expression change dramatically as the voice on the other end of the line buzzed in the receiver. Nelson appeared as though a weight had been lifted off his neck; his head snapped upright and he looked across the room with shining eyes, beckoning to Robert. He covered the mouthpiece a moment and said, "Brady's in New York." Into the mouthpiece he said, "Listen, Brady, I'm not sure I believe that. Say it again, slowly and clearly and let me think about it."

Robert had his head against Nelson's and was listening too. Pete Brady's voice, distinct and unmistakeable said, "It's true. They called off the contract. They found your friend with the haggis in his voice and they're working out a friendly deal, and part of it is I lay off. They've paid me and frankly, I'm just as happy."

Robert whispered, "It's a trick. Ask him what . . ."

But Brady was speaking again. "You there?"

"How do I know you're not around the corner, trying to get me to leave my cover?"

There was a pause, then Brady said, "Get a pencil."

Nelson beckoned wildly. Robert grabbed a pen and a sheaf of papers from beside the sink and handed them over.

"Write this down," Brady said. "I'm over on the Jersey side. Area code 201. 524-9155. Call me back and you'll know I'm really here, understand?"

The line clicked dead. With his hands shaking, Nelson hung

up and picked up again too quickly and did not get a dial tone and forced himself to wait ten seconds the second time, got the tone, dialled 1-201-524-9155 and waited in agony for the ring to start.

Three hundred and fifty miles away in Teterboro, New Jersey, Pete Brady picked up the phone.

"Convinced now?" he said affably.

Beside him another man watched keenly and glanced at his watch and out the wire-mesh window across the room, beyond which a red light was rotating and flashing every second on the windows.

"Good," Brady was saying. "Relax. Go home. Kiss the wife. Take a holiday. Your professor friend will call you at home in a few days ... No, I don't have his number, but he's okay. Take it easy ... Right. So long now, be seeing you."

Brady hung up and turned to the other man. "He fell for it. Let's go!" He patted the hard lump under his left hand breast pocket, picked up his raincoat, and ran out of the building.

Outside, on the tarmac of the Teterboro airport, the engines of the Gates Learjet had begun to whine. As Brady launched himself through the door and pulled it shut behind him, the pilot said, "We've got clearance and they say no delay for take-off."

"Move it," Brady said. "Still clear at the Island Airport?"

"It'll be clear for the next three hours."

The airplane was already moving down the taxiway.

"What's your estimate for Toronto?"

"I'll have you down at the Island an hour and five minutes after we put up the wheels."

Brady gave a satisfied grunt and settled back in his narrow chair.

At eleven minutes past ten, the wheels of the Learjet stopped rolling in front of the white clapboard terminal at the Toronto Island airport. Brady was out of the plane before the customs' official was out of the building.

He cleared customs easily and sprinted across the grass behind the terminal and jumped onto a small boat bobbing at the concrete stairs west of the ferry slip. The boatman let go his grip on the step, revved up instantly, and was docking on the other side, a few hundred feet away, in seconds.

By the waiting-shed was a green Dodge, the motor running. The driver was in the phone booth with the phone to his ear. When he saw the white-haired man, he hung up and jumped behind the wheel.

"All okay," he said.

They spun around in the parking lot and careened out into the access road.

It took nine minutes to make it along the lake shore, up Jarvis Street, across Dundas and up the crumbling alley between Seaton and Ontario Streets.

In the lane behind the barricaded house, the car stopped. A man stepped out of the shadows between two garages. "I've been here since dark," he said. "Your guy never came out. I heard the phone when you called at nine. He's still in there, all right."

Brady placed a wad of money in the man's hands and another in the driver's, who got out of the car. "It's mine now," Brady said. "You don't want to be anywhere around. Get a good alibi."

They were gone before he had backed the car into an adjacent empty garage. Brady moved slightly into the alleyway, into the shadows.

24

It had been a terrible week for Lucas Rankin. Despite the emotional comfort of his evenings' unburdening to Martha, his most dispassionate view of Emmanuel College and his ambition to receive the benefits of its blessing and certification, he grew more pessimistic. He went to lectures but stared into space. He read his Bible but the words ran together. Martha had disclosed cryptically that she had something to show him in the city, and had indicated that she wanted him to go walking with her, but irritably he had pleaded exhaustion and put her off, and had felt guilty when he saw her disappointment. Perhaps one night, he would go and see whatever it was she wanted him to see. She had taken to leaving the house early in the morning and sometimes late at night, and she wore a look of self-satisfied mystery that puzzled him.

There came an evening, after a seminar on human motivations that left Lucas thoroughly demoralized, when he decided to tell Martha he wanted to quit. A few blocks from his flat, he heard his name called several times. He turned and saw an old school mate from home; they had played high school football together. Briefly they had chummed around. Now, in a city grown more hateful to Lucas every day, his friend's unexpected appearance in the street seemed like a sign. Lucas felt an extravagant rush of feeling for this nearly-forgotten acquaintance, and allowed himself to be persuaded to go to a nearby bar for a drink, thinking he'd have a ginger ale.

But soon his friend's tireless sexual boasting and his complete lack of interest in Lucas's private bewilderment left the young preacher more lonely than ever. An edge of self-pity crept into his feelings, and he let himself be talked into tasting a beer, the first alcohol he had ever taken. He sipped it slowly and hated the taste. Suddenly he told himself bitterly that perhaps a dose of forgetfulness was what he needed, and he drained his glass in a gulp, ordered a second, and swilled it in three long belts. Then he ordered another.

Half way through his fifth beer, Lucas felt dizzy. Unsteadily he made his way to the washroom and threw up, splashing himself as he did so. When he looked at his face in the mirror he saw a haggard reflection that he scarcely knew. He shook his head remorsefully.

"Martha," he said to the mirror.

He did not even go back to the table.

Turning into the short walk in front of his house, he looked up and saw Martha at the window. He braced himself. When he walked in the room she came to greet him in her usual way, stopped short, wrinkling her nose distastefully, and looked him up and down – at his spattered pants, his bedraggled hair and hangdog look. She clapped her hands together angrily and stalked away from him. She turned at the other end of the room and stared a long time. Lucas just stood there. Then Martha shook her head, as if negating something, perhaps her anger. She slowly came back to him, searched his face solemnly for a moment, tapped her chest with her four fingers cupped, pointed to her forehead and nodded at him with an intent look.

"All right Martha," Lucas said. "I'll do what you say."

She smiled, and her eyes, which had flared open in anger, softened to her characteristic, half-lidded, tranquil expression. She took Lucas by the hand and led him to the bathroom and cleaned him up with a damp facecloth. She sponged off his trousers and his new white Adidas with their blue slashes – her gift, now spattered with yellow. Then she motioned him to put his coat back on. But Lucas held up an admonitory hand.

"Martha," he protested, "I said I'd do what you want, but it's near ten o'clock and I don't feel well."

Her eyes flared again. She stepped to the wall and stabbed her finger at the calendar hanging there. Stab! Friday. She shook her head, indicating refusal. Stab! Saturday. Another headshake. Stab! Sunday. The same.

Then, laying her finger softly on Monday she smiled as if it were already resolved, relaxed her face again, let her eyelids drop above her wide cheekbones, took Lucas's now unprotesting hand and led him out the door.

As they walked toward College Street and the streetcars, Lucas asked, "Where we going?"

She smiled and touched her eyes with both hands and hugged herself.

"To see somebody? Pretty late for a visit."

Martha closed her eyes and tilted her cheek against her hands, palms together, then opened her eyes and shook her head.

"Okay," Lucas said.

They stood waiting at the carstop. Lucas shivered. "Is it too far to walk, Martha? Walking makes me feel better. I might get sick on the streetcar."

They set out arm in arm, along College Street, Lucas frowning but not displeased, and Martha with her deepest, visionary and satisfied look of calm.

Jet engines shuffled hollowly above them. Looking up, they saw a small white shape, its wings and belly reflecting all the lights beneath, turn low over the city. As they watched, the clean-lined sleek machine opened dark spaces in its underside. Wheels emerged. Landing lights flared up at the wingtips. It disappeared from sight behind tall buildings to the south, toward the lake. Martha and Lucas trudged resolutely east, toward Ontario Street.

25

Robert and Nelson came out the back door of the barricaded house at six minutes to eleven. The call from New Jersey announcing their freedom had possessed so much of the quality of miracle, of deliverance, that for the first minutes after they hung up, everything seemed possible; the strictures and rules, the anxieties and risks examined over the past two months appeared insignificant: they had been given the gift of life anew and the experience was so heady that their judgement was jointly impaired for some time.

Nelson was buoyant, extravagant with triumph and goodwill. He suggested that their first pact, the division of past and present, might be reconsidered, and they discussed how they would go to Daisy together – Nelson first to pave the way, to prepare her for the strange encounter, and then ask for her collaboration in planning how they should work out the new life for all of them. The two men went around the house gathering up things with snatches of melody humming in their throats and loud laughs, and Nelson once jumped in the air and grabbed the molding over the door frame and hung there swinging his heels and crowing like Peter Pan.

But then Robert soon saw that his appearing in front of Daisy would be of emotional brutality. Sobering now, he knew that he had changed profoundly and that Nelson had not. He knew that Nelson would soon rediscover his resentment and, yes, maybe hatred, of this interloper, this unwanted partner. And so he knew he must go. He dimly thought of going to China or Africa, making himself totally the servant of whatever he found there, and he counted on Pinch to help him. He told Nelson only that, no, he had to leave as agreed, that it was for Daisy's sake, and he was lucid and persuasive. Nelson regarded him with admiration and ill-concealed relief. He said, "You're sure?"

"Yes. Don't worry. Pinch will help me get to where I need to go. If you like, I'll let you know, through Pinch. Nelson, I'm going to do some good things.

"I think I am too."

When they stepped into the alleyway, each with his kitbag of necessities, everything else having been dumped into the cellar of the soon-to-be-demolished house, the trap nailed safely shut and the power turned off, the air smelled clean and fresh. It smelled free!

But habits of secrecy remained. The existence of Robert must still be concealed and protected. They walked silently down the path to the teetering garage where the Volkswagen waited. A few stars showed above, occasionally eclipsed by broken clouds moving slowly. Across the alleyway there was a glint of moonlight on the dark window panes of another empty house; but the moon hung out of sight behind the houses on their side.

A window was ajar somewhere despite the cold air; they could hear a record playing, a clear voice from the early seventies:

> *I long to hear your voice,*
> *To see your smile again.*

At the garage, Nelson bent to lift the rusty overhead door, which grated abrasively on its tracks as he heaved up on it. Robert felt a thrill of apprehension – something from my old world, he thought – and a pressure on his bladder, and he stayed back in the shadows between the two garages and fumbled at his zipper.

Then he froze, listening.

The sounds of Nelson fussing at the car inside the garage were clear. He could hear the music still.

> *You used to need me near*
> *But all that's changed, it seems.*

The orange parking lights had gone on inside the garage and

a soft glow showed through the cracked board siding. But there was something else to be heard, or felt, something in the alley.

Robert tugged up his zipper again and peered across the alley into the unrevealing blackness in the breezeway between two houses opposite. There! He had definitely heard a footstep.

But the man with the white hair was not across the alley in the breezeway. He was on the near side of the alley, almost invisible in the shadows. The garage was between him and Robert. He squinted against the light into a crack in the garage wall as he tried to identify with certainty the figure bobbing up and down around the upraised front lid of the Volkswagen's baggage compartment. Presently he gave a low, satisfied grunt and raised a long barrel that caught a stray moonbeam and flickered briefly in the blackness of his concealment.

Four things happened almost at once. Nelson closed the baggage lid quietly and stood a moment outlined against a faint orange reflection on the rotting boards behind him; Pete Brady began to squeeze the muscle in his right index finger as he centered the sight on the black silhouette in the garage; Robert brought his head cautiously out between the garages and was just in time to see a lithe grey figure launch itself silently out of the shadows across the alley, white tennis shoes flashing in the moonlight, in a graceful flying tackle at the hidden gunman.

The gun went off with a flash into the garage and the bullet tore through the rotting boards inches from Nelson's head.

Pete Brady brought his pistol down with a crack on the head of the figure whose powerful arms were wrapped around his buckling bruised thighs. The grip on Brady's legs relaxed as the figure went limp.

Nelson charged out of the garage as the gunman's head was coming up again, but Brady did not see Robert grab Nelson, aim him at the breezeway across the alley and whisper "Run!" with all the imperative he could muster. It had been agreed: if anything came loose they would split and run, divide the chase.

When Brady stood again and slid his face around the edge of the garage, his heart beating hard in fury and the gun barrel shaking as he tried to get his half-paralyzed leg muscles back under control, he could see Nelson, now hesitating and looking back from the safe darkness of the breezeway; he could not see Robert, thirty feet down the alley toward the barricaded house, also in the shadow and moving slowly away, as silently as possible.

In the breezeway, Nelson was inching backward, his left hand guiding him along the brick side of the house. Suddenly he felt another hand in the darkness; involuntarily he gasped as he whirled and saw a strange woman standing there in the shadows – but not strange, rather, strangely familiar. She clapped a hand across her mouth and shook her head hard, and Nelson realized that whoever she was, she was trying to protect him, to silence him for safety.

The music from a nearby house had come to an end. In the black alleyway, slashed here and there with gentle moonlight, the echoes had died, and there was silence. Robert, hidden behind a jut of rotting fence, could clearly hear, from across the alley toward the breezeway, Nelson's sharp intake of breath, and then a muffled movement, and then another deep breath. At any moment Brady would hear it too, must have heard it already, must be moving out of his shadow, lifting his weapon.

And now Robert knew what it was he would do with the rest of his life.

He saw Daisy's face with perfect clarity then, smiling at him in the bed at Canopy Lake, radiant with loving him. He recalled Pinch's voice, *"And I you, Robbie."* He saw the sleeping face of himself as double, his Nelson, his partner. He heard the whir of nylon line over placid moonsplashed water.

He felt perfectly at peace and consumed with love.

He stepped decisively out of his hiding place into a ray of moonlight and said in a clear, easy voice, "Brady!"

In the breezeway, Nelson, faintly over the sound of his own constricted breathing and the blood pounding in his ears heard, and was chilled in disbelief as he heard it, the confident voice that saved his life. He saw a white head rise into view and, then a flash and heard a *whup*! He was congealed in indecision. He watched Brady run across his narrow field of vision at the end of the breezeway and disappear. The woman's hand gripping his arm, restraining him, seemed to tremble, but it was he who was shaking.

A car without its lights on pulled up just within his line of sight and stopped briefly while the passenger side door, opposite him, swung open and slammed shut again. Inside the car the gunman reached across the unconscious bleeding form of the man he had just shot and then pushed him roughly off the front seat and onto the floor of the car. He slammed shut the door that had swung open as he started to drive. He muttered, "I want some information before I finish you. Appolinari, Haig, and where the money came from. So don't fall out of the car!"

But to Nelson, watching from fifty feet away, it seemed as though the door had swung open again to eject something. The car leapt ahead. As it vanished, its lights flashed on and the red tail lights reflected back down the alley. Nelson glimpsed the legs of a man, prone, sticking out between the two garages. "Robert!" he choked.

Heartsick, he shook off the restraining hand of the silent woman and pelted back along the walk between the houses. Even before he reached the body he was puzzled by the bright white shoes. He rolled the groaning man over on his back and felt a shock at seeing the beard, which in the half-light made this stranger, his rescuer, seem like Robert before he had shaved. The woman pushed Nelson firmly aside and knelt and lifted the man's head. Her voice was a muted, whimpering, *Ah ah ah-ah-ah!*

The man opened his eyes and stared at the two people bending over him. "Someone' was going to shoot you," he said thickly.

"Ah, ah," the woman murmured. She took the edge of her stole and dabbed at the side of the man's head where the blood oozed thickly. He hissed with pain. "Can't somebody tell me what's going on?" he asked plaintively. And then, as he tried to sit up, he winced and groaned and said, "Oh Lord, I ain't worthy to gather up the crumbs beneath thy table!" He eased his head gingerly onto the woman's kneeling lap.

With those words of prayer, recognition began to form in

Nelson's mind. The alleyway was peaceful. Someone was playing the same song again.

> *I long to hear your voice,*
> *To see your smile again.*

Through the screen of his confusion and fear and grief, Nelson stared at the woman, then back at the bearded, pain-wracked man. "You're the preacher ... Rankin!" he said, in a kind of numb amazement. Lucas did not move. Nelson looked at the woman who nodded anxiously. After a moment Lucas sucked in a deep breath and said, "I'll be all right. Just wait a bit, then we can tell what to do." He gulped air a couple of times as if he were afraid to vomit.

Nelson let himself down onto the ground, feeling as though the world was spinning crazily. The space in the chill alleyway, which had seemed so free and open when he and Robert had emerged into it moments ago, now closed in black around him. Within his buffetted brain, swirled eddies of light and sound, half-heard words, images of Robert, of the flash of a gun, of Daisy, an echoing sentence *"One shall be taken ... Which one will you be?"* He struggled to breathe. Although his heart beat wildly, urgently, he felt like a storm-sickened passenger at sea who wishes for the peace of death.

For several minutes they stayed like that, a tableau, immobile except for the woman's right hand. With a careful rhythm she pressed the ball of her thumb lightly above the bridge of Lucas's nose and then stroked upward with a slow, healing caress.

Lucas braced his hands gingerly on the ground for leverage and eased himself into a sitting position. He looked at Nelson slumped beside him, then at the woman.

"Is this who you wanted me to see?"

Nod.

"You thought he needed my help?"

A nod, Yes.

"Did you think something like this would happen, Martha?"

Vigorous, angry headshakes. No. Oh no! No! No!

Nelson, vaguely aware of speech, opened his eyes.

Lucas looked hard at him. "Martha, my sister here, led me to the back of your house. There was a man watching. I think Martha knew something terrible was wrong. We hung back in the walkway there between the houses. Then this other white-haired man came and sent the first man away. Then I knew he was going to shoot someone in the garage. That was you."

Nelson stared blankly.

"We'll take you home with us," Lucas said. "Only I don't think I'm up to much walking. It's a long way."

The word "home" penetrated. Nelson yearned for light and warmth, the touch of hands, someone to tell him it would be all right. But part of him thought: be careful.

Still, these people, so improbably here on the killing ground, innocents in the midst of this nightmare, these gentle people promised rest. But he could not move.

He looked at Martha. "Can you drive a car?" he asked faintly.

A supplicating gesture, No. She looked from Nelson to Lucas and back again.

Nelson forced himself to sit up. He looked down the alley toward where a patch of moonlight showed a dark blot on the gravel. His stomach tightened. He bowed his head as if inviting a blow to still his conciousness.

But Martha, looking back and forth between her wounded brother and Nelson, seemed to be asking Nelson to take charge. He felt the old energy that challenge had always stirred. He stood up. His throat was terribly dry, and the muscles in his neck ached. His chest felt bound, clamped. He struggled for breath. His eyes were hot, but the release of tears was paralyzed.

"I can will this!" he thought.

He took Martha's hand again and licked his lips. He wanted to tell her to help Lucas to the car, but he could not speak. His throat would not respond. With an effort he subdued a flicker of panic. He tried swallowing but there was nothing to swallow and the muscles were stricken. Half gagging, he stared into the woman's eyes and pointed to his mouth and shook his head in desperation. He pointed at Lucas and at the garage.

Martha's eyes opened wide a moment, questioning; then she stooped and helped her brother up. She led Lucas to the garage, left him leaning on a fence rail and gave Nelson a hand with the door of the garage. Together they guided Lucas, stumbling, into the back seat of the Volkswagen.

Nelson sat motionless, his left hand on the wheel and his right on the ignition key, vainly trying to recapture his voice. *Make yourself!* But it was no use. *Drive, then.* Pure will. He started the car. The noise startled him, so that he looked wildly into the rearview mirror and around the dusty garage, cast into bizarre shadows and streaks of light as the headlights came on. Then the rumble of the engine began to comfort him, and he knew he had the strength to go on, at least for a while.

Martha guided them through the streets.

26

He sat in a kitchen warming his hands on a mug of tea without drinking it. His mouth was dry and yet when he tried to drink his throat constricted. But the warmth in his hands was a kind of hearth, a focus. Martha was dabbing softly with a wet cloth at Lucas's head wound. Martha – he remembered her dancing in the tent. The black stole lay over the back of the chair, draped and coiled.

Lucas said kindly, "You don't have to say anything at all, not 'till you're ready. But I could call the police, if that'd help?"

Nelson opened his mouth. Still no words would come. He held up a cautioning hand. Lucas frowned and shrugged.

Nelson drew in a long breath. Then a thought struck him: *I am Rob Nelson. I am not "Nelson" any more.* He began to tremble.

He had longed for the sanity of being one again, had been ready to cheat and betray for it. Now it seemed like coming home to an empty house. Robert had chosen to die. Why? A voice echoed in his head certain and soft: "Brady!"

That was all.

Rob looked at the two faces staring solicitously at him. They represented safety and rest while he tried to make the world around him stop shifting and turning, and yet he could not suppress an impulse to turn to Robert for advice. He kept at bay the knowledge that Robert had given him his life by offering his own; he would not examine that now. But he thought again, "Yes. I am Rob Nelson now."

Lucas said, "You can stay with us. There's a blanket and pillow and a couch in the front room."

Rob nodded miserably.

"You knew who I was. Have we met before?" Lucas asked.

Martha responded to this. She made some signs to Lucas, pointing frequently to Rob. In three deft questions, Lucas learned from her that Rob and another man had been to a prayer meeting.

"Was that the man who got shot?"

Rob looked at them beseechingly. If only Robert were here! Involuntarily, he turned and looked around the apartment, seeking his other self. The death he had once wished for had left him guilty, bereft.

But what if Brady had missed his shot. "Why do I have this painful sense of . . . of Robert? Of his presence?" Rob wondered.

"Can you say your name?" Lucas interrupted his thoughts.

Rob licked his lips. Of course he could say his name! He opened his mouth. Only a soft voiced breath emerged. He shook his head in impotent frustration.

Lucas said, trying again, "You need to get it out."

Rob knew that. Damn this preacher! How angry he suddenly felt; abandoned. Robert had left him. How could he talk to these weird people? He needed Daisy. His eyes narrowed as he hunched over the tea mug, his hands clasped tightly around it. But how could he even talk to Daisy?

Martha rose, came to the table and knelt, and searched Rob's face a moment – the tightened lips, the nervous, suspicious eye. He almost reached out his hand through his wall of watchfulness to touch her soft-eyed face, which had clouded with a sorrowing look. But he kept his hands clasped like armor, and Martha stood up and went to another room.

Lucas said, "Martha ain't quick. Couldn't go to school. Can't hear too great and can't speak at all. But she sees a lot of things I don't see or others don't see either. I don't know how. If you could only tell her – she has understanding in her heart."

Rob closed his eyes. The eyelid under the patch felt hot and he rubbed it through the cloth.

Lucas said, "Isn't there anyone you could talk to? Anyone we could find for you?"

Rob looked around the room and found the phone on the wall. He went to it tentatively and tried to remember the number at his house on Moore Avenue. But what would Daisy think? That he was insane? Tomorrow, if they found Robert's body

... he must protect her from that, but the task seemed beyond his grasp. He tried to form in his mind the first words he would say. But no words came. He felt paralyzed, unable to reach out to Daisy; he dropped his hand despairingly.

Lucas watched silently and waited.

Rob knew that he was badly shaken. Still functioning with a small element of detachment, a clinical, observing corner of his mind told him that he was not reacting adequately, that he was in a diagnosable state of shock.

He reached his hand up to the door frame and rapped softly with his knuckles and listened carefully to the sound. He sensed things he knew to be unreal. There was an almost physical voice, Robert's, calling his name – it wrenched at his heart. But the small dispassionate part of his mind said: classical hallucination of grief.

His head ached terribly. His eyepatch was wet with perspiration but he did not feel free enough in this house to remove it. He rubbed his neck and tried to slow everything down, to stop the whirling images, the pounding, the voices, to force part of his mind to take control of itself and think, as Pinch would do. Pinch!

This time he picked up the phone and dialled the 514 area code and the number at Pine Avenue; he thought he could muster that one word: Pinch. That would be enough! But the phone rang and rang. The answering machine must be disconnected. What did that mean? Bleakly, he hung up the receiver, leaned his head against the door frame, and shut out the light for a moment.

Try to think!

He was roused by a gentle hand on his arm. Martha stood there, searching his face again. Hers had lost its look of sorrow; he saw now a kindly eagerness. She handed him a block of notepaper; on the top sheet, in forceful capitals, one word:

TRUST

She made a little ducking motion with her head, thrusting it forward at the same time – a gesture of encouragement, "Come on!" she seemed to say.

How he wanted to! He searched her eyes in return. There

was no guile, nothing but that quiet eagerness, an eagerness on his behalf, he sensed, not hers.

Lucas had been watching closely. Now he came and stood beside his sister. Light from the kitchen cast their three shadows in a solid triangle on the hall floor beyond. The house was very quiet.

Lucas said, "Now, I don't guess you're my sort of Christian?"

Rob shook his head.

"Or believe in God."

Rob hesitated, and Lucas went on. "Whatever it is stopping you from speaking, the power to heal that's inside you – I call it God; you call it something else – is there. You believe that?"

Rob nodded tentatively.

"Well that's grand!" Lucas said. "People can help to heal each other, with caring and hands and being close. Do you know about that?"

Rob sighed, and wished tears would come to break the awful silence, the barrier between him and his grief.

Lucas said, "There. You're trying to tell your story. You need to. Won't you let us help?"

He held his hands out toward the anguished man, palms up, steady. Rob looked at the broad, work-lined fingers. He nodded dumbly and slowly brought his own hands forward. Lucas took Rob's hands and placed them on Martha's. Her fingers closed softly. Rob felt a calmness pass from her to him. Though his head still ached, the pain seemed less threatening, more remote.

Lucas placed his fingertips on Rob's temples. "What I'm doing now, I call prayer," he said quietly. "But it don't matter what you call it; if the hands feels healing to you, that's all that counts for now."

The pain in Rob's head receded further. He was still conscious of it, but more aware of knots loosening in his neck and shoulders, his mind slowing down, racing less. For the moment he had total confidence in Lucas.

He looked in the bearded man's eyes. Robert's image, bearded and kind, mixed in memory with the man he saw before him. But there was no conflict in the image now. Lucas moved his hands down slightly, and gently pressed the edge of Rob's jaw.

The relaxation from his shoulders and neck spread into his throat. He was not at peace; a distant and troubling pain throbbed somewhere in his head; but he felt strong for the first time.

Lucas put his hands on Rob's shoulders now, like a father sending forth a son. He said, "We still don't know your name."

Rob's heart beat with excitement. Martha folded his hands together and covered them with her own. The remaining tension in his throat seemed to drain down the extended arms into the warmth between her hands.

Lucas said, "But we'd like to."

Martha smiled at him, serene, heavy-lidded, confident.

He felt saliva run in his mouth; he worked his tongue and swallowed easily. His throat loosened. Lucas pressed lightly on his shoulders and nodded, as if to say, "You see?"

Rob drew breath easily in through his nostrils. He opened his mouth and said calmly, "My name is Rob Nelson."

Martha exhaled a long, happy sigh and squeezed Rob's hands tightly.

Lucas said, "You may not understand this, Rob, but you're doing something important for me right now. I'll try to tell you about it later, if you're interested, that is."

They sat over fresh cups of tea. Lucas and Martha waited as if they had all the time in the world. Rob still sensed Robert's presence, almost as if, from the corner of his eye, he could see him sitting in the kitchen too, but when he looked there was only a shadow on the wall.

He said, "I've been away from my wife for a long while, and part of what has been going on all that time – I'm able to see this now for the first time, telling somebody about it – has been trying to find a way back to her. I have to tell her things that no sane person is likely to believe, and she has to believe them or it won't work between us."

He sighed, a long release of breath. "I don't know if you've lived with many secrets in your life?"

Lucas said, "I don't guess so, no. At our house, people pretty well said what it was and that's it."

Rob said, "I thought about trying to live with her and not tell her, but I've been learning about the price of secrets. Too many secrets, up to now. The one person who might have helped me figure out what to do is the man who was shot tonight. I'm going to tell you that this man was my twin brother. That's not exactly true, and it's something I can't explain to you – not yet anyway – but twin brother is close enough. He ... he's really so much like me ... Oh God!"

His throat had tightened up again, but he made himself sip his tea and in a while he was able to continue.

"If they find his body, they'll think it's me. So will Daisy, my wife. You're wondering why I don't head that off. I can't. There are some very evil people involved – criminals from New York. There was a lot of money at stake and my ... my brother and I were in the middle of it. It had to do with an invention made by a physicist named Haig in Montreal. These criminals wanted a part of that invention and thought they had it. I was the one who got them involved in the first place. Now they blame me for the fact that they've been cut out, and because one of their top men has disappeared. And so they put a contract out on my life. And they think they've made the contract."

Martha shook her head and grasped Lucas's arm roughly. She looked from Rob to Lucas, then back to Rob and stamped her foot on the floor.

"I don't understand that either, Martha," Lucas said. "That contract, Rob. What does it mean?"

Rob explained. "And they'll think it's me they've killed, because they didn't know *he* even existed. We look exactly alike."

"Even that bad eye?"

"Even the eye."

Martha was frowning heavily, deeply distressed.

"Oh God," Rob said. "I shouldn't have started. It's a pretty tough story, Lucas."

But Martha touched his arm and composed her features and indicated he should go on.

It was past one in the morning. Fatigue was pulling at the corners of all their eyes. Rob said, "Do you see what a hideous thing it is I must do? I have to let my wife think I'm dead!"

"But if you're going back to her afterward, why not now? If

you can trust her later, she'll be ready to take whatever you have to tell her now?"

"It's me that's not ready."

Lucas tugged at his earlobe. "Why don't we get some sleep, Rob? Martha and me'll stay with you long as you need it. We'll work it out."

Martha took Rob's hand and laid it on the notepad.

TRUST

"I'm trying," Rob said.

Rob stood in the bathroom looking at his haggard face in the mirror. He removed his eyepatch and washed his face in cold water. His head pounded again and there was a hard pain in his chest, like a recent, half-healed wound. Would he ever be strong enough to retrieve, on his own, some of the wholeness he had known with Robert, some of the richness that they might have had together, that Robert had seen and wanted but he, as Nelson, had refused?

In the darkened living room, a blanket wrapped around his shoulders, Rob sat on the couch and stared through the branches of a maple at the wet street. A fine, steady rain shimmered on the pavement. Lucas and Martha were asleep.

Suddenly his back stiffened with an assault of pain. The next moment he was on his feet, half in a crouch, his arms wrapped around his head in desperate defence. A voice that he could hear and recognize as his, yet not as his, sounded in his brain as clearly as though it spoke beside him in the room.

It's over, Nelson. Good-bye. I loved you.

In that instant the pain in his head and back fell from him and breath rushed into his lungs. He exhaled in a moan of protest. Then he said aloud to the room, "He *is* dead. He was alive until now. I felt his pain. He's dead now!"

But still the tears he needed did not come.

What had done it? What had happened to Robert? Had the journey through twelve feet of space produced some subtle coloration in Robert's brain so exactly copied from his own? Or had the voice come from seeing the self from without – was that all? "If that's all, why have I not changed?" he asked himself. "The man who died tonight was, in every discernible way, me. But he had a view of life and a generosity that was something I always wanted but could only imitate."

Rob sat in the kitchen while the sun came up. He made tea and toast. The two unlikely people who had saved his life this night slept peacefully. He envied them their moral clarity.

"I've always been morally confused," he thought. "I only ever had one purpose: to move up. Love has always been elusive because I never really gave it."

And then he thought, "Why do I punish myself so much? I've been close. I've been on the trail. I've almost understood. I was always just getting ready. Maybe there's still time. There *is* still time. I always said that before but I knew I was kidding myself."

Six o'clock. He walked into the front room and turned on a little transistor radio. A voice said, "C F M T: News after this!" A commercial began. He could feel his heart working uncomfortably hard. He almost yielded to an urge to shut out what he feared to hear, but he kept the radio on. The commercial ended. The news that he was waiting for was the lead story.

"Good morning. Jeremy Klein reporting. A grisly murder and an armed man on the run top the news in metro this morning. Metro and provincial police had a shootout in suburban Ajax a few hours ago with a man suspected to be a professional killer working with American organized criminal interests.

"The suspect escaped following a one-hundred-mile-an-hour car chase from Ajax into Toronto, after he had been flushed from a supposedly abandoned house in Ajax. Neighbors had seen suspicious lights in the house and called police. Detectives entering the house after the suspect escaped in a green late model car found the body of an unidentified man in his late thirties. The body had been badly mutilated and police suspect torture. The only clue so far to the man's identity: one eye is blind.

"Drivers coming to work in metro this morning may have a long slow trip. Roadblocks have been set up on all arteries leading into the city, and . . ."

Rob switched off the radio. There was someone behind him.

He turned around. Lucas stood in the doorway of his bedroom in a faded brown robe.

"Was that it?"

Rob nodded.

"Can you sleep?"

He shook his head, deeply angry, unable to weep or speak or think.

"I'll get Martha up. We'll talk."

The day passed in a haze. One hour ran into another. Perhaps he ate something. The two people must have been with him all day. He remembered faces, lips moving, no words. At some point he felt his chin and noticed that he had shaved and thought, "When? What for?"

At dusk he sat by the kitchen window waiting for a sleeping pill to work. His brain was slow but still agitated, without peace or silence. His morale was vanishing. He was torn between desire to be with Daisy and fear of confronting her.

Lucas came and sat with him. "You couldn't listen to me a minute about Jesus?"

"I'm sorry. I don't think so."

"I'm sorry too. If you could hear that message about letting Him take your burdens, Rob."

Rob shook his head sadly.

Lucas said, "I guess I knew that. I've been thinking since you came. I've been troubled a lot about what I'm doing, in this school I'm going to. I don't understand all them people saying they're Christian, not doing anything about it.

"Heard a song on the radio, the other day: 'If you can't preach without going to school, you're not a preacher, you're an educated fool.' I've been turning that song over in my mind since you came here, Rob. And I know now I ain't meant to be in this school at all. And maybe I ain't meant to do what I was doing before, either. But I am meant to be helping people, and I got a whole lot to think about too, and I got you to thank for all that, so thank you."

Rob was comforted by Lucas's presence but depression and self-contempt had a firm grip on him. He began to talk to Lucas about his work, his doubts about his work, his speculations about the possibility of excellence in his life, his deep cynicism about his own morality of stratagem and control, and his envy of Lucas and Martha in their untroubled integrity.

Martha came in from somewhere; he had not known she was out. She had paper bags. Of food?

She poured soup in a dish. He ate it. There was no taste. The heat running down his throat made his heartbeat slow and ebb somewhat. Perhaps he could sleep, after all.

Rob lay on the bed in Martha's room – they had insisted he take it. After an hour he knew it was no good. He fought the risk of dreams; each time he closed his eyes threats of a fearful theater of blood and shadows began behind his forehead and he looked at the room again for support. Eleven o'clock; there would be some news. He got up. But he did not turn on the radio.

They sat in the kitchen until past three in the morning. Tired of talk finally, he urged Lucas and Martha to get some sleep in their own beds and promised he "wouldn't do anything foolish."

By seven the next night he still had not slept. Yet he was feeling clearer of mind and had decided not to take any more sleeping pills. Lucas had been out all afternoon. Shortly after seven he returned, carrying a borrowed portable television set.

"You better watch something here, Rob," he said. "They're doing a whole program about you. They said there won't be no obituary; you wouldn't have wanted that. They're going to run selections from the best of R.M. Nelson. Some fool must think your work was worth something."

They all watched. There were excerpts from films going back to 1959. There was nothing from *Sputnik and After*: the film had been lost and it was not his work anyway, though brief reference was made to his role in it. There were good excerpts from a 1961 film on investment rip-offs, *Make Mine Mutual;* scenes from *Rackets Don't Make Noise* ironically showing both Appolinari and Pete Brady; scenes from *Run For Coverage* on insurance frauds; from *Dying to Please You,* from *Nobody Wins;* and from *Lead Pipe Cinch.*

At one point Lucas said, with spontaneous, unfeigned admiration, "Did you really make all these stories? Ain't you proud of that?" Rob managed a half-smile.

At the end, a young staff announcer Rob had never worked with or even met, but had seen on the air, said, "For the next eight days R.M. Nelson's documentary films can be seen in the network's television theatre on Mutual Street. Tickets are available at our main reception desk. Admission is free. All films will be shown at their original length, uncut and unchanged. This is the journalistic legacy of a courageous man with an honest vision. Good evening."

Rob shut off the set.

Lucas said, "I think they had a better view of you than you allow yourself, Rob. Most people, it's the other way around."

"But it's not the truth, goddam it! I'm only getting ready to be something like what they said. If I could get another chance!"

He stood up and slammed his fist against the screen of the little portable, yelling "Shit! Shit! Shit! All shit!"

And then, the sharp pain of the blow on his knuckles triggered rage and release. The dam broke. He began to weep. Huge tears ran down his cheeks. His nose blubbered. He heaved with loose sobs. It went on for nearly two hours. The relief was nourishment to his spirit; with each sob he could feel strength returning and he gave in gratefully to the cries and the tears and knew what medicine they were.

When it was over he slept for thirteen hours and woke up calmly and quietly and with a sense of optimism pulsing in his chest. He told Lucas and Martha he was a changed man, that Robert had left him a legacy of new possibilities and the old world was dead. They did not understand what he meant but were pleased to see him so well.

Over breakfast he reviewed in his mind the overwhelming things that had happened to him in the last months and felt very strong because he had not been conquered by them. Now old ways of decision and action were once again within his grasp. He phoned Air Canada and booked two seats to Los Angeles in the name of Wilson, for the following day. The familiar sound of his nasal giving-orders voice resonating in the telephone receiver cheered him more.

Pinch would be his anchor now. Pinch and Daisy. Daisy for the moral anchor, Pinch for the future. He and Daisy would go away and hide, and when it was safe, get back with Pinch and then it would all be fine again.

He watched an early news film of the funeral. He looked in vain for Daisy on the screen. He could not contain his excitement. "No one else has ever seen his own funeral! I'm a free man now. It's time to begin. Let's get at it, Pinch!"

It was dark outside. Rob was restless, anxious to be off to Moore Avenue, very confident now in what he had to do, almost amused. Lucas took the Volkswagen to Moore Avenue and cruised past the house and came back to report on the state of the funeral supper. "They haven't all left yet," he said.

But finally it was time. Lucas drove. Martha sat in the back seat. They stopped a few doors away from the house. Though the lights were still on, no cars were parked outside and there was no shadow of movement on the living room curtains.

"I'll check through the kitchen window and go in that way," Rob said. His chest was bursting with anticipation.

He stepped out of the car. Lucas said, "I'll bring the car when you phone. Day or night, now. Don't worry. And Rob, remember I said I'd be praying."

Martha squeezed Rob's hand. She pulled him toward her and kissed his cheek.

He loped down the driveway of the house next to his and vaulted a fence into his own back yard. He stepped soundlessly onto the porch and peered through the window into the dark kitchen. There was a light from the living room. He slipped his key into the lock, turned it without a sound and opened the door.

His hand brushed against the dish rack at the side of the sink and some glasses clinked. He came to the archway opening from the kitchen into the living room and stared at his wife's back and saw in the mirror her downcast face and eyes closed tight. All he could think of was the great surprise he was going to bring her, the great gift. He was the old Rob, the boy wonder, the operator, the bagful of surprises.

He was actually grinning as he stepped forward silently on the rug and came up behind the grieving woman and said, "It's me, Babe."

27

"And the weird thing, Babe, is this: I didn't realize until I started telling you about Robert and what we had gone through, and what happened in my head the last three days in Lucas Rankin's apartment – I didn't realize how easily I'd slipped back. I actually came in here just about ready to shout, 'Surprise, Surprise!' I think I even expected you to jump up and down and applaud. The old me's alive and well. But I know I've moved on all the same. I've grown. I'm closer to being able to match me to my image. I watched that tribute on the network last night. Did you see it?"

"A bit blurred. But I saw it. I heard the end of it. That announcer."

"I knew what he said wasn't true. It was what I sold people. You knew I sold that image. You never confronted me with it, really; you never told me it was a con job, but –"

"I did, Rob. I remember saying to you, 'What would your admiring public think if they knew you were such a devious son of a bitch.' The great recorder of truth on film screws other men's wives and lies to the people who love him."

"Did you say that?"

"You don't remember, do you!" she accused.

"It's the kind of thing I wouldn't want to. I don't mind it now. If we can get ourselves into a space where we're safe from Brady, where nobody knows who I am ... I don't care where it is ... I'm ready to start again."

"Rob, dear Rob, are you asking me to believe all the old shit is finished – the screwing around, the disappearing acts, the lies? How can I believe that after fifteen years of it?"

"I'm not asking you to believe that. Listen to me, for Christ's sake. I'm saying it's still very much alive in me. And if all the things that happened in the last three months hadn't happened, we would have drifted into a rut where we put up with each other because it was convenient. Or we would've split. But those things *did* happen. Do you believe they happened?"

She made vague motions with her hands. That was no longer the issue; an issue, perhaps, for another time, when she could hear it from Pinch, when she could think about it in tranquillity, examine it all again, as she knew she would anyway for the rest of her life.

Whatever had happened, however he had experienced the things that he described, Daisy could say to herself now that there was more point in starting again than in ending. For her and for this man who had broken so many promises and told so many lies, *something* had happened that had put him within reach of the strength a man needs to deal with his vulnerabilities. She went over to him and kissed him fully, her mouth warm and odorous against the base of his nose; the first time she had done it in this night of strange homecoming, and she could tell from the gentleness of his arms around her then that he was very close to her and very moved.

"Daisy, Daisy," was all he said. He held her warmly, silently, for minutes. Then he said into her hair, "We have a chance now that we didn't have before. That's the best I can say. I think it's worth taking ... has to be taken."

She nodded against his shoulder.

"You know the whole story. You know what the risks are. *You* say what we should do. Where do *you* think we should go? We can't stay here."

She nodded again and eased back from him to sit on the chair.

"I've thought it as far as I can by myself," he said. "The tickets are for LA. Lucas picked them up today. We can go west from there, Hong Kong, maybe. You can get a fake Canadian Passport there for a thousand bucks. We could stay long enough for you to have Morley Stone wire out the life insurance money, get my passport, go to Australia, back to the States, London. Some place big and anonymous. What do you think? I'll change it any way you want, now that you know it all."

Daisy was stricken with a series of yawns. She tugged her

cheeks down with her finger nails and massaged her eyelids and tried to think about it. Her mind kept wandering from the arguments she was trying to pursue logically, arguments about safety from pursuit, sources of money, living under the lie of a changed identity in the face of a decision to build an honest life. She was still emotionally gasping from the long night's buffeting of bizarre stories, from the funeral, from the hideousness of the last three days, from the months of secrecy and rejection. And he was still self-centered enough to demand a decision from her, in her condition; a decision that would be hard to go back on. He might have won the capacity to see his faults but he was far from free of them.

"Rob, you took three days in that preacher's place before you could see what you had to do next, before you could even come and let me know you were alive. Three days!"

He looked puzzled.

"But you expect me to know what to do right away. Snap! Like that. After three sleepless nights and then this load you dumped on me tonight!"

He blinked. He had thought about that, but somehow had assumed he could *will* her decisiveness; create, out of the threat that Brady might still be in business for some perverse reason, enough urgency to move her. He had thought about it but not in her terms, despite his promise to himself that he would yield to her. He said, "You're right. I'm sorry. I was using the idea of Brady. It was because I wanted to get moving. It had nothing to do with you."

He went to the phone and dialled. "I told Lucas to expect your voice," he said, holding the handset out to her. "When he answers, just say, 'Daisy.' Then tell him to cancel your ticket, you're going to stay here for a few days. He'll know. Don't say anything about me, because the line could be tapped."

It was answered on the second ring. "Lucas," the voice said.

Daisy said, "Daisy. I won't be using the ticket today. Will you cancel it? I'll call you in a day or two."

"You bet ..."

"You better hang up," Daisy said.

There was a click.

Daisy softened then. Sleep was creeping over her. She said, "We're going to sleep now. We're going to take enough time to do it right for a change. All the time we need. We'll take our chance on Pete Brady. You think he's finished with you, and so do I. And he'd have nothing to gain from me."

She yawned again. "And I can't think of anything more now." They went upstairs together.

She said, "Rob, I'm glad to have you back in this bed. But I'm still distant. We've got a lot of work to do before there's real trust. We're gambling now. I am anyway. You'll give me time, won't you?"

Daisy dreamed and stirred on the bed. Out of the dream but not fully into wakefulness she felt the warmth beside her where for so many months there had been cool sheets only, where she had often wakened to find her arms thrown longingly around the other pillow. Freed from the injunctions of an unconsenting watchful mind, her body answered to the warmth of him; loosened, opened, flowed. Still between dreaming and knowing, she rolled against him and her fingers traced a welling anointment as she roused him, he too still nearer dreams than waking. Then consciousness came fully to them both at once and she drew in her breath with the ferocity of what she felt between them. She sprawled over him then, darkly, her mouth blindly on him as she drew her gown up to her shoulders and pressed down to envelop him. They did not speak. They moved only to be more intensely close.

In the street outside, the fog cleared away. Solicitous neighbors, passing the draped windows on their way to work, judged the widow had been enough disturbed by help and consolation and left the place alone. A newspaper appeared in the old milkbox at the side of the house. The mailman came. But inside, two people slept deeply, untroubled.

If a second mailman, tall, with long hair above oversized sunglasses and a face much older than the hair would suggest, came casually down the concrete walk at the side of the house, and as he reached into the milkbox reached simultaneously with his other hand up to the kitchen window and left an object smaller than a matchbox affixed by suction to the frame just below the glass, a fine wire trailing from it, nobody would have noticed – and nobody did.

By noon the clouds had thinned to a few wisps and by four o'clock a low November sun had turned the faces of the houses along the east side of the park a warm orange. The pace of traffic began to pick up again after the early afternoon lull, and the sound of the trollybuses on nearby Mount Pleasant Road was carried along the street by a freshening westerly breeze.

Rob rolled easily in the familiar bed and awoke. He looked at the sleeping face beside him, her arm thrown back over her head and her lips slightly open. There was the trace of a wrinkle across her forehead. He smoothed it softly with a finger tip. She did not move. Looking at her, he felt the rush of excitement and optimism that he had felt the day before.

"Careful, now," he said to himself.

He got out of bed and padded downstairs and took in some letters and the morning paper. He made coffee and read the front page. Presently he looked up over the edge of the paper to find his wife peering at him sleepily from the kitchen door.

"It's real?"

He knelt at her feet and hugged her legs and she bent over him and worked his back and shoulders with her square, comfortable hands: the litany of motion and position that was their unspoken ritual of thanks for each other's presence and existence.

They sat over canned soup and toast and cheese and looked at the last sunlight making beams through the tree shadows in the cemetery behind the house.

"When I woke up I smelled you," Daisy said. "I smelled *us* in that bed. I thought, 'It's a pity to have to leave this place. We could try to make it be what it was meant to be.' But now I look across that graveyard and I can't wait to get away."

"With me?"

"With you. I know what the risks are. They're better than they were." She squeezed his hand. "My body knew better than I did in the night. I'm glad. I'm ready to move.

"I'll feel up to it tomorrow. I'd better call Morley and tell him to look after everything, deal with my clients, all that. Will your friends drive us? Could they do some errands? Go to the bank?"

"What are you thinking of?"

"I think we should go to Detroit. In the car. It's easy to cross at Windsor. Early in the evening or early in the morning. We'll drive at night and go through customs in the morning with the work crowd. They don't look at anything. Say we're going shopping. We shouldn't try to fly out of here. Too many people in Toronto know you. People in airports read papers. But we could fly from Detroit to Chicago. I was remembering you took that polar flight to Stockholm. Nobody knows you in Stockholm. People speak English. There are no tourists in the winter, not from Canada, but there might be in Hong Kong. We can settle there for a while, get the financial affairs straightened out, figure out if we really want to go ahead with a new identity. Don't argue with me now, Rob. Give me time. Give us time. Okay?"

But he was angry; his life was at stake, after all. Then he realized that, in longer, broader terms, that was probably what she was talking about.

His moment of irritation didn't escape her. She said, "It's not a trivial thing for me, giving up a law practice, leaving a case in the middle of it – there are many threads to be cut and tied up again. I'm coming with you, and I love you, and I'm prepared for a lot of work on that. But I'm also going to have a great deal to say about what happens from here on. You understand, don't you?"

He blew air out hard between pursed lips. "Sorry," he said sheepishly. "It's going to take time."

"Yes, it is," she answered. "That's what I'm saying."

He said, "We'd better phone Lucas Rankin."

There was a thump at the milkbox by the side door; the evening paper had arrived. Daisy went to get it while Rob dialled the phone and then hung up again before he had finished, remembering that he was not taking any chances.

Daisy returned with the paper in front of her, scanning the front page. Suddenly she gasped. "Oh, Rob!"

He read over her shoulder.

McGILL SCIENTIST DEAD
FOUL PLAY SUSPECTED

Montreal, October 31. Special to the *Star*.

A badly decomposed body discovered by fishermen in a few feet of water near the Dorion bridge early today has been tentatively identified as that of physicist John A. Haig. Haig had been missing for some weeks.

Police told the *Star* that the body, partly wrapped in plastic, was too far gone to be physically identified. Parts of the jaw were missing, so normal dental verification would not be possible they said.

Det. Sgt. Alfred Lemoine said that a driver's licence encased in plastic had been found in a wallet on the body.

An autopsy will be performed tomorrow, Coroner J.P. Latendresse said.

It is known that Haig was closely associated with television filmmaker R.M. Nelson, who was murdered earlier this week.

Haig was honored during World War II for an invention related to electronic submarine detection devices, the Defence Department confirmed.

There are no known surviving relatives.

Science staff members at McGill were not available for comment.

Rob groaned aloud. Daisy turned to him. His face was white and frightened.

"Why the hell did they have to do that!" He moaned. "They had me, goddam it! He must've ..."

Daisy hugged him hard, and he slumped into a chair. "My darling, my darling!" she said "I had such a hope about Pinch too. You weren't the only one who loved him."

Daisy knelt beside him and put her arms around him. She

said, "Most of us are either bastards or dullards. But not Pinch. He was decent and brilliant. I used to hold on to that, all the time you were down there with him and I was lonely and lost and doubting. I would try to think, 'He's with Pinch. Something good will come of it.' "

Rob buried his face in his arms on the kitchen table.

Daisy said, "And last night after I began to believe you, and to see what a hell of a mess we were in, I knew that Pinch would bail us out in the end. That Pinch would know. Oh dear God!"

She was suddenly stricken with fear. "Rob!" she whispered. "You were right. We've got to get out of here. Now. I'll phone Lucas again."

She was trembling. "Rob! Let's go!"

He looked up at her, his face drawn and still very pale. "I don't think I can, Daisy." He looked exhausted. She stared at him in exasperation.

Then she said, *"Get up!"* in the voice of a sergeant major. The kitchen window rattled in its frame at the sound. The frame vibrated with the glass. A small grey box on the frame received the sound through its suction cups and turned the sound and the sense of all the words spoken in that kitchen into electric pulses in a tiny trailing antenna.

Rob got dully to his feet.

"Come on, my darling. I'll manage us until you feel better. Give me the phone number."

She dialled. Lucas answered.

"Could you drive me to Detroit and bring the car back here? Tonight?"

"You bet. What time?"

"Soon. An hour?"

"Need anything else?"

"Just a minute." She covered the phone. "Have you got money?" she whispered.

He looked at her flatly. He exhaled a labored sigh. He said, "I have enough. I've got my American Express Card. It'll be good for a while."

It took her twenty minutes to pack, find their passports, leave a key in the milkbox in an envelope for Morley. Rob paced glumly up and down in the dark living room while Daisy cleaned out the refrigerator.

"You could stop fidgeting and come and make a lunch while I clean up," she said.

He was wrapping canned ham sandwiches when the doorbell rang. Daisy opened it cautiously.

"Well, Daisy," Lucas said, stepping in quickly. "It's something to meet some one that you know so much about already." He scrutinized her face for a moment and she his. "I'd say something fine has happened," he hazarded.

"I'm prepared to gamble that it could," she said simply.

"Martha's in the car. She'll turn the lights out if we're not supposed to come out. Hello, Rob."

Rob nodded and finished the sandwich wrapping. Daisy took their two small bags to the door. Rob brought the bag of sandwiches and a thermos of coffee. They opened the door a crack and looked out. The headlights were out in the Volkswagen.

"Wait," Lucas said. He stood with his eye to the crack of the door and listened and heard several sets of footsteps going up stairs somewhere along the street. A house door closed and the lights of the Volkswagen came on again.

"Ready?" Lucas asked.

Rob looked around the house, trying to force his memory to check for anything essential he might have left. "Wait," he said.

He went back through the darkened kitchen and opened the back door. He stepped out on the porch and looked across the fence into the almost invisible cemetery. The bare trees were still and the city sounds faint and distant. He stood silently for a moment staring off into a far corner, remembering. "The thing is," he said quietly into the night, "while you were alive I wanted to be rid of you. Now I'm afraid I'll never be a whole person again. I'm sorry . . . Robert."

Then he stepped back in. He locked the door and went to Daisy.

"Let's go," she said.

Martha stood beside the car, her black stole wrapped around the lower part of her face, her arms hugging her body. As

Daisy approached she pulled the stole down from her mouth and stepped forward and took the other woman in a strong, frank embrace. "Ahhh," she said quietly.

Daisy looked at Martha for a long moment, then pressed the other woman's hand and slipped into the back seat with Rob. Lucas took the wheel.

Two hundred yards away, across the park, a man in a car with its lights off removed his headset and placed it by the windscreen on top of a small receiver which he switched off. It had done its work. The man put the car in gear and eased out of his parking spot, but did not switch on his lights until the Volkswagen had pulled out of sight, going west on Moore Avenue. Then, as the sedan came around the corner of the cross street, it looked like any other car. It let the Volkswagen get well ahead of it, and put several cars between them as they travelled south on Mount Pleasant toward the lake and the freeway west toward Detroit.

28

They crossed the border without incident at seven in the morning. Those who could, dozed in the cramped seats. When it was her turn to drive, Daisy asked Lucas to sit beside her, and went over all their plans with him in detail. She asked Lucas to contact Morley at Nicol, Nickle, Marcus and Hruska, in a couple of days, and to look in on the house.

"I know it's an imposition. I'm anxious that the selling of the house go quickly and smoothly. It's in my name so it should be all right. Morley Stone has signing power. And I think it'll help if there's someone there to ask if everything's all right. Partly so Morley won't worry that I'm off my head. You could reassure him. And Lucas, tell him not to claim the life insurance yet. Say I'll phone in a few days. We've got some things to work out on that."

Every kilometer sign passed on the MacDonald-Cartier Freeway put them in a safer frame of mind. By the time they were speeding across the western Ontario flatlands, they scarcely paid any attention to the few other cars on the highway. Slouched in the back seat, his collar pulled up and his head settled against the frame of the car, cushioned by his folded jacket, Martha dozing beside him, Rob tried to fight off despair, tried to feel as though the motion of the car was sweeping clean his life, tried to see, as Robert had seen, the possibilities of a fresh start. He yearned to achieve that excellence-of-being Robert had spoken of. In the old reliable stores of determination, Rob had found the will to go on, for Daisy's sake, as long as he had the energy and mind. But with Pinch and Robert gone, he could not make himself believe in a fruitful future.

He looked at the head of his wife bent over the steering-wheel. "Maybe," he whispered to himself.

He felt swept by affection for her. He admired the way in which she had taken over, and was making their escape operation smooth and intelligent. He wondered if he could find in her what he had lost in Robert and Pinch.

At Detroit Metropolitan Airport they made reservations through to Stockholm, and Rob nervously paid with his credit card and signed an unlikely looking signature which the agent did not even verify against the card.

"I'm going to send American Express that money," Daisy said in a whisper when they left the desk. "As soon as we have some."

Lucas and Martha were to take Haig's car back to Toronto and abandon it so that no connection could be traced, through Haig's Quebec licence plates, to any of them.

The flight was called. There was a moment of awkward silence. Rob fidgeted. "Let's go!" he said irritably. "Lucas, Martha, I'm grateful. You know that. I can't manage goodbyes very well, and I'd just like to say thank you and go."

Lucas took Rob's hand warmly between his own and nodded, his lips pressed together, between resignation and a smile of encouragement.

Daisy shrugged helplessly. "I can't . . ." she began, but did not say whatever it was she found impossible.

There was a cloud of speechlessness over the four of them. No one moved.

Martha broke the spell. Holding up her hand to signal *Wait!*, she quickly unwound the long black stole from her shoulders and body. In three or four swift loops she folded it into a neat bolt. She stepped to Daisy, pressed the stole into her hands, reached across to Rob without looking at him, pulled him close to Daisy, lifted her right hand, touched them both lightly on the lips, then took their shoulders and with a firm hand guided them toward the gate. When they passed the electronic security gate and turned around for a last wave, there was no one to be seen.

An hour and a half later they stood in the concourse at Chicago's O'Hare Airport drinking beer at a standup bar, waiting for the SAS flight lounge to open up.

Daisy pressed Rob's arm. "Try not to be obvious about it," she whispered. "There's a tall man across the concourse who's been watching us. A man with a beige raincoat."

Rob held onto the edge of the bar and saw that the hand holding his beer was trembling. He waited a moment, then turned and leaned back against the bar trying to look casual and as if he were simply observing the people coming and going along the concourse. The man across the way had large sunglasses, a broad brimmed hat and long fair hair. He was too far away to make out the features. There seemed to be something familiar about the body, the stance.

"It it Pete Brady?" Daisy said, feeling ready to give in and collapse. She looked around for a security guard or a policeman.

"No. Don't do anything," Rob said. "He's walking away. I think you were imagining it."

The tall man in the sunglasses had indeed started to walk briskly away down the concourse, and they saw him wave as if at someone a distance away.

"False alarm," Rob said.

"No, I'm sure he was watching us."

"Thought he knew us from somewhere. People do that a lot. People stare at my eyepatch."

That was true. She wanted to be reassured. She leaned against Rob and told herself her fears were empty; but then she saw how tense and distracted he was and the fears flamed again and she wished the time would speed by, that the hands of the big clock would begin to spin and the loudspeakers call for them to hurry on board the plane.

It was an hour before the electronic noticeboard told them they could check in for the SAS flight. They walked about the terminal, tried not to snap at each other and from time to time Daisy continued to search the moving knots and lines of people for the man in the sunglasses, but did not see him again.

When the flight finally boarded they got on early and strapped themselves in the wide seats of the first-class cabin. Daisy had argued against the extra charge for first-class, but Rob had insisted. They were already in near exhaustion, and a long flight in economy would drive them around the bend, he argued.

There was a maddening wait before the engines were started. Rob kept looking at his watch. A steward arrived, apologized for the delay and offered drinks. Rob ordered a double scotch and drank it too fast and ordered another and silently dared Daisy to tell him to stop, and then realized she wouldn't and perversely put his glass down on the holder in the armrest between the seats and left it there.

Daisy saw his predicament, and reached over and took his hand. Still perverse, he refused the gesture and kept his own hand hard and tense at first. Then aware of his game, and tired of it, he let the muscles relax, let her take his hand, looked at her with his reassuring crinkle, and said, "Sorry."

And then the relief when the plane pulled away from the terminal at last. They held hands and gazed out the window as the land fell away. The plane banked to take up its northerly heading and they caught a last glimpse of lake-strewn woodlands for a moment before they passed through a deck of cloud and the world went white and featureless below them. But Daisy remained glued to the window for a long time, staring down.

Then they both had drinks and more drinks and by the time the dinner began to appear they were almost merry. When the trays were cleared away Rob put the seat back and closed his eyes and scarcely felt Daisy stepping over him as she made her way to the toilet.

As she returned to her seat, the curtains separating the economy from first-class opened and a steward came through. Daisy looked past him curiously, to see how the other half lived. A tall man with sunglasses and a broad hat was standing with his back to her, talking to a stewardess, and gesturing over his shoulder toward the first-class cabin. The girl was nodding amiably.

Daisy dived into her seat and shook Rob awake.

"He's on the plane," she whispered angrily into his ear. "I told you. It's the same man. He's on the plane and he's trying to talk the stewardess into letting him come up here. Rob, where can we go? What can we do?"

"Cut it out!" he said crossly. "It's somebody you happened

to see in the terminal who's going to Stockholm on the same plane."

"I'm sure he's wearing a wig. And why would he keep sunglasses on in the plane?"

"Lots of people keep sunglasses on in the plane. Listen, we're okay now. Anything that could hurt us is a long way behind. Please!"

But she was not satisfied. She bit her lip and then she said, a little too loudly, "All right! If you won't do anything I'm going to demand that the steward take me to the captain. I'm going to get help."

"That won't be necessary," a familiar voice said from the aisle. Rob felt a hand press down on his shoulder. His arms and neck prickled as he turned and faced the big smile and the huge sunglasses of the man who knelt with his head at their eye level. The sunglasses were lifted. A pair of pale blue eyes looked out with a strangely bright expression. "That won't be necessary at all," the man said again. "We've got a lot to talk about, and we might as well get started right away. *Hut hut hut hut hut!*"

More About Penguins and Pelicans

Penguinews, which appears every month, contains details of all the new books issued by Penguins as they are published. From time to time it is supplemented by *Penguins in Print*, which is our complete list of almost 5,000 titles.

A specimen copy of *Penguinews* will be sent to you free on request. Please write to Dept EP, Penguin Books Ltd, Harmondsworth, Middlesex, for your copy.

In the U.S.A.: For a complete list of books available from Penguins in the United States write to Dept CS, Penguin Books, 625 Madison Avenue, New York, New York 10022.

In Canada: For a complete list of books available from Penguins in Canada write to Penguin Books Canada Ltd, 2801 John Street, Markham, Ontario L3R 1B4.

In Australia: For a complete list of books available from Penguins in Australia write to the Marketing Department, Penguin Books Australia Ltd, P.O. Box 257, Ringwood, Victoria 3134.